# AFTER LYLETOWN

# AFTER LYLETOWN

## K. C. Frederick

THE PERMANENT PRESS
*Sag Harbor, NY 11963*

For information, address:
    The Permanent Press
    4170 Noyac Road
    Sag Harbor, NY 11963
    www.thepermanentpress.com

*Library of Congress Cataloging-in-Publication Data*

Frederick, K. C.–
    After Lyletown / K. C. Frederick.
        p. cm.
    ISBN 978-1-57962-219-0 (hardcover : alk. paper)
        1. Secrets—Fiction. 2. Robbery—Fiction. 3. Graduate students—Fiction. 4. Nineteen sixties—Fiction. I. Title.

PS3556.R3755A69 2011
813'.54—dc22                              2011006882

Printed in the United States of America.

*Once more, to Toni*

*With special thanks to Dan Bancroft, for his help with the law.*

~ 1968 ~

**A**lan has already had enough of the bald guy in the black turtleneck: he's someone who wants you to know he's hip to the scene but too smart to be involved. "I don't know," the guy is saying to a woman wearing an Indian print dress with lots of beads, "sometimes it seems like we're just doomed and I think let's get it over with. You know: boom, end of world." He frowns theatrically before taking a drink, but he's talking again before he's fully swallowed his wine. "I was at the Pentagon last fall. For the march, you know. I think that's the last time I still felt any hope." He throws up a hand like a lawyer making a perfunctory appeal to a jury that he knows is dead set against his client. "So tens of thousands of us marched and people made speeches and guys burned their draft cards, and what happened?" He pauses for a second before supplying his own answer. "Nothing. The war just goes on."

The bead woman responds to his confession of futility with a soulful smile. "Still," she says, "it must have been something when they tried to levitate the Pentagon. Did you see any of that?"

The exasperated guy looks from her to Alan. "No," he pushes at his glasses with two fingers. "No, I didn't." He shakes his head again. "But that did it for me." There's only the slightest interval before he delivers his punch line: "I ain't marching anymore." He dives back into his drink, trying not to look impressed by his own cleverness, but the whole performance has the air of a shtick.

A sunshine guy, Alan figures after he's wandered off. Mr. I Ain't Marching went down to D.C. and for a while under the October sun he was probably excited to be among the throngs of pipe-smoking professors, smiling hippie girls holding flowers, well-scrubbed students carrying signs with the names of their schools, sober housewives in walking shoes, and freaks dressed as Civil War soldiers or caped comic book superheroes. He may even have felt he was part of something powerful as he moved with the mostly orderly crowds that were watched over by orderly police; it's possible he joined in the singing and contributed his applause to the speakers speaking words that were not only brave but true. But Alan is pretty sure he wasn't around that night when the numbers were much smaller and the hard core warmed themselves around bonfires as they waited for things to get nasty, which they did soon enough; so that before long you were stumbling through the dark breathing tear gas through a wet handkerchief you wore over your face like a bad guy in a Hollywood western, and even before the rabid marshals were upon you, you could hear the thud of their batons striking the bodies of others, and you were lucky if you were able to scramble away tasting only a bit of your own blood. He'd been too quick for that jowly white-helmeted marshal with his too-tight raincoat who tried to grab him, which was why he didn't have to spend the night in jail like a lot of the others, though he wasn't quick enough to escape getting whacked hard against the arm that hung so limply as he skittered back through the chilly night that for a time he was sure it was broken. Even thinking about it now produces a distant involuntary neural memory.

Yeah, he could have told the bald guy, I was there too. The Pentagon is still standing and, yeah, the war is still going on. So what do we do now? Just give up?

Whenever somebody tries to tell him the protests aren't working, that they're playing into the hands of the government, he thinks about LBJ pulling out of the election. Something made that happen, didn't it? Though that's what he thinks on his good days. The truth is, there are plenty of times when he can understand the bald guy's disillusion, facile as it might be.

But he didn't come here to think about things, did he?

It was Zack who told him about this party. "Go, go. So you and Martha split. That's no reason to sit around and mope, no reason to seethe." That brought a sly smile. "Well, maybe seething isn't so bad. It could lead to something. You might punch somebody out, somebody might punch you out. Either way, you know, you're moving, you're doing something. Remember, the cistern contains, the fountain overflows." Zack, who likes to think of himself as an anarchist, has a fondness for quoting Blake.

The fact is, Alan didn't need literary, or any other kind of motivation, to wind up here: the idea of spending a couple of mindless hours among strangers is appealing in its own right. So far, though, as far as he knows, nobody here has punched anybody out and there have been neither cisterns nor fountains. But after listening to that last guy, he's looking for a bit of respite from talk and is content to find himself a quiet corner where he can watch those around him smile and frown at each other, lay hands on shoulders, laugh and shake heads. Occasionally a roving pair of eyes catches his. *Do I know you?* they ask before moving on, *Do I want to?* The stray contact is exciting: under all the laughs and shouts, he knows, there's a lot of hunger, and more than a bit of desperation as well. *Yeah,* he says without speaking, looking back at the dark woman who's cultivated a vaguely Egyptian look, *why don't we give it a try?* When she turns away he takes a sip of his wine. *So you lose,* he thinks.

Nearby a kid with Ben Franklin glasses seems to have found what he's been searching for, to judge from his blissful spaced-out gaze that looks upon everything and approves. Just now that gaze is directed at the posters on the wall: Dylan, Che, Stokely. Like the saints in old churches, Alan thinks, the measure of our dreams and aspirations, our doubts about ourselves. "You don't know what you want," Martha yelled at him the last time he was in her kitchen with its bowed floor and the ceiling fan that didn't work. "Or maybe it's just that you want too much so that everything is bound to disappoint you. I disappoint you, don't I?" I disappoint myself, he could have told her, but by that time no words would have made any difference. Maybe that wasn't such a bad idea, having the saints up there, reminding us of how far we still have to go.

The memory of that encounter provokes a sharp stab of dissatisfaction, and his eyes move restlessly across the room. He's ready for something—maybe not a fistfight, but something. Isn't that why he came? He knew what he could expect if he'd stayed at home and there was no appeal to that. Even though some of his friends keep assuring him that the break-up with Martha was the best thing for both of them, it hurt him badly, and he can't help feeling he failed somehow. At the same time, he didn't want to be tied down, he told her, and that's still true. But then, all that personal turmoil is so small and petty against the backdrop of what's going on in the world these days—you're always expecting the TV or radio to be interrupted by a news bulletin, and any time the phone rings, it could be someone you know who's decided to drop out and start a whole new life. It's hard not to feel you're stuck in neutral while important things are happening all over.

Alan is sure he's not the only one at this party who's waiting for something to happen. Certainly it isn't the coming election, now that it's come down to LBJ's stooge Hubert and the diabolical Richard Milhous Nixon. Still, here in the fall of 1968 it's hard to believe things can just keep going the way they've been going: the assassinations and riots, squads of helmeted cops with full body shields and billy clubs charging into crowds to restore things to "normal." What's normal anymore? The world he was part of only a couple of years ago—fishing in a flat-bottomed rowboat on Grass Lake with his Uncle Pete, who'd let him have a few swigs of warm beer as he told his nephew stories about old ballplayers like Walter Johnson and Pie Traynor—that world is as distant as Pompeii. These days Uncle Pete has a George Wallace sign on his lawn and a loaded gun in his glove compartment.

The times are spooky, which is just fine with Zack. "Rivers of blood," he's likely to say after a few tokes. "Flowing through streets of fire." Nothing excites him more than to see people on TV carrying appliances through streets littered with broken glass, engaged, as he says, in the redistribution of wealth, while flames dance on the horizon and sirens wail plaintively in the distance. "This is history," he'll say. "History is the sound of sirens and breaking glass." Looking at the images of rioters confronting cops, he'll smile like a banker contemplating a solid set of returns on an investment. "The rules are changed and all bets are off," he's said. "This is the greatest time to be alive." Zack has the true believer's certainty about the future. "Mere anarchy will be loosed upon the world," he's declared. "I say, bring it on. Look around you: priests and nuns have become troublemakers and convicts are heroes. Anything can happen these days."

That's why Alan is here, isn't it, hoping for something to happen in this room full of strangers? Though at first glance this doesn't seem much different from a dozen other parties he's been to, down to the plastic glass of Boone's Farm Strawberry Hill wine he holds in his hand. Give it time, he tells himself, something's bound to happen. It's enough to send him off on an exploration of other rooms.

As he's easing his way through the doorway, his path is momentarily blocked by an incredibly thin guy with a wispy beard who's wearing ratty jeans and some kind of South American poncho that looks like he's slept in it more than once, and not necessarily indoors. The man cocks his head and squints at Alan, who breathes in the odor of patchouli. "Hey, man," the stranger croons in an accent that Alan can't immediately place, his head and shoulders bobbing in time to his words, "don't I know you?"

Alan shakes his head. "Don't think so," he answers.

The guy blinks, still blocking the door, not aggressively, but with a sly persistence. His hair is long and dirty, his face is cadaverous and his teeth are bad. "You sure, man?" He leans closer. "Mendo, maybe? At Adolf's place?" The man is German, Alan guesses from his accent, or possibly Dutch, and older than he'd first seemed, maybe even over thirty. Though his brow is knit in apparently strenuous concentration, his eyes are glazed and it's not clear that what he's seeing is what most people would call the real world. "You sure you weren't with Marla and Doug in the Epiphany Bus? The Pigmy Forest?"

"Sorry, pal," Alan shrugs, mildly pissed off by the man's persistence. "No bus. No epiphany." He takes a sip of his sweet wine, which is awful. But then, he hasn't had a chance to get stoned yet. "I guess I just look like somebody else."

The stranger frowns, his eyes sharpen accusingly. "You weren't mixed up in what they did to Doug, were you?"

"Hey," Alan feels a surprising flash of anger. "I said I didn't know what you were talking about." He actually brings his face within a few inches of the other man's. Maybe he's destined to punch out somebody tonight after all. "No," he adds firmly. "That's spelled N-O."

The stranger backs away a half-step, suddenly deflated. "Huh," he sighs. "I could have sworn. OK, then, sorry. Sorry." His face sags in confusion and he looks at the floor. "Somebody's going to pay for what they did to Doug, though," he mutters to himself. "Somebody has to pay." When he looks up again his eyes are filled with a visionary gleam. "Amerika is burning," he declares abruptly, making the spelling clear with his pronunciation. He shakes his head as though in wonder, and chants, "Burn, baby, burn."

"Right on," Alan says, pushing past him. The room is heavy with the scent of marijuana, a throbbing bass punctuates the muted seashell roar of talk. He's glad to be rid of the guy but still surprised by his own sudden anger at the stranger's accusatory air. After all, he was a freak, he was stoned, he probably didn't even know where he was, and he'd gotten to Alan anyway. No, he'd never been to Mendo and as far as he's concerned, Doug and Marla can go to hell and take their bus with them.

That night near the Pentagon when the air was filled with the smell of tear gas and the marshal brought his club down on Alan's arm, he was able to jump away quickly, out of the man's reach. The guy was panting, he had no chance of catching Alan if it came to a foot race, but his ice-blue eyes made clear how much he wanted to hit this punk again, hit him hard, hurt him. Looking back at the man, Alan felt nothing but hate. If he'd had a gun, he would have felt no qualms about pulling the trigger.

He moves further into the apartment, a large, high-ceilinged space in the Mill area in a turn-of-the-century brick building that was probably once used for making large quantities of some indispensable household object in a short space of time, enriching a few bearded plutocrats through the labor of exploited immigrants. In the last few moments, Alan has glimpsed a couple of people he knows from school in the crowd around him and he feels a bit more at home here. The host, somebody named George—or was it Greg?—a burly bearded guy in a tattered gray sweater, is in one of the rooms he's left. He was holding court beside one of the few pieces of real furniture in the place, a sofa that was probably declared 4-F by the Salvation Army. An improbably sweet-faced man with granny glasses and rosy cheeks that clashed with his fiercely prophetic beard and his angry rhetoric, he was using the back of the sofa as a podium as he declaimed to a semi-circle of partygoers on the floor about Vietnam, about LBJ and the other fascists who are running the country, about the need to . . .

You hear it so much that after a while you just start to tune out automatically. It's like Muzak these days and like Muzak it finally subsides to a background hum that barely makes a claim on his attention. It isn't ideology Alan wants now, he needs something more immediate. At least it's more promising in this room, where the tall windows cut into the exposed brick look out onto wavering neon stripes of light in the wet street, and under the muffled thrum of talk he can detect the sound of Jefferson Airplane. All right! His irritation with the accusatory stranger falls away, as does his lingering gloom over the break-up with Martha. All doubts and misgivings disappear as the unmistakable opening notes of "White Rabbit" enter his blood stream and his skin tingles in anticipation of Grace Slick's voice joining the beat, climbing, climbing the ladder of sound that will culminate in her exultant declaration, "Feed your head," the ultimate invitation to mystery and change.

The music draws him on, into a narrow passage where he has to make his way through a crowded gauntlet of bodies: he grazes hip and shoulder, feels the brush of hair, encounters anonymous smiles and peace signs. Over it all Grace's voice soars: "One pill makes you larger . . ." So does touch, which is more nourishing than ideology.

Without transition he's become part of this assemblage, sliding in and out of conversations with strangers.

*Can you believe it? Greg pays a hundred and fifty a month and he's got more rooms than Versailles.*

*No way should Hubert Humphrey be on the ballot; he should be tried as a war criminal for supporting LBJ's policy.*

*He could rent out some of this space and make bundles of money but he lets people crash for free.*

*OK, I know it sounds paranoid, but this dude says he has absolute proof that the government is setting up concentration camps for blacks. In New Mexico, I think.*

*I'll tell you, man, it's totally liberating when you boost your first piece of merchandise and strike a blow against private property.*

*If Nixon wins it'll be the last free election before the U.S. becomes officially a fascist country.*

*Ellie and I are leaving for a commune in Colorado next month. We've had it with this bourgeois shit.*

*Of course we have to vote for Nixon because once he's elected we'll be that much closer to the revolution.*

The ambient sound of the party, rising and falling, blurs his sense of time. He's holding a glass of wine, but it might be his third or fourth and, moments after talking to a woman named Marnie who was vehemently denouncing classical music as an instrument of fascism ("Hitler is just the natural extension of J. S. Bach."), he's somehow by himself again. For the moment, he might have become invisible. "We're going to have to blow it all away," an older guy with immense dark eyebrows was saying a few minutes ago, "we're going to have to bring the whole fucking fascist state down with all its jails and police stations and Pentagons."

The morning after his night at the Pentagon, possibly moved by some vestigial Catholic instinct to make pilgrimages to holy places, he'd tried to locate the exact spot where the marshal had whacked him on the arm. The Pentagram, Zack's friend Sophia insists on calling the monumental five-sided building, the place where the evil forces converged, where brute matter suffocated spirit. In the Virginia daylight, though, you didn't need any occult references to scare you. All you had to do was to stand there and take in the structure's immense presence. That morning, with faint traces of tear gas still on the air, Alan hadn't been able to get near the place where the blue-eyed marshal brought the baton down on his arm, which was still hurting. Mostly, he just stood a good distance away looking at that massive edifice flaunting its five concrete sides and at the moment it seemed more ancient than the pyramids, indestructible, and he'd felt a spasm of despair.

Despair, the nuns had taught, was an absence of hope, and that was exactly what Alan felt as he looked at the smug gray solidity of that building. They're going to win, he thought, because they have the guns, the muscle, the money, they own the buildings with their thick walls and they have the machines that can make as many more of them as they want. It's useless to hope because this script has already been written. It was a passing feeling, but it went deep. "You might as well be dead," he told Martha after he'd come back, "if you can't anticipate some surprise in your life, some mystery." He was still fighting what he'd felt looking at the Pentagon. "Jesus," Martha said, "I know that. But you have to have some things you can count on, don't you, some things that won't surprise you?" Sure, sure, he nodded, but they weren't really connecting, it was clear.

Alan isn't here to replay old arguments, though. As if he has a plan, he's been moving from room to room until he's wandered into a relatively quiet space near the back of the apartment, and his heart races when, in the doorway of a long narrow room he glimpses Lily Culp standing near a wrought-iron floor lamp. Talk about serendipity! Framed by the pyramid of her dark blue cape, she's wearing a gold minidress with a wide black belt. A snatch of "White Rabbit" surges up inside him, infusing the scene with a lethal seductiveness. Lily's head is tilted, her jet-black hair falling on one side, and there's a smile on her pale face that's either amused or scornful, possibly both. One hand cups her elbow and a lazy anaconda of smoke twirls up from the cigarette she holds in the other. A weedy professorial type is sitting on a milk crate near her, his glasses glinting as he nods in the general direction of Lily's crotch, and Alan feels a spasm of rage toward this unknown character. Even he's aware of how crazy that is, since he barely knows Lily.

Then and there he determines that he's going to get to know her better tonight. "You want too much," Martha told him, and he couldn't deny it any more than he could explain what that meant. "You don't know what you want." That was true enough too. But just now, regarding the shimmering vision of Lily Culp, he knows exactly what he wants. Maybe it's because there's still a lingering memory of the Pentagon standing there in the morning light, supremely indifferent to the solitary onlooker cradling his hurt arm. He takes another sip of his wine before approaching the pair. He's encouraged by the welcoming nod Lily gives him as the man on the crate looks up at him with barely concealed irritation. "Alan Ripley," she greets him as if they're old friends. "Good to see you."

She introduces him to Trace Wilbur, who is indeed a professor, though not at the City U., where she teaches and Alan is a grad student, but at a tonier women's college just outside of town. Trace, a trim man in his forties, springs up with a polite smile and shakes Alan's hand. In deference to the occasion, his repp tie is loosened. "Well," he explains with an expression of deep seriousness, "you've just walked in on the start of a very interesting discussion we were having about gun control."

The look Lily gives Alan is clearly an appeal, and he guesses she'd be grateful for some relief from this guy who gives every appearance of being an earnest bore. "It's absolute lunacy," Trace directs his words at Alan, "to have all these guns around as if we're living in the Wild West. And we wonder why the U.S. murder rate is so high." He looks toward Lily and when she says nothing he turns back toward Alan. "What I'm trying to do is to organize a group to raise consciousness about gun control. You know: petitions, letters to Congress. There's got to be a way to stop the madness."

Alan gives the man a perfunctory nod. He can see that Lily doesn't share Trace's passion for getting guns off the streets, and he takes a sip of wine instead of saying anything more, struck by the incongruity of her opposition to his plea for disarmament. Thin, stylish and sophisticated, she's hardly the Annie Oakley type.

"We can't let the fate of the country be determined by yahoos with six-shooters," Trace declares, looking again toward Lily for affirmation. "Can we?"

She takes a deep drag on her cigarette and watches the tumbling smoke for a few seconds. "Trace," she says at last, "maybe if you'd have started this five years ago there might have been a chance you could do something." She shakes her head sadly. "It's too late now."

"No, no," he insists with a smile, "that's just my point. We have to do something now, before it does become too late."

Trace looks at Alan, hoping to find an ally, and Alan is about to give some blandly supportive response when Lily speaks again. "Look around you," she says. "What do you see? War everywhere, in Vietnam, in the streets here." She waves her cigarette. "I'm afraid it's too late for petitions and letters to Congress: all of us have to choose sides. Now." She stands there in the cone of light, unyielding. "Everyone can see what's going on in the cities: Detroit, Newark, even here. You haven't forgotten the riots after King's death, have you? And who were the principal victims? Black people are trying to liberate themselves and the establishment is resisting with every weapon in its arsenal. I couldn't," she says, her voice rising, "I couldn't in good conscience lend my support to the systematic disarmament of the black community at a time like this when the cops all over America have declared war on anyone who doesn't have white skin." Her eyes burn with moral indignation and Alan can't help thinking of her as Joan of Arc.

Trace sighs as if he's dealing with a student who just doesn't get it. "But it's exactly war in the streets that we have to try to prevent."

"You can't prevent what's already happening," she counters.

"But can't you see," Trace insists, "that things will only be more dangerous for everyone?"

Lily looks at him impassively. "Then so be it."

Trace smiles to himself and shakes his head. "I can't believe you're such a fatalist."

"I'm not a fatalist, just a realist," she says.

Trace is about to respond when his attention is diverted by a thin, harried-looking woman who's suddenly appeared in the doorway. "Ah, Jane," he acknowledges her presence. "Excuse me," he says to the others, a little guiltily. "It's my wife. We, ah, were supposed to leave a while ago." He looks at Lily. "I guess I got carried away. But it's an important issue, gun control." As he speaks, Jane, who's wearing a decorous wool dress and a string of pearls, can't hide her disapproving scrutiny of Lily. When Trace joins her and they've moved off Lily breathes an audible sigh of relief. "A smart man," she says, "but tiring." Alan basks in the casual sense of intimacy she's created. She takes a deep inhalation from her cigarette and expels the smoke through her nose, a gesture he finds incredibly sexy as well as very European. But then, she teaches European painting at the university.

As the smoke curls slowly around them, the rest of the party seems to be a thousand miles away, and Alan is excited by the fact that the two of them are alone together in one of the outer rooms of this poor man's Versailles. The air is charged, at least for him, since for some time he's had something like a crush on the older woman. He's heard plenty of stories attesting to her capacity to shake people up with her social as well as political behavior. Her ferocious championing of embattled blacks tonight, even at the expense of the general public safety, has done nothing to lessen his admiration for her. Without thinking, he drops onto the milk crate formerly occupied by the departed Trace.

Lily is in her own world for a time and he's content simply to be in the same room with her. "What about you?" she confronts him after a while, her voice pitched low. "What do you think about Trace's ideas?"

He looks at her. Her face is a pale oval with small but perfect features, framed in a dense mane of black. "To be honest," he says, "if you're going to take a narrowly rational point of view, what he was saying might make some sense. But I can see where you're coming from. Yeah," he says, "there are limits to what rationality can accomplish."

She smiles to herself, then turns toward him. "I like a man with an open mind."

He's drawn by the note of invitation he hears in her voice. "It's easy to have an open mind in the present company," he says.

Lily shakes her head, suddenly serious. "But we have to choose these days. We don't have the luxury of staying neutral. Don't you agree?"

He nods.

"God," she says. "People like Trace, well, he belongs in another era, doesn't he?" She looks at him. "I prefer to spend my time with someone who recognizes that the world has changed."

For a few seconds neither of them says anything further, but she looks at him as she draws in the smoke and her green eyes grow larger. There's no doubt that something's going on between them and Alan savors the satisfaction of having, just when he'd most wanted to, said the right thing at the right time.

"I heard you caused quite a stir at a faculty meeting the other day," Lily says.

The spell of longing is broken and Alan is on his guard. Truly, he doesn't consider that episode one of his finer moments. "Yeah," he laughs, "I think they may want to rethink allowing grad students to sit in on those events." He'd been part of a panel arguing for what he thought was a perfectly reasonable liberalizing of the reading list for Freshman English, and the discussion had been civilized enough until that supreme asshole, Charles Arthur Whaley, decided to take up the defense of All Things Sacred. It wasn't long after that that the discussion deteriorated into a shouting match—though to be accurate it was Alan who was doing the shouting while Whaley coolly lobbed epigrams in his direction—that culminated with Alan's storming out of the meeting, letting one and all know as he left the room that he needed to be out among the living. Apparently, the story had got beyond the department.

"You don't seem like the wild man type to me," Lily says.

He laughs. "I'm not," he says, then adds, "but I can be wild if I'm provoked, I guess." Whaley's supercilious "that's not the way we did it at Harvard" attitude had finally got to him. Didn't the man ever read the paper or watch TV? Couldn't he see what was going on around him? His studied lack of curiosity verged on the pathological. "*Bob* Dylan?" he'd exclaimed with arched eyebrows. "I'm still getting used to taking Dylan *Thomas* seriously as a poet."

It got the guffaws he wanted from the half of the department that thought the way he did, and after a few seconds Whaley turned up his hands comically—his timing was as impeccable as Johnny Carson's. He looked at Alan with a patronizing smile as if to say, "You little shit, don't think you can mix it up with the big boys," a formulation he'd never deliver aloud, preferring the statelier cadences of William Buckley. But the smugness of that final gesture was the last straw. Alan had been able to keep his cool up to that point, recognizing that throwing a tantrum would play into the hands of people like Whaley who felt the younger generation was too immature to participate in matters like these; but the fire that blazed up in his gut demanded some action, and leaving the room in a huff was preferable under the circumstances to knocking out a few of Whaley's teeth. Though Jack Stein and a few of the more liberal members of the department applauded him and sent up cries of "Right on," Alan wasn't very proud of his retreat, whatever heroic interpretation you could put on it after the fact. In fact, he'd let them down. The memory of that moment stings even now.

"So how does one provoke you?" Lily asks.

"Oh, it's easier and easier these days," he says. Even that guy who'd asked him tonight if he'd been in Mendo had managed to get to him, hadn't he? "Maybe it's getting too easy."

Lily shakes her head. "We need more of that," she says. "Too many people these days don't get upset about things that should upset them." It sounds like an observation but he can't help feeling that it contains some kind of appeal.

"Well," he shrugs, "I did kind of lose my cool."

"Of course," she says. "That's because you could see that if you kept playing their game with their Robert's Rules of Order and supposedly civil discourse, they were bound to win, since they created the rules, and you wouldn't let them do that to you."

He nods. It's what he's told himself, after all. Still, he remembers his last glimpse of Whaley as he prepared to leave the room. It was clear the older man felt pleased that he'd pushed exactly the right buttons to fluster his opponent. Christ, he thought in the corridor, if the asshole had been a ventriloquist he'd have made me say exactly what I said. "How can you trust anything important to those people?" all of Whaley's pals were no doubt thinking.

"Anger can be therapeutic," Lily says. Her pale skin seems to glow from within. "If we're concerned about being polite all the time, nothing is going to change."

"True enough," he says, hoping that he'd at least managed to ruffle a few of Whaley's feathers. Possibly at home over a scotch that night, the old Tory grumbled to his wife about the young asshole who dared to challenge him. Alan hopes so. Still, though Lily's intensity puts him to shame, it's true he did stand up to Whaley and his crowd, he wasn't neutral, he'd chosen sides, after all. At the moment the memory gratifies him and he feels the same quickening of the pulse he'd felt as he'd looked at the lines of soldiers, cops and marshals and thought, You may have the weapons and the power, but we're right.

At the same time, even as he feels the warmth of Lily's moral approval he senses that a chord change has come over her. In the lengthening silence her face softens, her passionate conviction giving way to a thoughtful expression that by degrees shades into something more playful. After a few seconds Joan of Arc is long gone and an unmistakable naughtiness has entered her eyes. "Do I assume correctly that you might be up for a little cannabis?" she asks with a smile.

Yes, yes, he wants to shout, his heart suddenly racing at the prospect of sharing a joint with Lily; but he tries to keep his answer cool. "Sure," he says, "you can count me in." I've died and gone to heaven, he thinks. Smoking dope with the lovely Lily Culp. Is this a dream or what?

"I know a place that's a bit more private," she says. "It'll be more fun that way."

He springs to his feet and makes a mock bow. "I'm at your service." He has no problem at all with more fun.

He follows her through a couple of rooms and up a flight of narrow stairs, knowing that the recently departed Trace would kill to be in his shoes. "What is this place?" he asks when they reach a room whose purple wall hangings and canopy bed suggest something out of a harem. "Are we in Xanadu?"

"This is the secret garden," she says with a smile. Taking some cigarette papers and a baggie from her large purse, she ceremoniously packs and rolls the paper, then lights up and takes a deep drag with her eyes closed. She passes the joint to Alan, who feels the dope from the first hit. "Wow," he says, "this is potent stuff."

"The best," she smiles. "The gold standard."

He takes another hit. "I believe my mind is ready for a little vacation."

Her fingers brush his as they pass the joint. "Isn't mind the problem so much of the time? It just gets between us and real experience."

The purple wall hangings seem to breathe. "This is some place," he says. "Right out of Ali Baba." Carried away as he is on a surge of pleasure, he still can't help marveling at the change between the militant Lily, impatient with Trace's modest ideas of reform, and the woman who's with him right now, committed, it seems, to the most ancient of pleasures. "I'll bet that's a magic carpet."

Lily's eyes are closed, her smile is loose. "We don't need a carpet to fly," she says. "Not with this stuff." She takes another hit.

"I believe I'm levitating already," he says.

Her eyes stay closed. "All you have to do is want to."

Things speed up and slow down after that, moments detaching themselves from the flow, blending, bending. Somehow a candle has appeared on the carved end table. The quivering flame twists slowly, pulsing, then becomes still; it's transformed into a solid object, a tower of frozen fire that draws you in and cloaks the rest of the room in a darkness that abolishes boundaries, a darkness where you can lose yourself. For a while it's a sweet, beautiful feeling. Then, all at once he feels the need to hold on tightly, clenching, resisting the pull into that darkness. At the Pentagon that night they'd advanced on the building together, chanting, and for a time he'd lost himself completely, he was part of something larger, something truer than the uniform mass of cops with helmets and shields. The earlier tensions were gone and he'd felt no fear, he was part of a wave, a huge, cresting wave that was going to crash against the shore and cleanse everything in its path. Later, though, when they were scattered and he ran panting, hurtling through dark, unfamiliar streets, he knew he was alone.

He focuses all his attention on the candle. He can't let his gaze stray from that point of flame. Where is Lily? Where did she go? Is he all alone here? Will he ever be able to find his way back?

"Hey, where'd you come from?" Time has collapsed on itself suddenly and the candle is just a wax column supporting a flame.

"I've been here all the time, you silly boy." Though she laughs, there's a deep sadness in her voice that he recognizes has been there all along, even when she's seemed to give herself wholly up to the weed. He wants to comfort her, but he remains motionless, watching her long white arm, her white leg, candlelight playing on the gold of her dress. "Where have you been?" she asks, her hair spilling softly as she moves.

There are figures carved into the bedposts, stars on the canopy above the bed, sequins glitter across the room near some kind of altar with the figure of Buddha. He turns when he hears the swish of cloth. "Jesus, Lily, you're beautiful."

"You're a silver-tongued devil, my friend." Her hand moves through the air with the graceful underwater motion of seaweed. Toward him, taking his. "The world is back there in all those other rooms. Listen. Can you hear it?" But sad, under it all, sad.

Now they're kissing, her warm tongue explores his mouth, his own traces the ridges of her teeth. He can taste the sweet marijuana on her breath.

They pull back for a second and Grace Slick's voice is in his head again. "Hey," he whispers, "just like the song."

"Yeah, like the song," she murmurs. "What song?" Her dark hair swirls.

"Any song, all songs." The music moves in his blood. "God, you're gorgeous." Pitch black hair, skin so white. "You could have stepped out of a Botticelli," he says. "Or Modigliani."

"Sweetheart, I'm supposed to make the allusions to art." Her smile could make you cry.

She takes his hand once more and gently moves it downward, under her dress, under her panties, where his fingers touch the dampness.

"Oh, Jesus." His erection is pushing against his jeans.

"Mmm, oh, yeah."

"Jesus."

"Yeah. God, yes." Then just sounds, no words.

His breath is coming fast when she suddenly pulls away, falling back against the pillow, her face hidden behind her black hair. When she turns her head he can see the tears coming from her closed eyes, her mouth clenched tight. "What is it?" He looks at her, watches the silent crying change, become harsher, harder. "What? What?"

She shakes her head, her lips are trembling. "I'm sorry," she says. She draws back and swallows. "I can't."

"OK," he says, "OK," unsure of what's happening.

After a moment she says, "It's just . . ." He waits for more. "When I think about what's going on . . ." She shakes her head. "Somewhere right now cops are hunting down black people."

~ 1988 ~

"Oy," Sam Wasson groans softly, running his left hand along his other elbow. "I fear my tennis days may be nearing an end."

Alan shakes his head. "I know your tricks, you old dog. You're just trying to get an edge for the next time we play. You didn't look hurt out there a half hour ago. It's just that you played a shitty game today." He leans toward his recent tennis partner, who's squinting into the sun. "Come on, you know that if you had the least excuse, you'd be making an appointment to see the lovely Doctor Leslie."

Sam breaks into a radiant smile at the prospect. "Hey, you may just be on to something. This pain is my unconscious giving me a nudge, isn't it?" He rattles the ice in his glass of iced tea, takes a sip and frowns. "Do you think I have a chance with her, though? After all, she handles the ligaments of so many studs. Why would she be attracted to my old bones?"

"Don't be so fainthearted," Alan says. "From what you tell me about her, I wouldn't be at all surprised if she has a fetish for old bones. I think she's just been too shy to tell you, after all." He shapes his hands into a crystal ball. "I can see her in her office wearing her clean white coat. There's a sad look on her face. Why doesn't that cute Sam Wasson call, she's wondering."

"Tell me more, tell me more," Sam says. "I need some solace after the way I played today." He lifts a single potato chip from his plate, puts it into his mouth and chews it abstractly for a few seconds, apparently caught up in a private rapture, then takes a sip of tea. "Well," he says at last, settling back against the wrought-iron chair, "time to return to the real world."

Alan settles back as well. The sun warms his bare arm and he feels a wave of gratitude: he's pleasantly exhausted from a pretty good round of tennis on a glorious June day in this leafy suburb of Boston that he calls home, enjoying a nice lunch here at one of the outdoor tables at Ollie's with pleasant company, Julia and Tommy not a mile away. "Hey, the real world ain't so freaking bad, my friend," he says. The low hum of traffic around them is a soothing chorus.

Sam gives him an arch look. "I'd feel that way too," he says, "if I'd just got a bottle of bourbon from the tenants at Meaney Gardens. I hope you haven't drunk it all already."

That brings a smile to Alan's face. Meaney Gardens had been tough, but he'd finally managed to evict the drug-dealing Sharkey brothers whose noisy parties had brought their dangerous friends to the Cambridge project at all hours, terrorizing the other tenants in Building C. When the case was settled and the Sharkey boys were out, a group of tenants did some research about Alan's alcoholic preferences and chipped in to buy him a bottle of expensive bourbon. It was a gesture that touched him deeply, since he knew how much of a sacrifice that had to have been. "Don't worry," he says, "I'm saving some for you."

"That's a relief." Sam looks out into the street and sighs. Both of them listen to the rustle of the nearby leaves. "God, I love these summer days," Sam says. "I mean, after all the ice and snow we have to put up with around here in New England, we've earned them, few as they may be."

"I'll drink to that." Alan lifts his glass and takes a swallow of the cool, refreshing tea.

"You going to Connecticut this weekend?" Sam asks.

"Yeah." Alan smiles at the prospect of being at his summer place in the Berkshires with his family.

Sam continues looking down the street in the direction of his neighborhood not far to the west. "These days it's a pleasure to walk to the train stop," he says, a wistful quality entering his voice. "I'll let you in on a little secret, pal. I take my time walking to the train in the morning because I like to look at all the long-legged little girls on their way to that ballet school on Warren." When Alan responds with a look of mock horror he's quick to add, "Don't get me wrong, this isn't the confession of an old lech—in fact, it's just the opposite. What I'm saying is that it just seems so . . . nice. The morning light coming through the leaves, all those sweet little girls dawdling along in their tights and colorful leg warmers, carrying their big bags, their ponytails bobbing—it's like suddenly coming upon a bunch of exotic birds in the middle of town and, the best part of all is that everything seems to happen in slow motion." In his silence he seems to be seeing it again. "As far as I'm concerned, those girls don't have to go to any class to learn grace, they've already got it. You know what I think every morning when I see that on the way to the train?"

Alan has been enjoying this lyrical outburst. "What?" he asks.

Sam is beaming, a man who's touched the Holy Grail. "I think, life is good. I think I did OK for myself."

"I know what you mean," Alan says, amused to think that Sam and he have drifted dangerously close to the region of sentimentality usually reserved for old duffers. "Still," he says, "don't look at those girls too long. I don't care what's inside your head. You could get yourself into trouble."

A rueful expression crosses Sam's face, his eyes glint with muted irony. "Don't worry, I told you I'm not in danger of becoming a Humbert Humbert." He's silent for a moment and the sound of a bus shifting gears drowns out everything else. "Now Doctor Leslie," he croons when he continues, "that's another story." His lidded eyes are alert. "Or, for that matter, the lovely Arabella," he adds after a moment, with a curt flick of his head indicating the waitress at one of the other four outdoor tables whose hoop earrings glitter in the sun. When Alan says nothing, Sam adds, "I do have my yearnings."

Alan isn't sure how seriously to take him. "Even though life is good? Even though you've already done OK."

The look Sam gives him is unsettlingly clear-eyed and direct. "Yeah," he says. "Even though."

"Well," Alan concedes, "maybe we all do." At a loss for where to go from there, he turns his attention to what's left of his sandwich, biting through the crusty bread to the chicken brushed with Dijon mustard.

But Sam is obviously not finished with the subject. "OK," he says, more quietly, "don't get worried, pal. I'm not likely to start cheating on Annie." His eyes narrow. "It's just . . . hell, there are moments—this has happened a couple of times lately—when all at once it's as if there's a shift in the wind and I . . . I'm in touch with the way things were when we were all younger, you know, when everything seemed possible. . . . And then it's gone . . ." He's silent for a couple of seconds. "When that happens it can feel like all my horizons have been pulled in pretty tight, I feel this sense of loss . . ." After a moment he asks, "Do you ever feel that way?"

Alan isn't quite ready for this quick transition from the good-natured banter of a couple of minutes ago. There's an unmistakable urgency to Sam's question, but then, he's an intense guy who can get as passionate about a ball game as he can about more weighty matters. "Well, yeah, maybe," Alan shrugs. "But when it happens it's just momentary, just an itch. I scratch and it goes away."

Sam laughs soundlessly. "Lucky you." He leans back and looks into the distance. "Still, don't you sometimes wish you could have some of the old wildness back?"

Alan can see that he isn't going to be let off the hook. "The old wildness?"

"Come on, you can't kid me." Sam's voice is even lower now, as if they've moved into the realm of the most personal of secrets. "I'm sure you feel it too."

Alan turns up his hands as if to deflect a blow. It's an instinctive reaction, but he recognizes that he's on his guard. Something has darted through his memory in the last few seconds, an obscure shape glimpsed under water for the briefest of instants so that you can't be sure, moments later, whether you saw anything at all. He looks around him and reassures himself that he's here at Ollie's on Wellington Street, enjoying a lunch after some tennis with his friend. No, he thinks, I don't want that old wildness back, it almost finished me. When he's aware that Sam is waiting for some response, he says, "Remember, some people never survived that wildness, old friend."

Sam can see that Alan doesn't want to pursue this question. "Yeah," he nods solemnly. "You're right about that." He sighs, and possibly he's remembering friends and acquaintances who failed to survive their wildness. When he looks at Alan again, he doesn't seem to be thinking about those things anymore. "But who could believe we'd survive to see this," he says, "two terms of Ronald Reagan?" He contemplates his own statement for a moment. "Remember when we thought Nixon was as bad as it could get?"

"Hey, now you are going to depress me," Alan says. "I thought just a couple of minutes ago we were congratulating ourselves for having achieved a pretty good life." He lifts his glass, feeling the damp, cool condensation against his palm. "Let's accentuate the positive." He smiles. "I think you were a lot better off thinking about your long-legged young ballerinas."

Sam gives him a grateful smile, then his eyes tighten. "You're right. I sure don't want to sound like the old cynic who'd tell those little girls to enjoy themselves now because things are only going to get worse when they get older."

"No," Alan insists with comic earnestness, "we know you're not that kind of guy."

"Thanks," Sam says. "I hope I'm not."

Alan likes the idea of Sam giving advice to the ballet students. "What would you tell them," he asks, "if, say, you were the commencement speaker at their ballerina school graduation? What kind of grown-up wisdom would you offer them?"

"Don't grow up," he says with exaggerated emphasis; but he dismisses the statement immediately with a shake of his head. "No, no, but," he pauses a moment, searching, "but I suppose I'd want to tell them to enjoy their dancing, only not to pin all their hopes on becoming ballerinas." His brow creases. "God, I wonder what percentage ever do? It's got to be even lower for them than for the hot-shot high school quarterback who thinks he's going to get into the NFL."

"Tell them to keep their options flexible," Alan mimics the motivational speaker.

"Hell," Sam says, "it's a cliché but it's true. It's the only way to survive." He runs a hand across his balding head. It's one of those times when he looks astonishingly like Captain Stubing on *The Love Boat.* "I'm sure if I were able to go back into the past I'd never convince that long-haired freak I was, the skinny kid back in Philly who wanted to be the next Eric Clapton, that twenty years later he'd wind up managing public housing, wearing a suit and tie to work." He smiles to himself. "And actually liking his job."

"True enough," Alan says, moved by his friend's heartfelt admission. "I know the last thing I imagined myself being at that time was a lawyer, especially one who'd sometimes be helping management evict tenants. And liking it," he adds with a laugh. "I guess I'd want to tell those girls not to foreclose the possibility," he says, "of being pleasantly surprised by life."

Sam is clearly caught up in the mood. He nods enthusiastically, though he doesn't say anything for a while. When he does speak at last, it's with a quiet seriousness. "That's certainly true," he says, "but, you know, I owe a lot to that long-haired kid in Philly, and I'd want to tell those girls that even after they leave their old selves behind—which they will, which they'll have to—they should never completely disown them. After all, life's a long and winding road and you'll need all the friends you can find as you make your way around all its twists and turns."

"And detours," Alan adds.

Sam nods in agreement. "Detours and roadblocks." His expression is benign and generous, Captain Stubing presiding over a multiple wedding on the Pacific Princess. He takes a sip of tea and nods to himself. "Yeah, even though you and I are such wise guys now, we can't be too arrogant. There's a certain amount of forgiveness we have to bestow on our old selves."

"Amen," Alan says, though in fact he isn't as enthusiastic about the idea as Sam seems to be. Yeah, he thinks, forgive. But up to a point. In his mid-forties, he feels he's come to a pretty good place in his life, and he couldn't have got there if he hadn't been able to survive some of his earlier selves, forgiving, maybe, but also forgetting, even erasing. From his present vantage point, it isn't exactly magnanimity he feels toward the passionate but confused graduate student he'd been twenty years ago. That earlier version of Alan almost got himself into a huge amount of trouble and was only saved by luck. From that time onward he's been acutely aware of the importance of chance in the affairs of human beings, and he hopes it's given him a better understanding of people who are down on their own luck. But what he feels toward the person he'd been then is mostly relief that he's been able to move beyond him.

He feels a little more charity toward that graduate student's successors, like the misplaced English teacher who'd demonstrated spectacular bad judgment by getting back together with his old girlfriend Martha and marrying her, which brought misery to both of them, a misery that was only bearable because it was brief, though it wrecked his marriage and ended his academic career. In the end, it says something about that person's judgment that he was able to accept the fact that neither the marriage nor the career was working, and he made the right decision by getting out of both. The self who followed took the hermit's path, choosing to hole up in chilly Vermont, not only dropping out of the world but becoming insufferably contemptuous of it, for the best of reasons. At this distance, that whole episode seems like little more than a licking of wounds. But the licking of wounds had been necessary after all. When the hermit was succeeded by the earnest law school student with a fire in his belly for social causes, that was an improvement. The subsequent mutations that have brought him to his present place he regards as little short of miraculous. No, he has no yearning for the old wildness.

"You never look back?" Sam's brow is furrowed.

"I try not to," he answers. It's far too simple an answer but he tells himself that little good is likely to issue out of indulging Sam in his nostalgia.

His friend laughs to himself softly. "I'm not sure how much of that I believe," he says. "Sometimes you get a look: it's like you're sure there's someone behind your back."

"Do I?" Alan says, feeling suddenly accused, and exposed.

Sam's eyes light up. "I think I just struck something," he says. "I saw that look again. It was the look of a man who was afraid that someone was going to take away his bottle of bourbon."

"I sure wouldn't want that to happen," Alan says, recognizing as he says it that he most definitely wouldn't want to lose that bourbon, or the gratitude of the tenants who felt he'd fought for them. That booze is a testimony to his skill and satisfaction with what he does for a living, his whole way of life. "Yeah," he says, rapping on the table, "knock on glass, I wouldn't want to lose my bourbon any more than you'd want to lose your young ballerinas."

Sam smiles. "I guess we're just a pair of lucky guys, then."

"Don't knock luck."


Alan remembers that conversation a couple of weeks later when he gets a phone call at his office.

"Who is it, Sally?" he asks.

"He says he's a friend who knew you when you were in graduate school."

That gets his attention. Why would anyone he really knew in school be so coy as not to give his name? As he picks up the phone and puts it to his ear, he's prepared for somebody who's going to try to sell him something. "Yes?" he answers impatiently. "This is Alan Ripley."

The quiet laugh on the other end of the line is irritating, as is the silence that follows. "Well, well," says a raspy, distantly familiar voice at last, "sounds like you're doing OK for yourself, man." Still, the caller hasn't identified himself, clearly challenging Alan to do so. Alan, who's been put on the defensive, searches his memory, trying to make the connection, convinced now that he knows the speaker whose name continues to elude him. "Your secretary sounds expensive," the man says.

"Who is this?" Alan asks, hearing the testiness in his voice, though it's himself he's angry with for not having been able to come up with the caller's identity.

This time the metallic laugh unlocks something in Alan's memory, even as he recognizes that the laugh is a somehow diminished version of the original he first heard twenty years ago, forced rather than natural. Even in its mutated form, though, it's enough to establish a link, and the realization brings a silent thunderclap. "Rory?" he asks, incredulous. "Rory Dekker?"

"Good for you, dude," Rory says. "I was worried about your memory for a while."

Even in the compliment, if that's what it is, there's a quality of insinuation to the voice that Alan remembers, a sense of challenge. In the old days just lounging at the end of a sofa, saying nothing, the long-legged Rory seemed to be daring you to some sort of competition, and his expression made it clear that he was pretty sure he'd come out on top. Though Alan can hear somebody in the next room using the copy machine, the past is suddenly as close as the tips of his fingers. Jesus! Rory. Too many things are happening at once. Buffeted by the rush of sensations he can't control, Alan couldn't possibly describe what he's feeling. But he's back there and, strangely, the thought of it excites him. It doesn't take long, though, for things to fall back into place and, even as the excitement of this surprising contact subsides, he feels the incursion of something dark and disturbing. "Are you in town?" he asks guardedly.

"Yeah, I'm in town." Rory gives the answer an ironic emphasis, as if it's the punch line to a stale joke, and waits a second or two before going on. "I'm just passing through, you might say."

That brings a modest sense of relief. Alan is still trying to get used to the fact of this surprise reunion—it certainly isn't anything he's been looking forward to, though he's thought about the possibility often enough in the years since he'd first known Rory. Still, with the passage of time, the likelihood that the man would actually get in touch with him had retreated into the realm of the wildly improbable. Rory, Lily, Lyletown—he'd hoped all that was safely buried in the past. Now, with Rory's abrupt reentry into his life, the old apprehension has come flooding back. At the same time, the sense of some looming threat is hard to disentangle from the rush of wonder that the man should suddenly show up like this, reconnecting Alan to a part of his life he's managed most of the time to keep at bay. Just these few seconds of contact have already brought it all back, Lily Culp wielding her cigarette like a conductor's baton, himself and Rory listening, competing even in the quality of attention they're giving her. He remembers Lily's apartment on Chatterton Street with its profusion of colorful pillows, the smell of an exotic incense that came from somewhere in southeast Asia, the heavy hang of the drapes, the seemingly happenstance arrangement of the furniture, the mixture of great art and kitsch on her walls—a momentary refuge from the world outside that was on the verge of explosion. In a single instant it's all there, Ben Fraley, Bobby Pelham, Serena, an improbable assemblage come together to play their parts in bringing about the inevitable and overdue revolution. That heightened sense of possibility, that mixture of fear and expectation he felt in those days is momentarily here with him in the office like a taste in his mouth.

He can't quite come out and ask Rory how long he's been free, but of course he would be by now, wouldn't he? They were lucky, if you can call it that, that the only person killed in the fiasco was one of their own. Still, Rory, the only one of them who'd actually been caught, got an especially stiff sentence from a grandstanding judge who'd wanted to set an example for anyone who was even thinking about threatening law and order in a time of national peril. Arguably, other than Bobby Pelham, Rory paid the greatest price, though you could hardly say any of them got off scot-free. But Alan isn't going to be the one who makes the first reference to that period. "Well," he says, as if talking to Rory Dekker is just a normal part of his work day, "you here for long?"

"Just a day or two," Rory answers, and once again Alan is pleased that whatever contact he has with the man will be brief.

As the silence lengthens, he realizes that the next move is his. "What are you up to these days?" is the best he can come up with.

"Well, that's a delicate way to put it," Rory says, an edge entering his voice. "Yeah, what have I been up to? Let's see."

"Well, I mean . . ." Alan lets it drop. On his desk is a picture of Julia and Tommy, taken on their recent trip to D.C. He remembers the cherry blossoms, the small hotel near Dupont Circle, little Tommy in his green and black-striped rugby shirt running with lots of arm motion beside the reflecting pool, and momentarily he's back there watching his son, his wife beside him, a happy man. At the same time he's here in his second floor office at Ripley and O'Shea just outside of Boston. He hears Barney calling to Karla from his office across the hall, "Karla, can you get me the Pemberley papers?" There's something comforting in the sound of that: the Pemberley papers. In the next room, Sally is typing at her usual furious pace.

"You were the smart one in the end, weren't you?" Rory's voice breaks into Alan's reverie. Alert now, he waits for more. "Smart and lucky," Rory says, and laughs to himself. "Things turned out pretty well for you, didn't they?" Once more the man is silent and Alan's concern rises. What is it? he thinks, What do you want from me? "You've got a nice business, I'll bet," Rory continues, then adds, "a nice family." The last words bring a chill, as though the unseen Rory has somehow glimpsed the picture on his desk and touched it. Don't, Alan wants to say, though he remains silent. "You're married, right?" Rory goes on. "And you've got a kid." Leave them out of it, Alan thinks, trying to beat back the sense of alarm that threatens to engulf him. Hell, he reminds himself, Rory could have found that information reading the alumni magazine. Still, he's on his guard. Don't give this guy any more than the minimum, he counsels himself.

When Rory speaks again, though, it's in another tone entirely. "Ever think about those days?" he asks. The question is posed almost wistfully, with no hint of threat or challenge, all aggressiveness gone from his voice. He seems frankly curious, and even sounds younger.

"Sure," Alan answers neutrally. "Every once in a while, sure."

The voice on the other end of the line is silent for a time. "Christ," Rory says at last, "who would have known, eh?"

Alan suddenly feels ashamed of his earlier suspicion of his old friend's motives, and he experiences a genuine moment of empathy for the man on the other end of the line who, no more than he, could have had any idea in those days where the flow of time would carry him. Who would have known indeed? It's certainly an understandable enough sentiment. "Yeah," he agrees. "You said it."

In the silence that follows he savors this recovery of an easy companionship. For all his instinctive competitiveness and his theatrical California attitudes, Rory wasn't a bad guy. And, hell, they were all so much younger then.

"Hey," Rory says, suddenly almost cheerful, "what do you say we get together for a drink?"

"Today?" Once again Alan is on his guard.

The sounds of the office assert themselves for a few seconds until Rory answers, "Today or tomorrow. Like I said, I'm just passing through town."

Alan considers the proposition—it isn't something he has the luxury of turning down, is it? Of course, he'll have to go. Maybe all Rory wants to do is to talk about old times. It's true, Alan is excited and curious at the prospect of actually seeing him again. But he can't pretend that talking about the old days is all they're likely to do, can't pretend that he completely trusts Rory. This doesn't sound like an invitation to a social visit, and Alan has to be ready for anything. At the very least, Rory might try to hit him up for a "loan" that he isn't likely to be able to repay. That will have to be a calculation for Alan to make, and any such "loan" might be cheap, given that there are other things, weightier matters, the two of them might talk about. In the end, though, this isn't exactly an optional meeting. "I might be able to work it in tomorrow," he says. "Where would you want to meet?"

"I'm staying with friends," Rory says. "I don't have a car. It would have to be down here in the city."

"No problem," Alan says, relieved that Rory won't be making any incursions on his turf. "Give me an address."

"Why not here, from the place I'm calling from? It's a bar called Fred's." He gives an address that Alan recognizes is in a run-down section of the city. That gives him a moment's pause—he'd rather meet somewhere in the Back Bay, somewhere brighter, more open—but Rory's calling the shots, after all. "OK," he says, "I can pop into town during lunchtime. We can get in maybe an hour to talk."

"Great, great," Rory says. "It'll be a reunion of what's left of the Lyletown Six," and Alan immediately regrets having agreed to see him. Well, he reminds himself, an appointment, even after it's been made, can be broken off. Something could always come up. And it wouldn't be the first time Alan failed to keep an appointment involving Rory.


The Lyletown Six, Rory had called them. Those three words triggered a seismic jolt deep in Alan's psyche that abolished all his ideas of security. If it had turned out that way—and it so easily might have—he knows that there would be no law firm of Ripley and O'Shea, no Julia and Tommy, no tennis with Sam Wasson and talk of young ballerinas. It's one of the scariest questions to haunt him: where the hell would he be if he'd have been the sixth member of that group? Blessedly, he'll never know.

He knows this, though: there would never have been a Lyletown without Lily. It was Lily around whom they'd gathered, Lily who'd inspired the episode that brought together politics and guns, a handful of university revolutionaries and a pair of street-wise ex-cons—Lyletown was a political thesis gone botched and bloody, like more than a few others in that time, and it was Lily who'd launched it. And yet, for all the swirl of ideology and talk of revolution that surrounded her, from this distance it seems to Alan that a good deal of what happened could be explained by sex. Though he'd seen Lily Culp at the university and heard countless stories about the pale dark-haired beauty of the Fine Arts department who could scandalize the respectable members of the academy with her indifference to moral and political norms, it was at the party in the Mill section of town that Alan had first gotten an intimate glimpse of her intensity and passionate commitment to radical politics. As Trace Wilbur discovered that night, Lily was determined to do something more than petition Congress about guns. It was too late, she'd insisted to him, the struggle between freedom and repression in the country had reached a desperate, apocalyptic stage, and the forces of repression were on the verge of winning. "I was on the Pettis Bridge in Selma in '65," she told Alan later. "Believe me, that was scary and dangerous, but that was a lot more hopeful time, maybe a naïve time. Look what's happened since. The days of peaceful marches are over."

From the beginning, Lily's capacity for total conviction had fascinated Alan. She was so cool, so sophisticated and articulate on the surface, but underneath she was impelled by a hunger even she probably couldn't understand. A child of privilege from Philadelphia's Main Line, she'd felt a grievous sense of responsibility for the injustice in the world. In her professional life she might conduct herself as she'd been trained, studying paintings attentively and analyzing them with care, reserving judgment; but outside the boundaries of her discipline, she wasn't able to just watch, she was driven to act, and she was capable of acting impulsively, a gambler willing to risk everything on a double-or-nothing wager. How, Alan wondered, did she manage to reconcile the contending forces in her psyche? It was just one of the questions about Lily about which he had an insatiable curiosity.

But Lily wouldn't ever have gotten involved in the Lyletown business if it hadn't been for Serena Beltin, the daughter of middle-class Catholics from Attleboro, Massachusetts. Serena, a recent B.A. with a sociology degree and a consuming mission to change the world, had been instrumental in setting up a program at her university that brought teachers to prisons and ex-cons to school. In her mid-twenties, she might have been half-attractive, but she worked hard at making herself resolutely plain, using no makeup, her hair cut brutally short, dressing like a Russian peasant. Solidly built, she was strong: she could do heavy carpentry and wasn't shy about manual labor. The key to Serena, Alan always thought, were the intense blue eyes behind her horn-rimmed glasses.

Those eyes revealed an open and naked need to believe totally in something.

The story that as a girl she'd wanted for a time to be a nun was entirely credible. Though she'd emphatically given up religion and would therefore have despised the nuns' blind faith, she was clearly looking for its equivalent. Alan's friend Zack, who was no fan of hers, said that instead of becoming the Bride of Christ Serena chose to be the Bride of Marx. But analyzing and criticizing the status quo wasn't just an ideological exercise with her. "We're enemies of the state," she'd say. "We're all criminals in their eyes." She was a fighter who admired other fighters. Ironically for the once would-be nun, the highest compliment she could imagine was being called "unrepentant." Point me in a direction and tell me when to go, she seemed to say.

Lily needed Serena because Serena put her in touch with her convicts, as she was accustomed to calling them. Serena needed Lily for all sorts of reasons, though from what Alan was able to observe, the most important reason may have been that she was in love with Lily. Her emotional life was as passionate as her ideology and she was never content with half-measures. She must have quickly sensed something similar in the other woman, ostensibly so different from her. How Lily responded to Serena in private was something Alan had no way of knowing; but Lily had a way of making people believe she was reciprocating their response to her. He knew he'd been in love with her and he was certain Rory had been. Possibly they all had been.

The two women met at a peace rally a couple of months before the party where Alan had encountered Lily debating guns with Trace Wilbur. Serena told Lily about the prisoners she worked with at the university. "The guys who are incarcerated get to see the real America," she said. "They have a lot to teach us." Lily said she'd like to meet some of them and Serena was glad to oblige by introducing her to a pair of her prize students.

Ben Fraley was an ex-con who'd served time for killing a man in a bar fight. It hadn't been Murder One, but according to Bobby Pelham—who claimed that Ben had confided in him—it had been a very violent affair. "He's killed other guys," Bobby said. "He told me." In the writing program Serena oversaw, Ben proved to be a skilled and vivid storyteller, one of his most memorable efforts being a first-person account of someone who beats a man to death with a tire iron in the parking lot of a bar. "I watched him die," the narrator said, "and I was surprised at how little effort it took to kill somebody. Hell, I'd worked up more of a sweat cutting down a scruffy little pine tree on my granddaddy's farm." Who knew whether it was invented or autobiographical? A big, gregarious, bearded man in his forties, Ben could be personally charming but in the end he was intensely private. Alan doubted that he'd really confided in Bobby, or anyone. In the middle of one of his funny stories, his eyes could go steely for an instant and you had no trouble believing he'd beaten somebody to death with a tire iron and reflected on how easily it had been accomplished. On the surface he was a sweet-talker with a touch of a drawl who spoke a lot about going back to Alaska, where he said he'd spent his happiest times. There was something of the actor about him; it was clear he had an itch for the spotlight. It obviously flattered him to be made much of by these college types.

Over the course of time, Alan learned that Ben had gone to bed with Lily, and though, in keeping with the spirit of the times, neither Ben nor Lily made a big deal of it, it upset Alan. He wasn't being macho or proprietary, he told himself, but it did bother him to think that for Lily his own interrupted sexual interlude with her must have meant very little, since it was never resumed. It must just have been the dope, he thought, or a passing mood. They were supposed to be beyond thinking of sex in proprietary terms; still, it could drive Alan into a rage to imagine Ben, after the act, smiling and stroking his beard with immense self-satisfaction.

Bobby Pelham was another story. He was a small-time crook who'd met Ben in prison. Bobby, a weasely balding guy in his thirties with Elvis sideburns, liked to affect con attitudes, like carrying his pack of cigarettes in the sleeve of his tee-shirt. He had an endless supply of colorful tales of his hard times in prison. Bobby didn't need any college, Ben said, because he already had an advanced degree in bullshitting. He liked to present himself as an insider who knew how things really worked. Everyone, in his version of the world, was on the take, and all the major sporting events were fixed. He laughed a lot but his temper could flare up unexpectedly, and Alan was always dubious about his ability to carry a thing through on his own. While Ben strutted even when he was sitting down, Bobby seemed able to slouch when standing perfectly erect. Alan thought of Bobby as the eternal sidekick who needed someone like Ben to hang on to; but Bobby was important to the group because he had a number of local contacts, and it was he who'd gotten the information about Rick's Guns'n'Ammo in Lyletown.

By the time Alan came into the picture, the scheme was already well into the talking stage. Lily, for all her intellectuality, put a high value on her intuition, and it was clear she decided from the start that Ben was Robin Hood and Bobby was one of his Merry Men. After all, the two cons eagerly chorused their amens to all her characterizations of American society. "You're pretty sharp about the world for somebody who hasn't done serious prison time," Ben told her with one of his winning smiles. "That's the most flattering compliment I've been paid in a long while," she said, her hand going to her hair. Lily and Ben clicked from the beginning, and it wasn't long before she was voicing her frustrations to him about not being able to do as much as she wanted to change American society. One of her recent causes was that blacks needed guns to protect themselves. "Black people don't need any more white people marching for their rights. They need guns. If only there were a way to provide them with weapons for self-defense."

Alan hadn't been present at this scene—it had been related to him—but he could easily imagine Ben's response. "You need guns?" he'd muse, stroking his beard and falling silent for a moment before answering his own question, "You can always get guns."

"But they'd need a lot of guns," she'd counter.

"You could get a lot of guns," Ben would say quietly. Then he'd flash that smile again, the smile that made you believe that only he and you were in on a secret. "You know how they say the first step toward being rich is wanting to? Well, you have to want to. Do you?" He'd be looking right at her. "I do," she'd say, like a bride, and he'd just keep looking at her.

What was in it for Ben? Alan has often wondered since. Why would he want to get hooked up with a bunch of dreamy amateurs? Certainly there was a sense of power, of sexual domination, even a pedagogical impulse being fulfilled in directing this motley crew. He was a bit of a Civil War buff and possibly he saw himself as a battle-toughened Reb officer shaping a group of skinny recruits into a band of seasoned guerillas. But there was a hard-headed streak in him as well, so that it wouldn't just be ego games he was playing. It was no secret that he was getting tired of being here in the lower forty-eight, tired of just talking about Alaska. Something, maybe a birthday, an anniversary of an important event in his life, had made him suddenly impatient to get there; and it's possible he was hubristic enough to feel he could make a quick score, skip parole and then disappear in the northern wilds, only to resurface as someone else. All he needed was a bit of money. In fact, for that kind of money he didn't need to get involved in an elaborate scheme like the one they were planning, but it must have appealed to his imagination to do it this way, possibly it had even become crucial to his sense of who he was.

The plan they'd got to talking about involved a gun store in Lyletown, a dreary settlement in the boondocks north of the city. Bobby's sources told him that the security there was pathetic. "Strictly amateur hour," he told them more than once, bursting into high-pitched laughter every time he said it. That was the beauty of the situation, according to the cons: it would be like picking fruit from trees and there would be no need for violence. The group could look forward to quite a haul, enough to satisfy both sides of this alliance of convenience. The anticipated booty would be taken to Lily's cottage on a nearby lake. Lily, who wanted to have her share of the weapons conveyed through a middleman to some people she knew on the radical fringes of the black community, would keep her half; while Ben and Bobby would fence theirs, the proceeds to send Ben to the Yukon, while Bobby could spend his money as he pleased.

"Do you want to do something to help change things?" Lily had asked Alan after that first night. "Do you want to be part of the problem," she quoted Stokely Carmichael, "or part of the solution?"

"Of course, I want to help," he said, hoping he sounded determined enough. What he wanted to do most of all was to impress Lily.

Lily's pale beauty was wreathed in smoke. "Good," she said. "Because if we work together we can move history along, we can give it a shove. We can change things." Alan remembered his uncle Pete telling him, only once, about being part of the D-Day landing. "What I saw," he said and then stopped. A long moment later, he shook his head. "I seen hell, I'll tell you that." After a while he said, "But we changed history. They'll never take that away from me."

If Lily was thinking about history, it wasn't about D-Day. A more compelling precedent for her was John Brown's raid on the federal stores at Harper's Ferry in 1859. "Imagine the courage that took," she said, "to challenge the government that way, to force society to look at what it didn't want to see. Imagine the dedication." Of course the episode was a failure on the surface: the slave insurrection that Brown had hoped for never materialized and he himself was hanged. But his radical action hastened the Civil War and, ultimately, emancipation. "It wouldn't have happened by itself," she said. "Someone had to act. Someone had to resist the inertia and go beyond petitions and prayers and take action, even violent action. Someone had to be willing to be impolite, to cause trouble, because John Brown knew that people in power are never going to surrender that power willingly, it has to be taken from them." She closed her eyes. "And the strength of the man was enormous. Is it any surprise that at the gallows he didn't regret a thing he'd done?

"How can anyone who looks at America today just stand by and not act?" she demanded. Alan remembered Arthur Whaley's smugness, his clever put-downs, his sense that his kind would never be dislodged from their privileged positions. How could you not take sides?

And, of course, what they were planning wasn't exactly another John Brown's raid.

Away from Lily, his doubts about the relationship of the proposed theft of guns to the larger issues he believed in sometimes threatened to get the better of him, and he'd need to reassure himself. Hadn't he, like everyone else, had plenty of experience with government lies, with police cover-ups? Hadn't he, on a more personal level, encountered federal marshals a little too eager to carry out their duties? In the end you had to do something, to strike back, if only to prove that you existed, though it wasn't just something you were doing for yourself—that was the point. It was certainly better that blacks have guns with which to defend themselves than that armed white vigilantes should freely roam the city streets looking for unarmed ghetto dwellers to kill. Though the operation in Lyletown was designed to be quick and surgical, you couldn't absolutely exclude the possibility of violence, which was a troublesome issue to Alan. It eased his conscience a bit that his only role in the affair would be to watch, to make sure there were no surprises—he wouldn't be doing any rough stuff. In retrospect, he realized that he could have asked Lily how she could be sure the guns were going to get into the right hands. He could have asked her how completely she could trust a pair of shady characters like Ben and Bobby. He could have asked her if she really thought the operation was going to go as smoothly as bullshitter Bobby claimed it would, whether she was really so indifferent to the prospect of somebody getting hurt. But he didn't.

The craziness of the plan should have been evident in Ben's willingness to let people like Rory in on it. Rory just turned up one day and managed to talk his way into the group. A friend of Serena's brother, he came east that summer and crashed for a time at her place. With his long blonde hair and his fringed jackets and cavalry hat, he gave off an aura of some glamorous western hero like Buffalo Bill or George Armstrong Custer. In those days he moved with a kind of loping majesty and an air of confidence that only a very handsome man could have carried off, a man who was used to his devastating smile opening all doors. He'd been living on the margins, like a lot of people in that time, selling a little dope, listening to music, even resorting to occasional panhandling; but it took only a few minutes' conversation with him to realize he'd always felt destined to do something important. He'd been kicked out of a dozen high schools out west but, as he was quick to tell you, even as his teachers reluctantly expelled him from class, they reminded him that he was "exceptional."

Rory, if he was to be believed, was the son of a maverick lawyer in L.A. who defended the indefensible, an open atheist who loved nothing more than pulling the beards of authorities, so Rory's scholastic misbehavior might well have been transmitted genetically. When he was kicked out of one school after another his father cheerfully took his side. "They need that kind of shaking up," he'd declare when his son described the prank that brought the fire engines to the school. "It keeps them on their toes." His father died in a car crash under questionable conditions that Rory never spelled out when he told the story, though it had clearly been a shock to him, as was the discovery that the man had left his family with nothing but debt. His mother, stoic to the end, did her best to repair the damage her husband had caused, and Rory never forgave her for that. He dropped out of college, cut his ties to his family and began to wander the American earth until he turned up at Serena's place. He was bored by the bespectacled revolutionary types who showed up there spouting their ideological jargon, but he was immediately drawn to Ben and began to mimic his manner. What could be more natural than for him to see himself as an outlaw?

Ben was flattered by the appearance of a potential new disciple, though Bobby was clearly jealous and there were obvious tensions. But Ben was amused by Rory and even seemed to like him in a fatherly sort of way. It was Ben's word that was final and it was Ben who decided to cut Rory in on the deal.

The plan as it had been worked out called for Ben and Bobby to drive north in a van with Serena, arriving after the store had closed. The two cons would do the actual work of boosting the guns and ammo, while Serena, who was the best driver in the crowd, would be at the wheel with the motor running in the nearby parking lot, ready to bring the van around to the back of the store when she got the flashlight signal from the successful thieves. Alan, who was to drive up in his own car, would be posted as a lookout at a nearby intersection where he could command a view from another angle than Serena's. If either of them saw something potentially disturbing, they were to signal with a blast of the horn. Meanwhile, Lily would be up at her cottage on Moon Lake, waiting for the loot. Having overheard some of the planning, Rory talked his way into the deal by volunteering to run a diversionary activity to distract the small-town police force: at the time the robbery was taking place, he'd use a borrowed car to execute a bit of very visible reckless driving that would take the cops in another direction.

"We don't need that, Ben," Bobby protested the proposed wrinkle in their plans. "It's getting too complicated."

"No, no, I like it," Ben declared. Bobby scowled and Serena shook her head.

As a plan, it was no more foolish than a lot of actions taken during that superheated time. The thing was, the Caper, as they'd come to call it, was no sooner articulated than it was put on hold. There had been the rush and thrill of committing oneself to something risky, something that, though it could keep you awake at night, you could convince yourself you'd be doing for the greater good; and then, at least for Alan, there was the possibility that in the end it might be just talk, which was comforting to him, since his level of courage about the planned action, he'd found, could oscillate wildly. So for a time everyone waited. Meanwhile, Ben would tug at his beard. "Timing is important in something like this," he counseled his fellow-conspirators; and Alan could believe that, having gotten them all to agree to his fantasy, Ben was satisfied enough—maybe he was even getting cold feet. "What about the Caper?" Lily or Serena would urge him. "It's coming along," Ben would tell them. "We're working on it." Alan could see the tension growing between Lily and Ben. Had she been taken in by this con? she might have begun to wonder.

Later, Alan sometimes tried to convince himself that it was another person completely who let himself be caught up in an enterprise so clearly shady, so dangerous as the Lyletown business; but he knows that looking backward at a particular moment in one's life inevitably falsifies the story, since the person who's remembering knows how things are going to turn out, while to his predecessor, living in the uncompleted moment, everything seems possible, even something as chancy as the Caper. So of course it wasn't unthinkable for him to join a desperate, patched-together plan with dubious possibilities for success and undoubted illegality that clearly, for all of Bobby's happy talk, held at least the possibility of winding up with somebody getting hurt, or worse; a venture in which he was willing to put his trust in people he didn't know very well, including a couple who'd already been judged by society to be criminally untrustworthy, a venture he'd joined to a large extent because he was dazzled by a woman. To realize how close he came to being caught up in all this can give him a chill even today. And yet in his moments of conviction he'd believed, because he'd wanted to believe, that this crime would hurt nobody and would actually wind up helping an oppressed group of people defend themselves. His views on all sorts of things were in flux at the time. Even as he was considering the Caper, if someone had asked him about how things were likely to be changed for the better in America, he might have said he was an advocate of non-violence, like the late Martin Luther King. Yet the truth was that he believed all sorts of things, some of them contradictory; and in the end it was possible to be morally bullied by someone like Lily, with her unshakable sense that the moment was desperate and desperate measures were called for.

Alan doesn't believe in fate but he certainly believes in chance, and it was the luckiest of chances for him that just at the time when the on again-off again Caper was switched definitively on, he started experiencing stomach pain and nausea that led to an emergency appendectomy and hospitalization, with complications that prolonged his stay. He's assured himself countless times since that appendicitis isn't psychosomatic, but he still wonders.

The others weren't so lucky, since the plan went disastrously bad. Ben, probably pressured by Lily to put up or shut up, finally had all his ducks in a row, he told her, though now the group had to act on short notice. Alan's sudden illness wasn't going to be allowed to change things in any essential way: Rory would simply take his place and the diversionary drive would be scrapped. In some ways it would be better to keep the whole operation tighter, Ben had said at the time. As he lay sedated in his hospital bed, the sounds around him blending into the dim oceanic roar inside a shell, Alan wasn't thinking about any of this. Had he been, he probably would have breathed a sigh of relief.

It would have been a sigh well-justified. The Lyletown Five, as the papers quickly named them, started out as planned, with Lily going to the lake and the other four driving a stolen van to Lyletown. It was a clear moonlit night, which made concealment more difficult—but of course no one had thought about that. Rory, who'd come up in the van and was posted at the intersection near the gun store, must have felt exposed, which would have made him nervous. Meanwhile, according to the news reports, Ben and Bobby had more trouble breaking into the place than they'd counted on, and things went much more slowly than they'd planned, which had thrown off the timing of events. When an off-duty cop named Rossi came up one of the streets that neither Rory nor Serena could see, he slipped past the watchers and, suspicious about the half-open door in the alley, started poking around. It would have been about then that Rory, disturbed by the lengthening time of the operation, went to the van where Serena was at the wheel. He wanted her to give some kind of hurry-up signal, like a blast of the horn, but she refused, since that wasn't what the signal was supposed to mean. Probably as unnerved as Rory, she insisted on staying at her post as planned and waited for the appearance of the flashlight in the store window. That was too much for the impatient Rory, who decided on his own to find out how things were developing.

Meanwhile Rossi, who was by now convinced there was some mischief going on, went around to the back of the building. When he entered the gun store, he surprised the two ex-cons. Bobby, who certainly hadn't told anyone he was carrying a gun, panicked and started firing at the cop, hitting him in the leg; but Rossi, though wounded, managed to shoot Bobby, hurting him badly. In a few seconds the deal was suddenly off—there was going to be no huge haul of weaponry, no complicated division of the booty, it was just time to try to save your ass—and Ben gave the signal to Serena, who quickly brought up the van, into which Ben managed to drag his wounded partner. The police sirens may already have been sounding when Rory, who'd managed just at the wrong time to make his way to an observation point behind the store, recognized that things had gone awry. From atop a dumpster in the alley, he saw Serena drive up quickly and he realized there was a real chance he might be left behind. In a desperate attempt to catch up with the van, he jumped off the dumpster, breaking his ankle. According to Rory's testimony, Serena didn't stop for him, and the van apparently headed straight for the lake as planned, though the fugitives were carrying no cargo but the mortally wounded Bobby Pelham, who'd received a shot to his stomach. Nobody knows for certain what happened on that ride. Either all three of them got to the lake together, or, just as likely, Ben jumped ship somewhere along the way. In any event, none of those who survived, including Lily, was heard from again. Bobby's body was found near Lily's cottage, and the bloody van was discovered the next day in a neighboring state. Back at the site of the attempted robbery, the police quickly arrested Rory who, being injured, hadn't been able to drag himself away. In the only good break they got, Rossi hadn't been badly wounded and would soon recover. Rory cooperated sufficiently to identify the others, but he was the only one of them who had to do jail time.

The days following the Lyletown affair were dark and fraught with anxiety for Alan. No amount of attentive nursing or sedating chemicals could suppress his sense of how awfully things had turned out for his comrades. Bobby Pelham was dead—it seemed incredible. Sure, Bobby was a loudmouth with an inflated sense of himself, but to bleed to death from a gunshot wound in a van that was hurtling through the night-time roads in a panicky flight seemed too horrible a fate for anyone. And Rory, crippled, taken by the cops who no doubt treated him roughly—that didn't match up with any of Alan's images of Rory. As for the others, would they too eventually be caught and brought back in shackles? Even if they eluded capture, they were now outlaws, branded as outsiders by the society they'd been trying to change. Because of the botched robbery, Lily was no longer the person she'd been a few days earlier. When she'd made her passionate declarations about the need to move history along, had she ever imagined that it might turn out this way? Maybe among the survivors it was only Ben and Serena for whom the role of fugitive seemed natural or appropriate. Alan had little trouble believing that the two of them had clearly imagined the possible outcome, that they'd been ready for it.

Appalling as it was to contemplate how the deeds of a single night had changed everything for these five people who were such an important part of his life, Alan couldn't help being aware of the consequences of that action for himself. When the cops pursued their investigation, would they eventually come around to him? It was certainly possible, he realized with a shudder of dread, and when that happened, his life could change the way the others' lives had. He hadn't been there and yet they could still get him, they could send him to jail for the part, however small, he'd played in the planning of the Caper. Would Rory identify him? Would the police track down any of the others? What would they say? As he recuperated in the hospital he eagerly scanned the papers, he paid attention to the TV, all the while waiting in terror for the other shoe to drop. In his hospital bed, his stitches healing, he felt an overwhelming sense of injustice. He hadn't even been in Lyletown, and still it was possible they were going to make him part of what happened that night.

Back in his apartment after he was released, he waited, entertaining wild thoughts of fleeing to Canada, of turning himself in to cut a deal, but he could settle on no course of action. He didn't pray exactly, but he promised himself that if he escaped being implicated in the Lyletown affair, he was going to put all this behind him. He realized now that he should never have let himself get involved in the first place. Really, all he wanted was another chance.

Eventually, a couple of bored detectives who were impatient to get to lunch, came to the apartment and asked him a few questions about the fugitives; but in the end he wasn't connected to the attempted robbery.

When one radical leader after another dismissed the Lyletown affair as amateurish adventurism rather than a legitimate step toward the revolution, the Caper's failure was complete. That didn't keep it from scaring the hell out of a lot of people and, incidentally, shutting down Serena's program for ex-cons at the university.

Alan is restless when he gets home. It's been a long time since he's been so consumed by images from that period. It's over, he's told himself again and again. It was a major misjudgment to have let himself get involved that way but, thank God, he'd been lucky enough to escape the consequences of what could have been the worst mistake he'd ever made. The life he's created for himself since then has been a way of turning that good fortune into something positive. Still, moral questions aside, he can't deny that he'd once had a stake in the Caper, and he's been endlessly curious about what really happened that night. Why did Ben and Bobby have so much trouble at the gun store when it was supposed to be such an easy job? Did they take out their frustrations on each other? Were they too distracted by that to notice Rossi snooping around? When did Rory, lurking in the alley, first realize that the robbery had gone bad? What did it feel like to recognize that he might be abandoned by the others, that he might be left to take the fall? And what about Serena? Did she want to stop for Rory, or did Ben force her to keep driving? As much as he wishes he weren't meeting Rory, maybe the man has some of the answers, or at least guesses, about those questions.

On the screened back porch of the rambling Victorian he bought last year, he savors the first sip of bourbon—not the expensive stuff the tenants gave him, which he's saving, but good old Jack Daniel's. As the liquor warms him, he runs his hands along the back of the wicker chair and is pleased, as he often is, with his house. "It's more space than we need for now," he'd told Julia after the building inspector had given his favorable report. "I know," she said, "and there's a bit of work we have to do with the upstairs." But both of them knew they were just talking, they'd already made up their minds. Closing his eyes, he breathes in the smell of wicker that evokes both memories and promises of summer; and yet, like the faint buzz of a mosquito that's heard on the summer air, part of his consciousness keeps getting pulled away from the present, attentive to the fact that Rory has turned up.

"What's the matter?" Julia asks. "Looks like you've got something on your mind."

His eyes travel across the green, sloping swath of his backyard that runs all the way to his neighbor's weathered stockade fence. "Sorry," he says. "Just stuff. You know: stuff from work."

Julia's glass of wine is on the table. She stands a few feet away, clutching her elbows. "Anything serious?" she says. "Anything that's causing problems?"

He shakes his head and gives her a bright smile. "Sorry to be such a drag." He's never told Julia about the Lyletown affair and the role he played in it. There are times when this has bothered him, and on occasion he's been tempted to tell her, but never enough to overturn his decision long ago to disown that former self and bury it deep. The fact is, even he has a hard time thinking of himself as the kind of person who came so close to getting involved with guns and cons in an affair of questionable morality that wound up with somebody dead and might well have produced even more casualties; it would be impossible to explain it to anyone else. It's better, he's decided, to keep the different parts of his life in separate layers, like geological strata. My Pleistocene era, he sometimes thinks.

His secrecy about those times is a measure of his determination to distance himself once and for all from the person he'd been twenty years ago. To be truthful, though, his motives for keeping the past past aren't just a matter of psychic rehabilitation, since Lyletown is hardly a dead issue. He's well aware that if his connection to that episode, however indirect, were somehow to come out, there could be all sorts of nasty legal as well as professional complications.

"You sure there isn't something you want to tell me," Julia says. "You've been a little different lately."

"Different. How do you mean?" He gives her his full attention.

She smiles sadly. "I don't know. It's like maybe, you aren't completely happy with the way things are going between us?" She's careful to make it sound like a question. "I mean, I'm spending a lot of time at school, I know."

He takes a quick step toward her and pulls her to him. "Don't ever think that," he says, squeezing her. "I'm the luckiest guy in the world and I know it. I've got a great wife and a great family. What more could I want?"

"You'd tell me, though," she says, pulling back with a tentative smile. "You'd tell me if you did feel that way?"

"Yes," he says. "Absolutely." He's running his hand along her back, when suddenly the sound of the phone ringing alarms him, and he pulls away from Julia to answer it.

"It's for you," he's relieved to tell her. "It's Janet."

As she talks to her colleague from the college, Alan wonders about what she'd said. Is she on to something? It's true he's felt a bit of restlessness lately—Sam's confession a couple of weeks ago about vague yearnings was something he could understand all too well, even as he quickly changed the subject. And what had Sam said about a sense of loss? Of course, you were always losing things, weren't you, saying goodbye to things? Is it possible, Alan wonders, to be simultaneously very happy and dissatisfied?

Even that bottle of bourbon from the tenants. The other night, he hadn't been able to sleep and wandered into the dining room, where the bourbon was on a shelf on the breakfront. He picked it up, the cool beveled glass pressing against his palm as the liquid inside sloshed pleasantly, and in the midst of his sense of gratification, he suddenly felt a stab of melancholy. Was this what his life had come down to in the end, a bottle of booze? It made no sense, he knew, but once again he was stirred by a sudden restlessness.

Looking back on it now, he can't deny the power of the feeling—it bordered on the uncanny. Could it be that his agitation came from his awareness somehow that Rory was about to reenter his life, complicating everything? That's impossible, he thinks, but that doesn't keep it from seeming true anyway.

"She wanted to have lunch with me tomorrow," Julia says when she comes back, "but I thought maybe you and I could meet somewhere in town instead." She winks. "Sort of like a romantic tryst." She laughs. "I love that word, tryst, don't you?"

"Damn it, honey," he says, "I just happen to have plans already for tomorrow at lunch time."

She frowns comically. "I should have known. I was just trying to keep my options open. But I guess Janet will still be available if I call her back."

"Hey, we'll have our tryst anyway," he says. "Maybe next week." Even as he says it, though, the sense of betrayal weighs on him.

Later, by himself, he's still remorseful about having to choose Rory over Julia, if it's fair to put it that way. But then, meeting the man who took your place and went to prison isn't exactly the kind of thing you can just blow off. Alan can't refuse. The sheer power over his circumstances that Rory holds makes this obligatory. There's no use trying to kid himself that he has a choice in the matter. When Rory calls, Alan has got to go, because this is important—more than important, it's dead serious. From the moment he heard that voice on the phone, he felt himself being drawn into an area of risk, even danger. The words the two of them exchanged were banal enough; still, in the very fact of Rory's making contact there was some kind of challenge, even the hint of a threat. Alan can't help thinking about the fairy tales he reads to Tommy, where an honest woodsman might be visited by a strange creature—a troll or dwarf or talking bird—he vaguely remembers encountering once deep in the forest. All too soon the woodsman comes to realize that he's made some kind of promise to the creature that puts him under a terrible obligation.

No, Alan tells himself, Rory hasn't asked for anything, has he? Why not just take him at his word, that he wants to get together and maybe talk about old times?

The fact is, there's no way Alan can pass up this chance to look his old friend in the eye. Who knows? Maybe Rory has answers to some of his questions about what happened that night in Lyletown. But it isn't just information that he's looking for. Underneath whatever else might be motivating him, there's one particularly nagging concern: Alan has never known how he'd have acted had he had a chance to play a role in that bungled robbery. Even though he has no doubts today that the episode was ill-conceived and not justifiable on any grounds, ethically or politically—if he had the chance to do it all over, he's convinced, he wouldn't touch it with a hundred foot pole—the fact that at one point in his life he'd actually consented to it and then been prevented from taking part has left a kind of blank space inside. He'd signed up for a test that he ultimately didn't take, and that's left some things unresolved to this day. Would he have been brave or cowardly in Lyletown, how would he have acquitted himself? He'll never know, of course, and talking to Rory isn't likely to settle any of those questions; but maybe sitting across the table from him might bring him closer to the answer. In the end, the opportunity having presented itself, he can't fail to take it.


It's warm in Boston the next day as Alan pulls off the Pike and makes his way along the fringes of the new South End. Within its tidy pockets of gentrified row houses, it isn't unusual these days to see a baby carriage or two of the white middle class stopped beside a small park enclosed by a nineteenth-century fence with wrought-iron railings. If the sixties were about revolution, the eighties are certainly about real estate. Not long ago it was gay pioneers who were rehabbing these old houses, paving the way for the white professional families that would later move back into the city. The bistro on the corner, the nearby coffee shop and the florist bespeak a benign version of urban life. You'd have to slow down and look more closely at some of the handmade signs on lampposts and store windows to get a sense of just how much AIDS has insinuated itself into every corner of this area, casting a pall on the neighborhood of red brick, gaslights and bay windows.

As Alan moves south on Columbus Avenue, this well-tended enclave gives way to other blocks where buildings of the same vintage are considerably more rundown, the sidewalks speckled with broken glass. On the fringes of Roxbury, trash litters the pavement, storefronts that house barbecue joints and churches, bars and liquor stores, smoke shops and corner groceries sport metal bars, grating and rolling security gates. The population here is darker, and amid the stir of people going about their daily business, there are occasional islands of solitary men in wrinkled pants who stand looking vacantly at the passing scene. This is exactly the kind of community Lily Culp was hoping to help toward its liberation by giving not alms but arms. In 1988, there seems as much need for liberation as there had been then, though Alan would guess there are plenty more guns around these days.

The address Rory gave him is harder to locate than he'd expected and he takes several wrong turns trying to get there, which causes him to be a few minutes late. But he finds Fred's at last, tucked between a cleaners run by Koreans and a bodega from which music booms to an Afro-Cuban beat. Across the street a handful of kids of about twelve are standing around, trying to look menacing. This is definitely a lock-your-car neighborhood. Fred's is as nondescript as its name, a long narrow bowling alley of a space, the bottom half of whose front window has been painted black. Inside, a sign near the door depicting a group of ecstatically happy young professionals drinking vodka is a solitary gesture in the direction of enlivening the place. Otherwise, though it's midday, a dim, smoky twilight prevails; and it takes a moment to register that in addition to the bar itself, there's a row of booths along one side of the room. Behind the bar, a wary-looking middle-aged white man in a checked shirt with an ex-marine's crew cut is wiping glasses, while the few customers scattered about drink in a silence punctuated by the occasional hacking cough. A noisy fan does little to cool the interior, where the residue of old beer mixes with the ghosts of a million dead cigarettes and the trace of some astringent cleaning agent.

The silence is broken by the sound of that unmistakable voice coming from one of the booths. "Well, well," Rory says, "I wasn't sure you were going to come. I was starting to feel you were going to stand me up." When Alan glimpses him a few feet away, the word "wasted" comes to his mind. You can see it's Rory in the way he moves, even seated, in the way he leans forward, in the mocking smile that plays around his mouth; but with the old Rory these gestures were natural, the graceful motions of a healthy young animal restless at being confined, even outdoors. The thin, haggard-looking man in his forties who's seated before him seems like someone who's trying out moves he doesn't entirely remember.

"Hey, sit down, sit down," Rory commands, and Alan takes a seat across from him. The former golden boy's hair is still blonde and longish but thinner and dirty-looking. His face, once strikingly handsome, has been whittled down to the gaunt starkness of a medieval carving, and its ruddy color has given way to a pallor that's accentuated by his dark brown shirt. There are deep pouches under his eyes, and you could believe he'd been sick recently. "What are you drinking?" Rory asks. He himself has a glass of beer before him.

Alan had set out thinking he'd just have a coffee but, facing the man himself, it's suddenly important not to seem to be withholding anything. "I'll have one of those," he indicates, and Rory calls out the information to the bartender.

"Well," Rory says, sizing him up, "you're looking prosperous. Life seems to have been treating you well."

Alan isn't sure the statement was meant to be a compliment. Still, what can he say in response? "I'm doing OK," he nods, surprised by the degree of his uneasiness.

Rory shakes his head slowly. "So you're a lawyer." He laughs to himself. "You don't defend guys like me, do you?"

"No, no," Alan says. For the briefest of instants he wonders if Rory has called him here because he's interested in his legal services. But that's hardly likely; he's probably just curious about the kind of work Alan does. "We're a small suburban firm," he says. "Actually, my office is close enough to my house so I can walk to work if I'm not in a rush." Rory looks on, his hand on his glass of beer. "We do general stuff like wills and divorces, property disputes," Alan continues. "You know, kind of bread-and-butter legal work. But we specialize in real estate law. I work a lot with public housing, for instance . . ."

The longer he talks, the more uncomfortable he feels—going on like this as if he's at a job interview. For his part, Rory's response is hard to gauge: he makes little attempt to feign interest in what Alan is saying, he just nods absently. Alan finds himself wondering if Rory holds it against him that he never visited him in prison. It wasn't as if they were childhood friends or anything like that; and, given the temper of those times, he's sure Rory can understand that Alan's visiting him probably wouldn't have been a smart idea. "So, yeah," he cuts himself off, "I do law. But what about you? What are you up to?"

Rory's mouth twists into a smile that's close to a sneer. "You don't really want to know, do you?" He laughs mirthlessly and looks into his beer for a few seconds. "I've been out for a couple of years now," he says. "They've given me shit jobs, so that's what I've been doing, the kind of jobs you'll give an ex-con." He spits out the last word. "I'm just treading water, you might say. Treading water."

Rory's opening salvo of complaint has done little to put Alan at ease, and he's having second thoughts about having come. He can't help taking Rory's quick dismissal of his own working life as an indictment of Alan's good fortune, and he wishes he hadn't gone on like that about his job. The memory of his lengthy description of his law practice brings a stab of guilt, but he knows he has to get beyond that. He regrets their having started off on the wrong foot. He's sorry for the way Rory's life has turned out, but that isn't why they're meeting here, is it? Though that does raise the question of what exactly they've come together to talk about. Alan's relieved when the bartender puts his beer and a glass on the bar and he has to go get it. When he brings it back to the booth, he's determined to move the conversation away from that awkward opening. He pours the beer into his glass and takes a sip before asking, "Do you know anything about the others?"

Rory wrinkles his nose. "The others?"

"You know," Alan says. "From the Lyletown job."

"I should give a fuck about those bastards?" He's suddenly angry. "They got off and I'm the only one that had to pay for the whole fucked-up scheme."

Alan drinks a little more of his beer. Well, he wants to say, Bobby paid with his life, who knows whether Ben is alive or dead, and the same can be said of Lily and Serena, who, even if they're still around, might not be thanking their lucky stars for a couple of decades of exile from everything they'd known, an erasure of their identities, not to mention having to accept the bitter truth that at this late date the revolution to which they committed their lives is very definitely unrealized. But, of course, Rory has a point: who would have traded places with him? "I just thought," Alan says, "that there might have been some contact."

Again the sneer. "The Lyletown Five was a media creation. It was just five separate people, each playing his own game." He shakes his head. "Those lezbo broads just abandoned me," he says. "She was so hot to get back to Lily. And as to that bearded phony Ben, I don't know if he ever got back to Alaska. Christ, I can't tell you how many times I've imagined him lying in a snowy ditch somewhere with a broken leg while the wolves were gathering around him."

The animus in his voice suggests that imagining terrible fates for his fellow conspirators may well have been one of Rory's chief pleasures in prison. Surprisingly, his words have depressed Alan. What happened in Lyletown was bad enough. To have it all come down to a middle-aged ex-con bitching and whining about his fate is a dismal deflation. Because one thing is evident after only a few minutes of this reunion: that the guy who, in his twenties, seemed, in his instinctive grace and brash confidence like one of the blessed of the earth, has lost all his flash and charisma, has become ordinary. And that's sad.

Still, Alan reminds himself, you have to try to put yourself in Rory's shoes. It's certainly understandable that after all those years when he could only tell his story to strangers in prison, he now has a rare opportunity to vent to someone who actually knows who he's talking about. It must have been frustrating for him to go over those events again and again to a changing cast of characters, railing against phantoms named Ben and Bobby, Lily and Serena, to listeners who could have no understanding or appreciation of the people he was talking about, and were probably only waiting for him to finish so they could start telling their own sad tales. Maybe that's one of the reasons why Rory wanted to meet with Alan, to have a listener at last who spoke the same language he did, who'd be able to give faces and bodies to these names he'd been throwing at strangers all these years. It's an appealing thought, and for a moment it seems enough to justify Alan's being here. But it doesn't quite wash, it can't be the only reason Rory wanted the two of them to get together. There's got to be more. For one thing, from all he's seen so far, he wouldn't be surprised if Rory has asked for this meeting so that Alan could see with his own eyes precisely what the Lyletown Five—or Six, as he'd put it—has been reduced to. Unsettling as that possibility may be, he can imagine taking things a step further: might Rory even be implying that things had come to this pass precisely because Alan had abandoned the rest of them? But that would be crazy, of course: he got sick, that's all, he didn't abandon anyone.

"I'm going to let you in on a little secret," Rory squints through the smoke of his cigarette. "That place where I spent more than a dozen years isn't exactly a five-star hotel." He laughs. "Even though there were lots of honeymoon suites."

Alan can only guess what it must have been like for the blonde, handsome kid in his early twenties who'd been thrown in with a population of hardened convicts. "I can imagine," he's tempted to say, but that would just invite the rejoinder, "No, you can't," which would be fair enough.

If Rory's aim is to make Alan uncomfortable, he's succeeding, and he seems to be enjoying that. There's a glint in his eye as he waves his cigarette. "You're a lawyer," he says. "You've probably run into your share of shady types."

"Well," Alan shrugs, "yeah."

Rory waits for a moment before going on. "Where I was," he says, "shady doesn't begin to describe it." The smoke curls up from his cigarette and as his cuff slides down, Alan notices for the first time a small tattoo of a spider web on his wrist. From another part of the bar comes a series of abrupt coughs, like a balky engine trying to start on a cold day. "I mean," Rory says, "there were some real mean sons of bitches in there." Again, he squints into the cigarette smoke. "There was a guy named Stoney," he says, and falls silent for a moment. He shakes his head. "Stoney worked in the laundry and his preferred way of killing someone was to garrote them with a wire. The best time was when he did it once in front of a mirror, he told me. That way he could see how scared the guy was."

"Jesus," Alan says.

"Stoney said the killing was the fun part. After that it was all business. When he'd finished the guy—snitches, mostly, to hear him tell it—he and his buddy Richie would use a pair of garden clippers to cut off the fingers and toes to keep the body from being identified. Then they'd yank out the teeth with pliers before putting the body in a pit that they filled with lime. I asked Stoney if he had any regrets about any of those jobs and all he said was that some of them died too fast." Rory takes a slow, meditative sip of his beer. "A guy like Stoney could get into your nightmares," he says. He laughs to himself. "Talking to him, I knew I didn't really have the criminal mentality." He sets his glass back on the table carefully. "You live in a tiny space in prison, but you'd be amazed at some of the people you run into there. As the song says, those were the days, my friend."

When Rory exhales, his face is veiled behind a scrim of smoke like someone lost in a fog. That's it, Alan thinks, that's what's different about him—he's lost. He went to Lyletown with the others twenty years ago and when he came back to the world, he found he had no place in it. It's possible that prison, where he's spent most of his adult life, is the place he knows best. Even now, how can he keep from thinking about those years inside, a period during which his world was reduced to a few square feet he could pace off with his eyes closed, the bars on the single window high in the wall, the leaky toilet a few steps away, the constant sounds of his unseen fellow inmates calling to each other, cursing, singing hymns, the cellmate who talks and farts in his sleep, the prying guard, all his privacy abolished with his freedom? Does he wake up with the smell of the place in his nostrils? Does he dream of being jumped every time he turns his back?

Alan has no way of knowing what that experience was really like, but just trying to imagine it is unsettlingly claustrophobic, and he doesn't want to think about it any longer. He'd rather pursue the question of what happened to the others who went to Lyletown. At least they're real for him, people he once actually talked to, touched. And one night twenty years ago they just vanished from the earth. For all he knows, Lily, Serena and Ben might have been abducted by aliens. Over the years he's wondered about them, but always within the confines of his own mind. Here, in this space where it's possible to talk out loud about these phantoms, his curiosity has suddenly been inflamed. "Look" he says, "you must have some ideas about what happened to the other three, don't you? I mean, I'm sure you're just as curious as I am. They didn't just disappear from the face of the earth, after all."

Roused from his private thoughts, Rory looks at him bleakly, his mouth moving as though he's chewing something unpleasant. "Sure," he says after a while. "Sure, I've thought about it." Some of the edge is gone from his words, as if a portion of his rage against the world has been spent in what he's already told Alan. "I assume Lily and Serena got help from the underground," he says. "Both of them had a lot of contacts. My guess is they probably managed to make their way to the coast." He takes a deep drag on his cigarette. "But if you think about it, getting away could have been the easy part, because I don't think it would take more than a month or two before Serena would have started to get on Lily's nerves, and I don't suppose it would be too easy to break out of that relationship, since your partner could always rat on you." He smiles wickedly. "It's like a punishment out of Dante, isn't it?" Alan nods: Rory's speculation sounds plausible enough, but he feels a shiver of dread. Isn't he in something like the same situation with the man he's talking to? "At least, that's what I hope happened to them," Rory says. The two of them are silent a moment before he speaks again. "As to Ben, I'm sure he was very disappointed with the way things went down, because my own feeling is that the son of a bitch was planning to take all those guns for himself and fence them. I don't think he ever had any intention of splitting up the haul."

Amid all his thoughts about the Caper, Alan has wondered about that himself. It's certainly believable that Ben got involved with the likes of Lily and Serena and the rest of them because he expected to fleece these easy marks. Once more, though, all his speculation comes up against a blank wall, the fate of the others remains a mystery. Still, just to be talking about all this with someone who knows about it has set Alan's mind racing. "Jesus," he says.

"What?"

"Nothing. It's just that . . . hell, Lily and Serena, Ben and Bobby. I haven't said those names out loud in a long time."

Rory nods. "My favorite fantasy for old Ben," he goes on, actually smiling now, "is that he makes his way to Alaska, but without his swag he has to keep working at different jobs, and that he loses a finger to a chain saw, he gets his foot crushed by a steamroller, and when he's working as a short order cook, some hot grease blinds him in one eye. Maybe, the cherry on the sundae, he loses his hearing after a dynamite blast at a construction site. I like to think of him as the incredible shrinking Ben."

Recounting the imagined fate of his former colleague has energized Rory; and when he pulls himself erect, he seems to have left behind the hunched complainer who'd sat in his place only a few minutes ago. His eyes are clear as he takes a long drag on his cigarette and exhales. "You had to be strong in there," he says, as if to himself. "You had to be strong or you wouldn't survive." When he falls silent Alan says nothing, waiting for more. "I learned a lot," Rory says simply. "I learned what I had to."

The words carry an undeniable authority. The man in the brown shirt sitting across from him, a totally unflamboyant version of the person he used to be, looks like someone who must have encountered challenges in prison that Alan can only guess at. At the moment, though, he can believe that, whatever toll those challenges may have taken, Rory managed for the most part to weather them. There's little trace of the mercurial golden boy of old in this battered, wiry man with an air of achieved calculation about him. The guy Alan is talking to looks like someone who's learned through hard knocks to quickly size up all the angles in a new situation, to figure out what he needs in order to survive. No doubt Rory has many more stories to tell than that of the Caper, narratives from which Alan would be totally excluded, though he's not particularly eager to hear any more about Stoney and the tools of his trade. He watches the ash fall from Rory's cigarette to the table. Though he and the other man are separated by only a couple of feet, Alan is aware of the immense distance between the two of them. Rory looks across the table at him, his thoughts a mystery. When he takes a swig of beer and runs the back of his hand across his mouth, the gesture seems to separate them even more.

"That must have been something," Alan says, aware of the inadequacy of his words.

Rory lets out a sigh. Whatever he's been thinking seems to have tired him out. The strong, time-hardened ex-con of a moment ago has given way to someone else. "Ever think," he says, his mouth turned scornful again, "ever think how different all that would have been if just one or two details of that Lyletown business were changed? Like, for instance, if you'd actually showed up and been the lookout? The way it was supposed to be."

"I got sick," Alan shoots back, surprised by how defensive it sounds.

Rory holds up a hand, an ambiguous smile on his face. "I know that. Still . . ."

He leaves it hanging, but the smile stays there, accusing, and it reaches deep within. What does the bastard think? Alan wonders. Does he think I somehow willed appendicitis out of my own doubts? Because the fact is, even up to the minute he started getting sick, Alan wasn't sure whether he was actually going to be able to go through with it. The truth was, whatever pledges he may have made, he kept going back and forth about that decision, moved by equal parts of moral concern and fear; and from this vantage point it's easy for him to believe that he might eventually have backed out of the Caper, or at least tried to, if he hadn't gotten sick. Did Rory somehow guess that back then?

Rory exhales a cloud of smoke and stares into it. "From time to time," he says, "I've wondered about how things would have gone if I'd have been able to work my original plan."

Alan looks at him carefully. "You think that would have changed things?"

He shrugs. "It could have distracted the cops, slowed them down. I don't know. It sure would have changed things for me, though," he says with a laugh. "I'd have shaken those cops up a bit and even if they'd have caught me, I might have ended up just being charged with reckless driving." His tongue plays with a piece of tobacco on his lip. "At any rate, I wouldn't have been the lookout, I'd have been out of it, wouldn't I?"

Alan tenses at the implied accusation. *And I would have been the lookout, is that what you're saying? I'd have ended up in prison. In your place.* It's not as if he hasn't wondered plenty of times whether he'd have behaved differently if he'd been the one standing on the corner of Webb and Broad streets that night in Lyletown. The fact is, from what he's learned about the event, it looks as if Rory panicked, and it's possible Alan would have been cooler under fire, even with Rossi, the off-duty cop showing up, throwing a monkey wrench into their plans—though that's easy to say from this distance. In the end, probably nothing he'd have done would have kept the job from going bad. It's fair to think, though, that if he'd been there he might not have gotten caught—Rory had terrible luck in that regard, there are no two ways about it. That's another thing that's puzzled Alan: why didn't Rory just run when he had the chance? There was no reason for him to try on his own to get a closer look at what was happening. Once it was clear things weren't going the way they were supposed to, there was at least the possibility for him to just take off and save his own skin. Maybe that's what's bugging him even today. Of course, if he'd been there, Alan might have acted in exactly the same way. But that's something neither of them will ever know.

"As you're well aware," Rory says after a moment, "if I'd have given the cops your name, they'd have been very happy to connect you to the deal." He smiles. "They'd have said that you were as hot for it as the rest of us. And they'd have been right, wouldn't they?"

No, he wants to say, I wasn't really that hot for it, not at all. Ambivalent, sure—how many times had he stared at the ceiling in the middle of the night wondering if this was the right thing to do? In the end, though, he can't deny he'd let himself be talked into participating in Lily's wild and desperate plan. He'd signed on, hadn't he? It would be impossible, though, to convey to Rory the complex mental gyrations he put himself through in order to justify that decision, just as it would be impossible to convey the immense relief he felt when his illness exempted him from having to go through with it. Still, in spite of that, Rory is right: however much he may be able to speculate about alternatives, the fact is, if he hadn't gotten sick, he most likely would have gone along. And then where would he be today? The very notion brings a chill as he looks at the middle-aged Rory Dekker across the table from him. "Yeah," he says quietly, answering Rory's question. "I guess I was." The admission costs him something. It's as if he's just conceded that it had been the Lyletown Six, after all.

Rory simply nods, a surprisingly understated response, and looks into his beer. "Ever think," he says after a while, "that it might have been you sitting on this side of the table if things had gone differently?"

"Yeah," he admits. "I have. Quite a few times, in fact."

Rory takes a deep, slow inhalation, as if he's a practitioner of a kind of yoga for smokers. He speaks more quietly now, insinuatingly. "Well, if you're inclined to speculation, I'll bet you've given a little thought to what would have happened to you, to your life, if yours truly had decided to spill the beans about the guy who wasn't there that night."

Now the hair on the back of Alan's neck bristles. At last they've stopped beating around the bush and have stepped into the territory of threat he sensed in Rory's phone call. He has a sudden longing for his ordinary life, the back porch with its wicker furniture, a glass of bourbon, the long green backyard running toward the Perlmans' fence. Instead of being here in this sleazy dive listening to Rory, he could have been having lunch right now with Julia, their tryst. It isn't fair, he wants to say, for all this to come back. He thinks of the phrase, "washed clean in the blood of the lamb." Everything he's done since that time can be seen as a penance for that mistake. I've played by the rules since then, he wants to say, I paid and I shouldn't have to pay anymore. Across from him, Rory waits, his eyes intent and probing. "Yeah," Alan says. "Yeah, I have thought about it." He takes a sip of his beer and feels surprisingly light-headed. For a moment he can imagine an outsider looking at this scene of two men talking in a dingy bar. What's going on, that onlooker might think, is this some kind of drug deal? "I've always wondered about that," Alan says at last, trying to calm himself, "and I've got to ask you: Why didn't you tell the cops about me?"

Rory leans back, his expression vaguely smug. "What would have been the point?" he says. "They'd already got the main stuff out of me, about Lily and Serena, Ben and Bobby." Alan can see now that it isn't smugness but a kind of detachment, as if Rory is speaking about a group of strangers, himself included. He shakes his head. "I don't know. The cops were pretty rough and they cracked me early." He frowns as he remembers that interrogation of long ago. "Maybe it was a point of pride that there was one name I wouldn't give them." He draws on his cigarette and exhales.

"Besides, you weren't actually there, were you? In Lyletown. In the end, you were just involved in the talking stage."

"That's right," Alan says. And it's true. He can convince himself that he was innocent because, as things turned out, he'd only given the plan a kind of theoretical assent but he hadn't actually done anything, though the nuns in grade school might not have seen it that way. Or the cops, for that matter, or any judge or jury. "Anyway," he says. "I'm really grateful you didn't say anything. That was . . . pretty strong of you. Thanks," he says. "And I mean it."

Rory looks into his beer and shakes his head. "I don't know," he says quietly, "maybe that was the last thing I had, all I had. Maybe hanging on to that piece of information was one way of keeping my self-respect. I don't know." He's silent a while. "By that time it was pretty clear how things were going to wind up for me. I didn't have any bargaining chips. Why throw another body under the train?" He looks at Alan with a mocking smile. "Let's just say you owe me one."

"Yeah," Alan says, "I guess I do." He feels a huge sense of relief, as if some complicated knot has come undone at last. So that's out in the open after all. In a sense, he does owe his freedom to Rory, his freedom and everything he's accomplished with it. "Jesus," he says, "imagine calling it the Caper."

Rory laughs dryly. "Yeah," he says. "Like some kind of kid's game. Some game." He draws deeply on his cigarette and expels the smoke. For a long time he says nothing. "Still," he says at last, "it's reasonable to wonder, isn't it, if you'd have been in my shoes, would you have kept quiet about me? Like I said, those cops could be pretty persuasive."

Alan doesn't answer right away. When he does, he shakes his head slowly. "I can only hope so."

The sound of the fan seems to become louder and both of them listen to it for a while. "Jesus," Rory says at last, not looking at Alan, "after I finally got used to the fact that I was going to be in there for a while, after I actually believed I might be able to survive, that I was strong enough . . ." His voice trails off. "Well, that was one thing, one hump to get over. But to think then that I might get out some day, older, all those years gone down the drain, I'd think that for all I had to give up, what do I get for that?" He shakes his head.

Alan has a sudden sense of wonder at finding himself here, in this red vinyl booth with a crescent-shaped rip on Rory's side that's awkwardly covered with masking tape, this table sticky with old drinks. Yet in the aftermath of Rory's prison memory, he's aware that there's still something hanging in the air between them, and the relief he felt a few moments ago is gone. What does Rory want? he wonders. After all, he came all the way to Boston, he chose to renew this contact. I'd want more if I were Rory, he thinks. After spending more than a dozen years in prison and working at shitty jobs after that, I wouldn't be satisfied just seeing one of my old pals from the good old days and shooting the shit with him, would I? I'd think the world owed me a little more. No, with all they've said, it still seems as if they've just been nibbling around the edges of something.

"This is a pretty shitty place," Rory says with a flick of his head.

Alan nods. "I'm not going to disagree with you on that." All of which is true enough, but they haven't come together here to pass judgment on Fred's, have they? Rory's reminded Alan of the huge favor he did for him. Is it possible, by bringing up the subject of his keeping quiet in 1968, he might be hinting that he's threatening to talk about it now, or sometime in the future? He's got to know that he could still cause serious trouble, that he's holding a hammer. He has to know that, even twenty years after the event, Alan could still be in legal jeopardy for his role, however minor, in a felony that resulted in a death. Certainly any belated revelation could be very damaging professionally, not to mention the toll it could take on his personal life. Alan had made up his mind long ago to keep that part of his life from Julia, and he's gambled plenty on keeping it a secret all these years, hoping that each passing day would put more distance between the person he briefly was and the man he's since become.

What do you want then, he wants to ask Rory, why don't you just come out and say it? He hasn't come here completely unprepared to deal with various possibilities, after all. "Hey," he says, looking pointedly at his watch, "I'm going to have to go pretty soon."

Rory slowly takes a drink of his beer and sets the glass on the table. He looks at Alan, his expression inscrutable. "Well," he says, "I'm glad we could get together for as long we have. I wanted to see how you were doing, and I have to say you seem to be doing OK. More than OK. It's good to see one of us made out so well."

Alan keeps waiting for the other shoe to drop. Gradually it occurs to him that maybe there isn't going to be any other shoe. Not this time, anyway. Though that might not be the end of things. He gets up and reaches for his wallet. "Let me get your drink."

Rory waves it away. "I'm buying this one." He chuckles. "You can get the next one."

Alan isn't quite ready to leave yet. "Do . . . do you need any money?" he asks. He's brought a couple hundred in cash with him, just in case.

Rory's look is dismissive, but friendly enough. "Oh, no, I've got a few bucks."

"Well, then," he reaches for Rory's hand. "It's been . . ."

"My sentiments exactly," Rory says, and his smile could mean anything.

"And you're just in town till . . ."

"Tomorrow."

"What's next for you?" Alan asks.

"I'm keeping my options open," he says. "I've got some irons in the fire. But not around here."

"Hey, good luck, then."

When the two of them shake, Rory says, "Good luck. That would be a change."

Alan is grateful that his car is still where he parked it and that it hasn't been vandalized. He turns the key and starts back toward the suburbs, a man who's dodged a bullet. What was that all about? he wonders. A vague sense of disappointment washes over him, as if he'd failed to get something he'd expected from this encounter with Rory. But what could that possibly be? There's no question, the meeting has left him drained and unsettled: maybe it isn't so much that he didn't get something, but that something was taken from him. Well, he's glad to be out of there. Possibly that was all Rory wanted out of him, after all, to see him squirm a little as he relived those days and contemplated other ways his life might have turned out. If so, he got his wish.

When he's back in the suburbs he doesn't go directly to his office, but takes a short detour to the street where he lives and sits in the car for a moment in front of his house. He had a vague hope that Julia might already be home from her lunch with Janet, but her car is nowhere to be seen. Wildwood Street is sunny and still, but a gentle gust stirs the leaves in the stout old beech that stands on his front lawn like a sentinel. Then the wind settles and everything is quiet again. Could you tell, he wonders, just looking at the gray Victorian with the quirky cupola, that nobody's home?

For no reason, he finds himself thinking of fairy tales again. I've had the talk with the creature I met in the forest, he realizes, and he didn't make any demand, or none that I could name. It seems as if I got away in one piece. Suddenly, looking at his house, he experiences a transport of elation. He'll call Julia from the office later this afternoon and tell her to find a babysitter for Tommy, and the two of them will go somewhere special for dinner tonight. Their belated tryst. Maybe they'll try that new place on the river, where they could get a table by the window. They'll go late, and in the candlelight's glow they'll lift their flutes of champagne to toast their future. As for the past, it will be somewhere in the suburban darkness, flowing away from them like the unseen river.

~ 1989 ~

Alan is getting closer, he's sure. Outside the car the day is clear, dry and comfortably warm, birds are singing. On a day like this, how can you feel gloomy? Though it isn't so much gloom he feels as a nervous apprehension, the sense that in an instant things can slip beneath your feet, that everything you value could come unraveled all at once. Some of that feeling, he knows, is left over from the quarrel he and Julia had a couple of days ago about going to the summer house this weekend. "I'm not ready yet," she kept saying, and he had a hard time staying patient, thinking when, when will you be ready then? They were in the kitchen, across the table from each other, and he reminded himself to take a deep breath before saying anything more. "Come on," he urged her gently. "When's the last time we were there? More than a month ago."

"Yeah," she shot back. "And remember what happened then."

Neither of them had to spell out what she meant. "Right, right," he agreed. "Maybe it was still too close to your father's death."

"It still is," she insisted. Her hands were clasped, her elbows on the table forming a hard triangle of resistance.

This wasn't something rational, he knew. It couldn't be solved rationally. Still, he felt, she needed to push herself or the thing would snowball. If she continued to let herself feel this way, who knew when she'd ever be able to go back there? "But the summer's passing," he said. "And think about Tommy."

"Why don't you think about me every now and then?" she snapped, a sudden desperate look in her eyes. The two of them were silent for a beat or two and she let out a long exhalation. "I'm sorry," she said. She looked exhausted. "I didn't mean that. I know you're trying to help me and I'll have to go back, eventually."

"Well," he said, disappointed. "Maybe it is too soon."

"No, no," she countered. "You're right." She reached across the table for his hand. "I'll have to go back there sooner or later."

In the end she'd agreed to give it a try, but he couldn't completely abandon the notion that he'd forced her into it. The whole episode had left him feeling frustrated, but what did it amount to in the end? What had he won, after all? And why should he believe things would be better this weekend than the last time they were there?

Still, there doesn't seem to be any connection between that quarrel with Julia and the impulse he'd felt at work this morning to see Sam today. Sam wouldn't be able to help him with his domestic situation, would he? Whatever the reasons, though, he's here in Sam's neighborhood, and that's actually settled him down a bit—though not being able to find the place on the first pass is irritating. The car moves at a crawl through the lush green surroundings as he searches for some familiar landmark. It's somewhere around here, he's sure, with the pond on his left and the land rising in a gentle swell on the right, where the stone markers of various shapes rise up from the grass; but he'd been just as sure he'd found the place a few minutes ago. Now, though, he spots something that he recognizes: among the memorials to the dead on the rising land to the right, he catches sight of the ostentatious marble vault with the name "Bekarian" chiseled into the ivory surface. He remembers that, remembers speculating during the service about the source of Bekarian's wealth, which must have been considerable, given the imposing monument that had been erected to mark his earthly tenure. Alan knows he's in the right neighborhood now. To his left the grass dips toward the pond, which is black and still today in the summer heat. Willows droop into the water, a red-winged blackbird lifts off from the nearby rushes, sending an almost imperceptible wave through the lily pads. He pulls the car abreast of Bekarian's vault and stops, hoping that his spatial memory will start to kick in. Eventually he'll get the hang of the place, just as he'll get used to Sam's actually being dead.

Alan gets out, closing the door quietly behind him. He crosses the path and steps onto the soft grass, where he starts walking on a diagonal path that takes him closer to the pond, from which the splash of an unseen fountain is barely audible. It's impossible not to register the names on the tablets set discreetly into the lawn. Already in a few paces he's encountered a rich ethnic diversity: Christian and Jew, Irish and Italian, a Wang and a Shalhoub, Rosen and Ryan. American democracy beneath the sod! In contrast to the insistent verticality of the more ostentatious dead on Bekarian's side of the road, the occupants here have chosen modest memorials, simple slabs of brass or marble flush with the surface. It may be more tasteful, but it makes finding a particular grave difficult.

He stops to get his bearings. A breeze rustles the leaves on a pale birch that leans in a graceful curve near a heavy-headed willow. The place is beautiful and well-maintained, he has to admit. How a town takes care of its cemeteries must say something important about it. "We have to think about where we want to be buried," Julia said around the time of Sam's death. Yeah, he agreed, hoping that was the end of it. "What do you think about getting a pair of plots here in town?" she pursued. Sure, sure, he nodded. He knew it was the smart thing to do, but he didn't want to think about that just then. Truth be told, he'd still rather not think about it.

There it is at last, framed by a couple of bouquets of flowers that are turning brown. "Samuel Jacob Wasson, May 16, 1944–June 24, 1989." Modest, in keeping with the man. It's still a jolt to see that name there in stone, though, and to think that all that's physically left of that person is lying below. Christ.

A gust carries the heartbreaking smell of new-mown grass and, with it, a pang of hunger. Instinctively he glances at his watch: he's already consumed a good bit of his lunch break. He'll have to pick up a sandwich at Ollie's and bring it back to the office. Not exactly the kind of thing you should be thinking about standing over the grave of your friend. Feeling the need for a more appropriate attitude, he collects himself, straightening. Maybe if he just stands there quietly, he'll be more receptive to any presence that might emanate from this spot. Distantly, some kind of grass-cutting machine drones like an ancient biplane tracing lazy arcs in the sky of another time; and Alan has to pull his attention back to the slab in the grass. Well, he didn't expect to find Sam here. If he exists at all now, it's only in the consciousness of those who remember him. God, he misses the guy.

Pancreatic cancer ravaged him quickly, and none of them, Sam included, had any time to adjust to this new state of affairs. It was only a couple of months ago that Alan and Julia were at Sam's place, when it was at least remotely plausible to think that things might not turn out to be so dire. Annie and Julia were huddled quietly together in the kitchen while Sam and Alan were in the living room, talking about the collapse of communism, the Red Sox game buzzing faintly in the background.

"Jesus," Sam said, "it's absolutely incredible what's happening in Eastern Europe."

"I know," Alan said. "Not in a million years would I have predicted it."

Frail as he looked, Sam managed a comic smile. "A miracle has happened in our time," he said, assuming the voice of a stage rabbi. "An actual miracle, boychik."

"Amen," Alan responded, the familiar surroundings of his friend's house conveying a sudden pang.

Sam shook his head, a look of genuine wonder on his face. "I really always believed," he said, "believed for so long, that I was going to be incinerated some day along with everyone else on the planet." He managed a curt laugh. "And now . . ." He was still smiling but his brown eyes were moist. He struggled up from his seat. "Let's go to the back porch," Sam said, his voice reedy. When he had a difficult time managing, Alan came up to him. "Need a hand?" he asked.

Sam nodded, his mouth tense. Alan helped him and felt his surprising lightness. "I'd like to get a little sun," Sam said.

"Is that OK?" Alan asked. "I mean, with the drugs and all?"

Sam sighed. "We get so little sun here in New England. You won't tell on me, will you? I won't overdo it, I promise."

Sam, who'd never been mean, had gotten gentler with his sickness, though there were sudden intervals toward the end that showed a more jagged side. Alan came to see him a couple of times in the hospital in those last few days. His heart sank as he entered the bustling lobby, knowing that in Room 532 of the West Building his friend was living out his final hours. It was impossible not to be gloomy in this setting, where Sam's tenuous hold on life was inescapably visible in the green lines pulsing across the screens of monitors and in the steady drip of fluids from IV bags into his body; and where the muted bells in the distance sounded like signals in a European train station announcing imminent departures. Still, one had to pretend to be hopeful. "How are they treating you? Alan asked. "I hope you insisted on the gourmet menu."

Sam's bed was propped up so that he was half-sitting, but he looked as limp as an empty sock. From across the hall came a low moan and the two of them listened for a moment, then Sam redirected his attention to his visitor. He tried for a smile but it came out as a grimace, then he sighed and for a long time neither of them spoke. "I know I've had a good life," Sam said at last in what was little more than a loud whisper, "and there are a lot of people who didn't have as long as I did." He paused as if gathering strength. His pale face was cadaverous, his eyes hollow and hungry. "But I can't accept it," he rasped, "I don't want to let go of all this." His chest heaved. "Even this place, this hospital room. I don't want to go." He began breathing quickly, his face was moist. "Hell, man," he said, "I'm scared." Alan bent closer, a desperate smile on his face. "I'm angry," Sam said, "and so sad."

Alan looked into the eyes of his dying friend. Whatever those eyes were asking for, it was more than Alan could give. "It's going to be OK," he said at last, though both of them knew otherwise. At the moment he desperately wished someone else would come into the room, a nurse, a doctor, even a rabbi. He was surprised by his friend's bitterness, his pain and his strength.

"Sorry," Sam said after a while.

"No, no," Alan countered. I understand, he wanted to say, but said nothing. The silence that followed was awkward, but in a couple of minutes they were back to talking about local politics.

Here amid the beauty and tranquility of the cemetery, that's the Sam that Alan remembers, the momentary glimpse of his passion, his hunger and his need, and then his apology for the embarrassing revelation. No, Sam, he should have said, it's not your fault, you don't have to apologize for being angry and sad. How little the two of them knew each other in the end. Alan never told Sam about Lyletown, for instance, and he's wondered since Sam's death whether he should have confided in him. What would Sam have said if Alan had told him about his role in that episode? From this vantage point it's impossible to think Sam would have judged him harshly. Alan can imagine him saying that you have to forgive your earlier selves, even last year's self. He wishes now that he'd confided in him. It would have been a relief to have had someone else know about this burden he's been carrying with him all these years.

But that's a selfish line of thought, isn't it, regretting that he hadn't allowed his dead friend to share his burden? That can't be why he'd felt the need all morning to come here today. He stands there above the slab in the grass, aware of the full weight of his sadness. Sam is gone, that's the inescapable truth. Were there secrets he'd kept from Alan? Alan will never know, that's all irrelevant now. He remembers that post-tennis lunch last summer when Sam waxed lyrical about those young ballerinas, and insisted on granting forgiveness to the skinny kid in Philadelphia who'd wanted to be the next Eric Clapton. "I have my yearnings," he said then. Now those yearnings are beneath the ground with him. Alan's eyes are on the pond, he hears the distant splash of the fountain, and all at once he's gripped by a sharp realization that he's standing here alive among all these others who are dead. He watches a bird alight on a branch, which trembles under the bird's weight. *It's all over so quickly*, the words rush through him, *you can't just let it slip away.* At the moment, the life that courses through his veins is almost too strong to contain, and he takes a deep breath, trying to collect himself. He turns from the pond, his eyes running across the shapes that dot the upward incline of the land. Bekarian's pompous monument looks down on him from its height. *They're all dead*, he thinks, *and I'm alive.* Is this what he came here to learn? Is this what Sam has given him? He glances once more at the slab in the grass, feeling the need to make some gesture, like the sign of the cross, though how appropriate would that be? Finally, he crouches and puts his hand to the cool stone, brushes away a few stray blades of grass. "Thanks, Sam," he says. "So long for now."

The winding lanes over which he travels on his way out are for the most part named after trees—Maple, Oak and Elm, Willow and Sycamore—and the cemetery is in fact thickly sylvan. Everywhere there are bushes as well as trees, and colorful plantings of flowers, so vivid and abundant today that he can't help wondering how much their growth has been stimulated by the decaying bodies beneath the soil. Amid the rich vegetation the clustered memorials to the dead stand in bright sunlight and deep shade: urns, obelisks and pillars, grand mausoleums and lichen-covered Celtic crosses, dozens, hundreds, thousands. The cumulative effect is overwhelming: for all the variations on a limited number of themes, the sheer dense massing of the dead, their generations intermingled, is oppressive. *They're all dead and I'm alive*, he thinks again, and he's grateful when he glimpses the stone crematorium with its roof of red tiles, and the gatehouse a short distance away, with a view of the wrought-iron gates.

Back on the streets once more, he welcomes the accompaniment of the anonymous drivers around him who move among the familiar landmarks of the living. Only minutes from the cemetery, he's passing the high school and the thronged tennis courts where he and Sam used to play. Laura Wicklow from Legal Aid has been hinting that she'd like to join him on the courts some day, and he's not so sure it's just tennis that she's interested in. Laura is a very attractive woman; and the way things have been going between him and Julia lately, he's sometimes been tempted, but not that much. At the stoplight a few streets beyond the tennis courts, he faces the ballet school with its larger-than-life silhouettes of dancers in the windows, though none of the students are to be seen. Sam, he thinks, wherever you are, I hope at least that they have ballerinas.

A few minutes later he's back at the office with his sandwich from Ollie's. "I left some memos on your desk," Sally tells him, all business. Maybe she can sense that he wants to be alone for a bit, maybe she's even guessed somehow where he's been. "Thanks," he tells her, and closes the door behind him. He's feeling better than he had this morning, he realizes, as if he's accomplished something. Maybe that visit was helpful, after all. Squirreled away in his private space, he takes comfort from his surroundings, this suite of offices on the second floor of the Baker Building. Even with his eyes closed, the smell of the place, enhanced today by the mouthwatering aroma of Ollie's roast beef and horseradish, can evoke that tight community of himself and his partner Barney, Karla the associate, Audrey the paralegal, and Sally, the secretary, all working efficiently and with more than a bit of grace in this compact space into which are packed four offices, a front desk area, file room, and small kitchen, as well as the conference room they use for closings, meetings, and of course, the occasional birthday party.

Love and work, Freud said, are the cornerstones of human happiness. However true that may or may not be as a general dictum, Alan is grateful for the satisfaction his work brings, especially now, when Sam's death has put an autumnal cast on the world. Not that things were very cheerful before then. The death of Julia's father only a few months before Sam has taken a heavy toll on her. She'll get over it eventually, he's kept telling himself, and he wants to believe it, but that's little solace when he sees her sitting at the kitchen table looking out sadly at scenes that only she can see and he knows that he's powerless to do anything about it. He knows she had a very complicated relationship to her father, and she's told him about her feelings of inadequacy as the surviving daughter who never really made up for her father's loss of his favorite, the older sister whose death broke his heart. The sources of Julia's hurt come from a place that's far beyond Alan's reach.

Under the circumstances, it's a relief to be here in the office for a large part of most work days dealing with landlord-tenant issues, which, however tangled and volatile they may become, are at least for the most part soluble. And vastly interesting to Alan as well. Professor Leyland, who'd convinced him to go into real estate law, used to say, "Shelter isn't only one of the most basic of human needs; what people do in their quest to find shelter and to hold on to it defines them in fundamental ways: who are you, what do you want and what do you fear? What will you do to get and to keep what you want? All that comes to light when you're dealing with real estate."

As he works, Alan makes his way slowly through his sandwich, careful not to spill any horseradish on the yellow legal pad on which he's taking notes about the case of Otis Jefferson, who's fallen behind in his rent at the Feeney Street Projects. Otis is a pretty decent human being who sometimes has trouble keeping things organized. Up until now, people have cut him a certain amount of slack, but there's a new property manager at Feeney who feels he has to come on like a tough guy to gain respect. You gain respect, Alan wants to tell him, by showing up at two in the morning in January when the furnace goes out. Zimmerman, the manager, has been making noises about eviction and it's Alan's job to work out some settlement before things go to court. There's no need to evict Otis, he's hoping to show Zimmerman. Maybe he and Zimmerman can get together for a drink sometime soon, so that Alan can learn a little more about the man and possibly even educate him about some of his tenants. Alan's working assumption is that there's usually a reasonable way to settle most of the disputes he runs into.

A less satisfying outcome for him is the case of Zelda Laval, who's been living in a sober house and has recently tested positive for heroin use. There's no way she's going to escape being evicted this time. Alan is sorry to have to throw the big woman out, but she's had her chances and the other tenants, who, God knows, have plenty of other temptations, have a right to live in a drug-free environment. Zelda can be very persuasive when she wants something badly, and she isn't dumb. Alan expects her to fight hard, charging racism, sexism and anything else she can bring to her aid; but the fact that she lied after so many allowances have been made for her will be the deal-breaker this time. It's Zelda who's failed, there's no doubt about that; and Alan knows there's nothing more he could have done for her. That doesn't keep him, though, from wishing he might have.

Some of his lawyer friends like Bill Hartigan can't believe Alan actually prefers this kind of work to the more lucrative business people like him practice. "How can you spend so much of your time dealing with losers like that?" Bill asked him a few weeks ago at lunch at the Ritz in Boston. Bill, who tries to model himself on Arnie Becker of *LA Law*, was paying. "I mean, people in projects," he said, wrinkling his nose. "Druggies, alcoholics, people who can't manage their lives, basket cases of one sort or another."

"Bill," Alan said to his expensively attired lunch partner, "if I did the kind of work you do I wouldn't be able to afford the clothes budget." Bill, who has a sense of humor, smiled and shot his cuffs, flashing gold. There was no point in trying to explain to him that the very failings of Alan's clientele that he'd enumerated are exactly what's so challenging about the business for him. They're at least as fascinating to him as the Byzantine intricacies of tax law were to some of his law school classmates, people being, in Alan's experience, no less complicated than taxes. Alan knows that Bill thinks the situations he deals with are simple. "Hey," he can hear his friend saying, "what's so esoteric about the concept of paying your rent on time, especially when that rent is so low? It isn't exactly rocket science, is it?" The fact is that for some of the people Alan deals with, it might as well be. For them, making that simple payment can be a huge problem; Alan's job is to try to help them solve that problem, and it isn't always easy for him to get their trust. That requires listening to them carefully, knowing when to screen out the bullshit, to read between the lines, keeping attentive enough to what might seem like aimless rambling to find the thread of an individual story. Only then can he try to come up with a particular arrangement that will enable that person to stay in his or her apartment. To do that well, you have to be smart, sensitive, creative and canny.

There's plenty of motivation for Alan to do his best for them, especially since, whether or not you call them losers, for many of his clients there's really not much to win, considering that most often the major prize they're fighting for is their ability to continue living in the projects, hardly the most desirable of habitations. But the fact is, for a lot of them that's pretty much all they have, which means for them it's the fight of their lives. "Managing" is what he'd tell Bill he's helping his clients do. Sometimes all they've got is a kind of disaster. Nevertheless, there's satisfaction in helping them manage that disaster. In the end, he knows he can make a real difference in people's lives. At least that's what he tells himself today. At other times, when the troubles he's dealing with seem overwhelming, all he can do about it is keep his head down and continue working.

He finishes his sandwich and washes it down with Ollie's coffee. Given the workload and the fact that he and his family are going to the Berkshires this weekend, he'll probably be in the office till late tonight. He sits there at his desk enjoying a short break, satisfied, at least content for the moment, allowing himself to be soothed by the scattered sounds of work being done. All at once things go quiet for a second or two, like a sudden intake of breath. In that instant he's back in the cemetery standing over Sam's grave in the tranquil warmth of the summer day, the willows hissing in the breeze, and he feels a wash of sadness, a sense of things unfinished, of things that might have been said that were left unsaid. At the same time he remembers that powerful sense he had of being alive: *It's all over so quickly, you can't just let it slip away.* The feeling is a little frightening but it's exhilarating as well; and he wants to hang on to it a little longer, to savor it; but already the sounds around him have resumed—Barney and Karla are talking, the typewriter clacks and pings, a phone is ringing. The web of the familiar reassures him that there are briefs to be filed, court dates to meet, work to carry him along, doing what he can to make an imperfect world slightly less imperfect. Aware that near at hand is another batch of papers he has to read, he feels more at ease, and the void is a little further away.

The work week will be ending soon, and he has mixed feelings about going to Innisfree this weekend. He's happy that Julia agreed to give it a try, at least. That in itself is a significant step. Still, God knows how it's actually going to go out there. He's got to trust in his gut feeling that it's the right time, that Julia is ready to go back there. He knows that the history of the summer house they've loved so much is entwined around the memory of her father, and he can understand why it would be hard for the daughter to go back there now, after he's gone. Alan is sympathetic to Julia's reaction, but he's disturbed by what her father's death is doing to her. Mourning is natural enough, but the world should belong to the living, after all, and it pains him to see her suffering so much under the weight of the man's memory. Could that be why he felt the need to go to the cemetery today, after all? Was it a kind of acting out of what he feels is so necessary for Julia, the facing down of her own ghosts? He sure as hell hopes that returning to Innisfree can be cathartic for her. Once more he remembers that sense of urgency that gripped him at Sam's grave, that feeling that being alive is everything. Julia needs something to lift her from the gloom she's been feeling and going back to the summer house seems to be a necessary step. It's not fair that Innisfree should be transformed into something haunted for her. She knows, as he does, how important the place in the country that his grandfather built is to Tommy and, especially at this age, it shouldn't be kept from him. Alan thinks about the little shingled house on the top of a hill in the deep woods of northwest Connecticut. Yes, there was a lot of history to the place already when he saw it for the first time; but he and Julia, even Tommy, have given it their own mark as well. It's up to them to keep that history going.

Alan and Julia were both living in New York when they met at a party in the Village. He was feeling good, ready for something. Only recently he'd come to recognize that, at thirty-five, with law school ending, he was ready to take another chance at marriage. True, he'd been chastened by his experience with Martha, but that whole episode, he told himself, belonged to another era. He wasn't the same person anymore, he believed, and there was no need to be hampered by that person's mistakes, so he was all attention when he saw the tall, dark woman with the interestingly crooked smile, and he knew he had to find out if she was available. She was standing by the open window near the fire escape, talking to a large woman with hoop earrings and short gray hair. As he approached, he heard the woman he was interested in say "It's called Innisfree" and, recognizing the reference to Yeats's poem, he decided to file that away for future reference. He introduced himself and for a while the three of them talked about summer in the city. At last, the gray-haired woman, who was a painter, left and he had Julia, whose name he now knew, to himself.

It didn't take him long to work the fact that he was divorced into the conversation. "So am I," Julia answered coolly, and he smiled to himself, thinking, I don't have to push this now, I can take my time. He told her he was finishing law school and she said she was working on a Ph.D. in English, "in slow motion," she said, and teaching part time to pay the rent. "Working on the Ph.D. is a hobby," she said. "Not the Ph.D. itself, but working on it." He liked her humor, though he could sense a touch of uneasiness in her self-presentation; he guessed that she was anything but a dilettante. She was smart, he could see right away, she was passionate about things, he'd soon learn, and she was a knockout, all of which made it hard to understand how her ex-, according to the story she told him later on the fire escape, had had the nerve to call her boring before he dumped her.

"What's his standard? " Alan asked her.

"A trio of eighteen-year-old cheerleaders," she deadpanned.

"That's tough competition," he agreed.

"Siss-boom-bah," she intoned into her drink.

"Cheerleaders would scare me," he said. "I'd keep thinking about their ability to do scissor kicks." She smiled her crooked smile at him and he wanted to straighten it out with a kiss, but he'd already determined he wasn't going to rush this. He felt the cool night breeze and heard the distant wail of a siren moving somewhere among the night-time streets of the city.

"So what's Innisfree?" he asked her. "I heard you talking to Roxanne about it."

She leaned back against the railing of the fire escape. "It's my father's place in the country," she said. "In Connecticut. He built it in the woods."

"Are there woods in Connecticut?" he asked. It was the snobbery of someone who'd spent a year in Vermont.

"Oh, there are woods, all right. You should see them sometime."

"I'd like to," he said. "I'll bet that house has quite a story."

"It does."

"I like stories," he said truthfully. "But wait. It's called Innisfree. Is there a lake? Is there an island?"

She tilted her head and gave him a look. "Come on, mister, haven't you ever heard of poetic license?"

Already he wanted to believe there was some kind of future between them, and he was hungry to learn about the years she'd lived before they'd met. Later, it seemed important to him that one of the first bits of that narrative she'd surrendered had to do with the house in Connecticut. As she filled in the rest of the story in the course of their early times together, Innisfree held a special place.

Her father, Richard Mallory, was a central figure in her story. He was a sad man, she said, a man who was out of place. He'd been stationed in the Pacific during the Second World War and what he'd seen there apparently changed him. "I wouldn't know, of course," Julia said. "I wasn't born till later. But it's what my mother said all the time: 'He was a different man when he came back.'" An insurance executive, he did fairly well for himself but, according to his daughter, he had few friends, having chosen after his wartime experiences to retreat into his family. "He had some kind of emotional breakdown after the war and his doctor recommended that he find some outdoor work, work with his hands, that would keep him busy. That's how Innisfree got started."

The house was in the wooded northwest corner of Connecticut, about ninety miles north of the city, part of an association that owned several hundred steep, sylvan acres that abutted a state forest. "You'd never believe you're in Connecticut," she said. "You can wander for hours through the woods." The house, she told him, was small. "But it's special. Trust me."

"I'd like to see it," he said. "I'd like that very much."

He could tell from the way she told the story that her own feelings about the place were complicated. Her father had built it, she said, largely by himself, over the course of a few years in the late forties, when her sister Madeleine was growing up. "In 1950, when the house was pretty much finished, Maddy would have been eight." It was one of the places in the narrative where Julia's voice would trail off. "I always wondered what Dad was like then. I mean, I think he built the house as much for Maddy as for himself." Julia's mother was evidently no enthusiast of the rustic life. "But I think for Maddy, and for Dad, the place was magical. He'd take her to all these places in the woods and give them fairy tale names. You can imagine how a kid would love that."

Alan had to read between the lines and listen to the silences in her story. Julia was seven years younger than Maddy, as far as she was concerned, an entire generation behind, and her clear implication was that her father loved her sister more than he loved her. Still, she gave no hint of feeling sorry for herself. At least on the surface, she accepted the way the world was and made the best of it. But it was clear from what she said that her father couldn't accept what ultimately happened, his favorite daughter's death in a car crash during her first year of college, when Julia was eleven. "Maddy's death devastated him," she said. He apparently went into a tailspin for a while after that and became a kind of quiet, resigned alcoholic. "He went through the motions at work, he came home and started drinking before he'd taken his coat off." His wife kept urging him to get rid of the country place, which was now haunted for him, but he couldn't bring himself to do it, instead letting it slide into a kind of sylvan decadence for about a dozen years. "I went there with Victor once or twice," she said—Victor was her first husband—"but it made me nervous." Listening, Alan nodded and thought that it wouldn't have to be that way with him, if he ever got the chance.

"I suppose for all practical purposes my parents' marriage was over by then," Julia said. His wife didn't leave him, though, for a few years. When she died soon after, her father's life seemed to have become anticlimactic. "They carried him at the company, but I understand that he doesn't do much more than shuffle papers these days. It's all pretty sad."

One belated development, though, was that, more than a decade after his daughter's death, he took a renewed interest in Innisfree, going there on occasion for what must have been bouts of extreme nostalgia. "I think he's done a little clearing and cutting, keeping the forest back. But otherwise, he's left the place pretty much as it used to be, which, as I've told you, is pretty primitive." There was no telephone, she told him, no electricity either. "He wants me to have the place," she said. "He can't bear to let it go outside of the family."

"Are you sure you want it?" Alan said, after hearing her story. "Sounds like it's got a lot of history."

She gave him a smile. "Whatever history it may have, shouldn't I give it a chance at having a future?"

One day in June the two of them drove through the tidy towns of northwestern Connecticut, a land of wooded slopes and covered bridges, until they pulled off the highway onto a dirt path. Passing through an opening in a low stone wall, they followed one of three imprints of tracks across a grassy meadow that was bounded by a pine planting, though not a dwelling was in sight. He leaned out the window and inhaled the rich summery smells.

"OK," Julia told him as they approached another stone wall where the land rose sharply. "Here's where it gets tricky. You just have to have faith." Seconds later, the car was subjected to a punishing climb up a steep, twisting dirt road littered with stones, some of which clanged like bullets against the car's bottom.

"Jesus," he said, struggling to maintain traction as they made their jerky way upward. When the road leveled off at last, there was a field of high grass on one side and a small forest of pines set in rows as regular as bowling pins, their shadows making a pattern on the floor of brown needles, as the car moved across this friendlier stretch of road toward a pair of gray stone pillars. Her father had built them, Julia told him, and Alan was impressed. Beyond the pillars was a sun-splashed opening in the forest where the bright green grass ran to a terrace on which the house Richard Mallory had built was perched. Even at first glance, Alan could see that the place was everything she'd said it was: it was like something out of a storybook, it was tiny and intricate and hidden, an elegant statement in the midst of the wild.

He and Julia got out of the car and stood there a moment, basking in the green quiet that was such a contrast to their noisy ascent. He held her hand and the two of them looked at the little fairy tale house with white shingles and dark green shutters, dormers peeping out of a roof that was covered with wisteria, and not one but three stone chimneys. Bees were buzzing in the high grass of the uncut lawn and the two of them just stood there a while listening. "Wow!" he said and then she led him to the back where the forest crowded the house like the deep woods of children's stories. When they went inside, he bumped his head on the low kitchen doorway. Everything was built to her father's dimensions, she laughed, and he was a couple of inches shorter than Alan.

Indoors amid a pleasant musty smell that faintly suggested cedar, the surprises kept coming: the house had neither a phone nor electricity, but there was an elaborately tiled fireplace in a room with two built-in single beds (again, she pointed out, no longer than the man who'd built them); and at the other end of the house, an elegant little library with a parquet floor that you could cross in four steps, a marble fireplace beneath a gold-lined mirror, all in the Williamsburg style, as was the rest of the interior.

"Watch this," she said, then twisted a brass handle so that a panel under the bookcase dropped down to make a bed.

"Amazing," he exclaimed. To which she responded, "You ain't seen nothin' yet." Going to the bookcase again, she pulled back what had looked like the covers of a pair of books, brought down a wooden handle the false books had hidden, and a panel in the adjacent wall swung open. Soon they were climbing the smallest of twisting staircases to a tiny space with a cot, a small writing desk and a pair of many-paned windows. "Our priest-hole," she said. "You could hide up there for years and nobody would know you were there."

"Your father is a crazed genius," he said, the two of them breathing the hot musty air of the secret place where a tiny window framed a square of green. "He's half Thomas Jefferson and half Vincent Price."

Next Julia took him outside and led him up the wrought-iron spiral staircase to a bright little bedroom, tucked into the peaked angles of the roof, with the inevitable built-in beds and a tiny desk that seemed to open out of nowhere—there was a fanatical economy about saving space that suggested the nautical. "You can imagine," she told him, "how much fun this would be for a kid." Looking at the built-in beds, Alan thought of the dead Maddy and he felt again that there were places in Julia's heart he might never know.

When they walked in the woods behind the house after-wards they encountered stone walls that had been put there by settlers in the eighteenth century, who'd felled the original trees and established their community, built a church and a school, then strenuously tried to farm this steep land covered with boulders. When the Indians were subdued in the Midwest, the farmers, giving up the effort at last, left for the rich black earth of Ohio and beyond, and the silent farms and empty barns they vacated were gradually swallowed up by the returning forest, until finally only these stone walls remained.

"I'm glad you like Innisfree," Julia's father said back in the city, when Alan finally met him. In his gray suit, he was dressed like an insurance executive, but there was little calculation in his eyes, only a dreamy sadness. A glass of bourbon was close by.

"It's special," Alan said and he watched Julia smile.

"Do you know the Yeats poem?" her father asked.

Alan nodded.

"Well, everyone needs a refuge," Richard Mallory said. "Especially these days, when there's so much that's shoddy." He rattled the ice in his drink. "We have to preserve what's special."

Alan had taken a job with legal services in the city, and because things were tight for them early in their marriage, he and Julia spent their first vacation together as man and wife at Innisfree, so they could save money. There, by the light of the kerosene lamp they talked about their future. Alan had gone into debt to get through law school and he wasn't sure how he was going to pay it off. Professor Leyland had gotten him interested in real estate law and he was hoping that Leyland's good word would get him a job near Boston, though he knew that might take a while. Julia was still hoping to finish her Ph.D. in English, and she had a part-time job lined up for the fall at a community college. "Things are going to be fine," he told her. "Everything's going to work out OK."

She smiled at him across the table her father had made. "I know it is," she said. Her skin was golden in the lamplight. They lay on a large flat rock later that night, looking at stars through the shaggy encircling mass of trees and she said it again. "Don't worry, everything's going to be all right."

They did save money that summer: they lived simply, they read, they swam in the icy pond on the association's property, they took hikes on the trails through the woods. Alan looked through an old photo album and saw that the hillside below the lawn had once been bare of trees, so that you could see the conjunction of three distant hills from the house. He suddenly had a project: while Julia read nineteenth-century British novels and took notes for the dissertation she planned to write one day, he set out to hack his way through the forest, to recover the view. He only had an old axe that he had to keep sharpening, and he whacked away at trees small and large, pushing very slowly into the forest. Thorns from bushes cut him, limbs slashed across his bare back, his hands were blistered, they bled, and at times he was almost blind with exhaustion. When he gripped a cold can of beer between his raw fingers and flayed palm there was a satisfying pain. He was a man of talent and energy, unrecognized by the world, determined to drive back the woods.

They got some old boards from a lumberyard for nothing and, since Julia had learned the finer points of carpentry from her father, they were able to build a little shack in the modest clearing. Like Peter the Great's putting his new capital on the Baltic, this was a statement. Alan insisted on calling the shack a study. Though he was a lawyer, he didn't feel other possibilities were closed off—he was ambitious. He believed he had some literary talent and he started to write a novel about a group of radicals who'd gone down south to help with voter registration. Chopping trees, he'd be excited by his ideas: whack, whack—a scene was coming clear. Alone in the little study at the edge of the woods, he was often elated, like an astronaut in his capsule seeing a world that those back on earth couldn't glimpse. After the first chapter, though, the work became much more difficult: he revised, he rethought, and then the novel stalled. Finally he abandoned it, and when he cut down trees he thought about other things. Who needed to write a novel anyway? He was a happy man.

The next summer he got the job he wanted near Boston. Now, for a change, there was enough money, but there was less time for the country place: the extra hours of driving took up much of their precious weekends and that made Alan more impatient with the place's limitations. Why subject visitors to those cramped built-in beds? Sure, they could joke that if you wanted pleasure, you needed ingenuity and a capacity for a certain amount of suffering, but it wasn't all that funny. And why shouldn't there be a phone in the house? What if their friends had trouble finding the place, needed directions? It might have been all right for the fifties, but a phone was a necessity nowadays. Julia agreed but her father had always held off, she said, because he was afraid the poles and wires would spoil the view, the special serenity of the place. "It wouldn't be so bad," Alan said. "And with the baby coming, I think we'd both feel better."

In the end he and Julia got their way in the matter of phone service, but the first time Richard Mallory saw the poles and the cleared area that had been required for them, the scar of dirt on the lawn from the trenching where the wire went underground to the house, he stood a long time looking at them, shaking his head, like a man standing at the grave of a friend.

When they came to the country after Tommy was born, the small house suddenly seemed smaller, especially since Mallory, who'd recently retired, visited them more often, and the presence of four people in the close quarters could produce a combustive force: the walls pressed against Alan, the built-in beds were like straitjackets for sleepers. He'd wake up at night thinking about his job, trying to devise strategies to defend people the system was built to exclude; and his small, narrow bed seemed like part of that system. He'd come up with a plan in the middle of the night: if they moved the door of the narrow bedroom they could tear out the beds from under their canopies and create enough space to put in one larger double bed. But to do that would mean cutting off the view of the herb garden from the living room when the bedroom door was open; and he knew that Julia's father, nominally a guest and not the owner, cherished that view. He tossed and turned in bed.

He dreamed of another plan, more radical still. "We could build on it," he told Julia, "push out the whole back end of the house ten feet and we'd gain—a world, especially upstairs. And you could still have the view of the herb garden." He could see the excitement in Julia's eyes as she contemplated the vision of the enlarged house but she knew what her father's objections were likely to be. "The lines," she said. "He'll tell us it would destroy the lines." The lines would still be the same in the front of the house, Alan insisted, his voice rising as if he'd hit his head again on the low kitchen doorway. He suddenly heard himself. He didn't want to be arguing with Julia and he took her hand. "I'm sorry," he said. She worked her hand free. "Do you know what it's like living with somebody else's dream?" she said. "Especially if you're part of that dream?" She was near tears. "Sometimes I wish he hadn't given us this house, I wish we could just sell it." And so it was settled for the moment.

Electricity was invisible, though, it wouldn't affect the contours of the house, and now that they had phone service, not to have electricity was crazy, since the power would be carried by the same poles and its importation would require no extra cutting. Once more the new parents were thinking of Tommy: as he grew up and started crawling around, the thought of those kerosene lamps would make them nervous. "Let there be light," they declared.

And so there was light and the electric toaster, the vacuum cleaner, an iron—what luxury! Even Mallory didn't complain on his frequent lengthy stays, except to occasionally bemoan the loss of kerosene's warm glow. When the carpenter ants got to the kitchen roof and it had to be repaired, Alan seized the opportunity to extend the kitchen a scant eighteen inches. This, with the changed roofline, was just enough to enable them to install a new door that required no bowing of the head for him to enter. Savagely, he continued to work at his clearing, renting a chainsaw that brought down with a snarl trees it would have otherwise taken him days to fell. In a moment of triumph, he glimpsed at last the feline curve of one of the hills he'd seen in the old photo.

But now it was Richard Mallory's turn. One day he announced that he wanted to build another room in the tiny area at the top of the secret staircase, which would be the only way of getting there. It was mad, Alan and Julia thought, but how could they deny him? So the old man went ahead, with a surprising, ruthless energy, as if he'd sold his soul for this spurt of force. What he conjured at last was quirkier than any of the house's other quirks: in the cramped space at the top of the secret stairs he'd managed to create the tiniest of rooms, with a built-in bed, of course, a writing desk, an armoire and even a pair of French windows that opened onto a small balcony with a wrought-iron railing.

In the end, there was more to Alan's world than the summer house. He'd gone into law to make the world a better place and he was finding that he had to make compromises all the time. Was the world changing him? He was beginning to make more money, but he often wondered if he was doing any real good. After taking time off when Tommy was born, Julia went back to teaching, declaring that she was still going to get her Ph.D. some day. She had her frustrations, Alan knew. There wasn't any point in exacerbating things by pushing on Innisfree.

It was true, they could now afford to get a real builder to work on the back of the house, to push it back ten feet, so that they'd have an upstairs room of their own where Alan could actually stand up, they could have a double bed. It would be a house grown-ups could live in. It would give them a lot more space in the kitchen too. At last they could fit enough cooks to spoil the soup. The lines of the house would be maintained, it would look pretty much the same from the front. The little nooks and quirks would be there, all the fancy fixtures, they'd still have the secret door, the old man's little room, so everything that's special about the house would be preserved and at the same time it would be much more livable. It was all very rational.

But he knew this wasn't a rational matter. He knew, as Julia did, that they were waiting for Richard Mallory to pass from the scene, so Alan turned his attention to other things. He wasn't a barbarian, after all, he wasn't going to challenge the old man on this.

Later, when her father's removal to a nursing home made his objections moot, so that they were able to put in all of their changes to the house without its builder having to see them, Julia told Alan, "I'll always be grateful that you didn't try to ram things down his throat, that you understood his position, irrational though it might have been."

He understood. He understood that he too was part of the history of the house his father-in-law had built. He'd fought against the old man on point after point and, though he was now able to enter the kitchen without bowing his head, and though they had more space, the house was still essentially what it had been when it had been created. It was still small, it still looked like something out of a fairy tale, and it was still a treasure hidden in the woods. For all the modifications Alan had managed to achieve that made the house more livable, its genetic code had long ago been determined by its builder. What had happened over the years wasn't an argument that any one party had won; it was a process in the course of which he'd been affected as much as he'd effected changes.

Which was why now, with the old man dead, it was important that the house's legacy be continued.

T he weather today has been a blessing. Alan and his family have traveled under blue summer skies adorned with a few puffy clouds and now, near Innisfree at last, the sun shines brightly on a quiet green world. As he leaves the asphalt road and turns onto the path that will take them to the summer house, he can feel the change beneath him, the tires biting into the more yielding dirt. "We're here, we're here," Tommy cries excitedly from the backseat. "Yes, we are," his father assures him. Alan keeps his eyes on the tracks in the grass ahead, aware all the while of Julia beside him, but she says nothing. When he turns toward her, though, he sees no hint that she's upset. "It's going to be a great weekend," he says quietly, and she nods.

"Look at the deer," Tommy shouts as a doe and a pair of fawns lift up their heads, stand photograph-still for a moment, then bound across the tall grass and into the trees, scrambling up the slope.

"They're trying to beat us to the house," Alan says. When the car passes through a gap in the stone wall, he takes the middle tine of a three-pronged fork in the road, the others leading to the Gaines and Peltier properties, which are hidden by the trees; and after traveling a hundred yards or so of level surface, they're at the point where the climb begins. As Alan shifts into a lower gear for the drive up the twisting road, he notices some shapes in the nearby woods. "Turkeys on the left," he points out.

"It's beginning to look like the place has reverted to nature," Julia says. "I hope the house is still there."

"Maybe," Alan says, turning toward the back, "Papa and Mama and Baby Bear are living there now."

"No," Tommy protests. "It's our house. Grandpa made it."

At the top of the climb, they're back in the sunshine, the dust of their ascent trailing in the air behind them. A rich sweet smell comes from the pine planting on the right, and Alan can glimpse the place at last: beyond the stone pillars, a gable pokes through the thick foliage. The white house comes into clearer view as they approach. "Inn'sfree, Inn'sfree," Tommy sings from the backseat. The trees are densely green and the grass is overgrown—Alan can see that he'll have a lot of mowing to do. But the abundance of vegetation only adds to the house's sylvan charm.

"He would have liked what we've done to the place," Julia says, touching Alan's hand. He's sure she's right. From the front the house is essentially the same place her father built; such additions as they've been able to make are all in the rear, or inside. Even the most visible mark of change from this angle, the deck Alan and Julia built together and then turned into a pergola, has weathered sufficiently so that it looks as if it might have been part of the original plan; and Alan has no doubt that his father-in-law, if he were here, would spend a lot of time sitting in one of the chairs beside the picnic table, reading in the shade of the overarching maples and breathing in the rich scent of the grapevine he'd planted so long ago, now entwined around two of the pergola's columns.

As Tommy runs to the little grotto in the stone wall behind the house where the key is hidden, Alan pulls Julia closer. "We did OK by the place," he says.

She nods and says nothing, but he can tell she's feeling all right.

"No bears in the house," Tommy proclaims once they're inside.

"Are there any broken chairs?" Alan asks. He opens the top of the Dutch door to give the place some air. "Any empty bowls of porridge?"

"Daddy," the boy says, "we don't eat porridge."

Soon they're unpacking. Alan carries their bags to the upstairs bedroom, the one really spacious part of the house—in spite of the white trunk of the chimney that once stood outside before the room was built, and now rises like a tree in its midst. The air in the room, unoccupied for more than a month, is still and warm, and he pushes open a window, then crosses the floor and opens the door to the balcony, which sends a fresh breeze through this upstairs room. The balcony faces the cool green quiet of the woods behind the house, where the thickly forested slope rises in the direction of an abandoned settlement where he's taken Tommy on hikes, the two of them poking among the foundations for some mementos of the people who'd once lived there.

"I'm going to make some lunch, OK?" Julia calls up to him.

"Yeah," he says. "I'm going to go out back and see if I can start the mower." The old machine is in the unpainted shed in the back woods, another structure built by Julia's father. Alan pushes open the wooden door that slides with a screech on a metal track and he's greeted by the smell of gasoline and canvas, old wood and the dry dirt of the shed floor. On the wall hang an ancient bucksaw and a two-man saw, a pickaxe, a crowbar and other tools. He drags out the mower and pushes it across the uneven terrain out to the terrace in front of the house. Tommy is playing with a plastic spaceship on the pergola, waiting for lunch. It takes a few pulls but the mower finally coughs, belching smoke, and settles into a loud roaring that stops abruptly when he lets go of the handle.

There's no point in starting until after lunch, Alan decides. Once he gets going, it's going to be pretty sweaty work. Assured that the machine will start, he takes a stroll in the direction of the clearing he'd cut a few years ago and stops just short of the stone wall that separates it from the lawn. A breeze carries a sweet, fruity smell that takes him back to the time when he'd spend hours cutting down the trees that had once stood there. Now, staring into what had once been forest, he experiences a stab of unease that undercuts the buoyancy he's been feeling since they arrived. What is it? After his heroic effort of clearing this place, he's left it alone and already a tangle of undergrowth is spreading across the ground, prickly bushes and young trees have reappeared, occupying some of the cleared area; and he can all too easily foresee the time in the not too distant future when this once open and airy swath of land will be returned to the woods. Even now, from this vantage point, he can just make out the lines of his deteriorating study, once the site of so much hope as he'd set out to write his novel. Maybe it's the memory of that failed project and nature's patient, relentless undoing of his heroic efforts with the axe that have made him feel momentarily futile.

He resists the feeling. He's accomplished a lot, after all, not only here, with the improvements on the house, the restoration of the property, but in his career as well, in his life in general. Still, it's true he never finished that novel, will never finish a novel. It's also true that even if he were to go back into the clearing, equipped with a power saw now, and fell as many trees as he'd once brought down, others would grow back in time, eventually wiping out his achievement. Well, there are lives he'll never live, there are deeds he'll do that will be undone. Will he really be fifty in five years? It seems not that long ago that he'd first come here, young and impatient, feeling that he was bringing something new and forceful to this place.

"Need any help cleaning?" he asks Julia when he's back in the house. "Mmm, smells good."

"Actually, the place has weathered the last few weeks very well. There are no dead animals, as far as I can tell."

"That's always a plus." He gives her a gentle punch on the arm.

Julia smiles. "I'm glad you talked me into coming," she says.

"Hey, I hope I didn't talk you into it. I hope you came of your own free will."

She nods, "I did. I guess I needed a little push, though." She shakes her head. "Sure, it's a little sad coming back here, because everything reminds me of him, but why wouldn't it? And what's the alternative? Just to forget him? I'd have to come back sooner or later. And it's better that I did it sooner. Now, are you ready to eat in about ten minutes? We'll eat outside, OK?"

"Sure. I'll check your father's room for any dead creatures," he says. He goes into the library and pulls back the false fronts of the books, then brings down the lever, and the pale blue panel in the wall swings open. He climbs the twisting staircase, the air becoming warmer and thicker as he ascends. When he's at the top, he can tell there are no dead animals here. The only smell is a general mustiness as well as a hint of the sweaty work clothes Mallory used to wear. Alan isn't even sure they're up here, but some lingering traces of their smell remains, putting the man's stamp on the room as do all the little details he managed to cram into this six by eight space, like the brass fixtures, the built-in armoire, the French doors. Crazy, Alan thinks, absolutely crazy.

"I miss Grandpa." Alan turns to see Tommy's head at the top of the stairs. He climbs into the room, which is barely able to hold the two of them.

"We all do," Alan says, running his hand through the boy's hair. "You know, Grandpa would want you to think of this as your own secret room now."

Tommy runs his hand along the edge of the narrow bed. "He used to show me places," he says sadly. "Secret places in the woods."

Alan smiles. "When you grow up, you can show them to your children."

Tommy frowns. "I'm not going to have any children."

A fly buzzes nearby, bumping repeatedly into the window. "Well, you should wait and see about that. I think when I was your age I might have thought the same thing."

"Hey, you guys," Julia calls up. "Lunch."

She's put a bright yellow tablecloth on the picnic table on the pergola. A thick beef and barley soup sends steam from the pot that holds it and a plate of sandwiches is nearby, with a couple of cans of beer and a glass of milk, all of the food dappled in the shifting light of the moving leaves that's further filtered by the lattice overhead.

"Daddy says I can have Grandpa's secret room," Tommy tells Julia.

"Well," she says. "I think he'd want you to have it. You're not going to want to sleep there yet, are you?"

A sudden look of alarm crosses the boy's face. "N-no."

"I think Tommy might want it as a secret clubhouse," Alan offers. "During the daytime."

Tommy chews on his sandwich. "Is Grandpa still here?" he asks.

Alan and Julia look at each other. "You know he's in heaven," she says, a little quickly.

"His spirit is all around here," Alan says. "He built this place, so there's something of him everywhere around here."

Tommy's brow is knit. "Do you think he's in the woods too? Like maybe in the secret pirate cave?" This is a place in the forest behind the house that Julia had shown Alan the first time he came, where a skull-like gray outcropping rises in a clearing among the trees. The rock has a cleft near its base that looks like a cave. Richard Mallory had named it, he'd gone there with Maddy, Julia told him, and later with her. It was one of the magical places he'd created for his daughters.

"I suppose," Alan says, suddenly uncomfortable with the supernatural drift of the conversation. "Hey," he points to the sky. "Look at that hawk." They all lift their heads toward the dark silhouette in the sky, serrated wings extended, soaring in a slow, wide circle above them, its shadow gliding across the grass and rippling over the stone wall.

"What's he doing, Daddy?" Tommy asks.

"I think he sees something down there that he wants to eat. Maybe a mouse or a chipmunk. He has eyes that can see the tiniest thing moving down below. I think it must be his lunchtime."

"Do I have good eyes, Daddy?" the boy appeals.

"Oh, yeah. You've got very good eyes."

"If I was up there, do you think I could see a little mouse moving way down in the field?"

"I'm sure you could."

"Tommy," Julia says, "after lunch I want you to rest. You don't have to take a nap, but you should stay inside for a while, maybe look at one of your books."

"OK, Mommy," he says.

"What about Mommy?" Alan asks. "What's she going to do after lunch?"

"I've got some really fascinating material about curriculum change," she says, making a face. "I can't wait to get to it." Increasingly in her job at the college, she's had to give her time to administrative matters.

"Lucky you," Alan says. "I'm going to mow at least the terrace. Then I think I'll do a little digging in the swale."

After they clear the table, the three of them go their separate ways. Alan fires up the mower and cuts the grass on the terrace. There's much more grass to be cut down below but he'll leave that for tomorrow. Just now he wants to clear the swale in the woods behind the house. This trench, dug by one of the locals with his backhoe, redirects the spring runoff as it makes its way down the mountain, keeping the rushing water from flooding behind the house. In the couple of years since it's been dug, though, it's filled up with silt and underbrush so that its capacity to move water is considerably lessened. Alan makes his way through the woods behind the house with a wheelbarrow, a pick axe and a shovel, determined to clear out a significant section of the ditch, removing the underbrush and digging away some of the silt. Even in the back forest, which is shady, this is hot work and he's soon sweating through his shirt. But, as with the mindless mowing, he takes pleasure in the routine, in his body's involvement in the repetitive process. He doesn't have the prodigious energy of a few years ago when he hacked away at the clearing, but he still needs a fair bit of physical activity to keep him sane. It's gratifying that he can do the work. So what if he's getting close to fifty?

About a half hour into the job, he's removed the underbrush from a section of the trench and is at work shoveling away the silt when his shovel's blade strikes something hard. It's not wood, he can tell from the sound, and he's suddenly interested. Maybe it's a piece of an axe or some other old tool. He leans down to look at the shape, brushes away the dirt and realizes after a few seconds that what he's got between his fingers is an Indian arrowhead. The hair on the back of his neck bristles with the realization that he's holding an artifact from a distant time. He feels the weight of the object in his palm.

He's got to show this to Tommy. He can imagine the boy's excitement at being able to touch an old Indian relic, and he returns to the house, grateful for the break from work. When he can't find Tommy inside, he asks Julia if she knows where he might be.

She takes off her reading glasses. "No. I thought he'd be looking at his books."

"Let me check your father's room," he says. "Remember, I told him it could be his secret clubhouse. Maybe he went up there and fell asleep." But after Alan climbs the stairs, he finds the boy isn't there. He isn't alarmed, exactly, but his heart is beating more quickly.

"I went around the house," Julia says, her concern evident, "and I didn't see him anywhere. Tommy," she calls loudly. They listen for an answer that doesn't come. On the grass the shadow of the hawk glides patiently.

"OK, OK," Alan says. "Let's not let ourselves get carried away. There's really nowhere for him to go."

"What are you saying?" Julia bursts out. "There are hundreds of acres of woods for him to be lost in."

Alan is trying to keep things under control. "When's the last time we saw him for sure?" he says. "At lunch, right. Maybe an hour, an hour and a quarter ago. So he can't be gone any longer than that."

"Tommy," Julia cries. "Tommy, where are you?"

Once again they listen and hear nothing.

"OK," Alan says, "let's try to be reasonable. Tommy's a good kid. He wouldn't just run away for the hell of it."

"But where is he?" Julia pleads. "Tommy," she calls again.

Alan is getting close to panic himself but he knows he's got to keep it down. "What about the basement?" he asks, though he doesn't really believe Tommy would have gone there. Having said it, though, he imagines the boy having fallen down the steep stairs. When they get to the side of the house, though, they see, to their relief, that the bulkhead doors are closed. "I'll look anyway," he says. He lifts the doors and steps into the damp, cool space that houses the water heater and the circuit breakers, as well as the wine rack that's left over from the days when Julia's father thought of the little room as his wine cellar. "No, he isn't here," Alan calls up.

Back in the warm air outside, he feels the need to come up with a plan. "OK," he says. "Nobody snatched him. At least we know that." He wants to say that no wild animal attacked him, which is probable enough, but it's not a subject he's eager to introduce. "I guess we have to figure he might have wandered off. But where?" He tries to control his galloping apprehension. "Everything's going to be OK," he says.

Julia is crying now. It would be totally understandable if at that moment she was regretting having come here at all. "And I was so caught up in those damned reports on the changed curricula," she says.

"No," he says. "Don't blame yourself."

"But where is he?" she sobs.

"Wait a while," Alan says. "I have an idea. Wasn't he talking about the places your father used to show him, and didn't he mention the secret pirate's cave?"

She nods. "Stay here," he says. "Keep looking for him here. I'm going to that cave."

He sets off at a trot toward the pine forest planted by Richard Mallory just after the war, and cuts through an opening in a stone wall. His breath is coming faster, and not just because he's laboring uphill. Please let him be there, he prays. Branches snap and brush against him as he pushes his way upward, the land rising more steeply now. At last he can see the gray shape of the outcropping. His steps are hurried as he labors up the slope and when he's come to within twenty yards or so of the bone-colored rock, he catches a glimpse of red—Tommy's tee-shirt. "Tommy," he calls softly, and the boy turns toward him. It's clear that he's been crying.

"Hey, what's the matter, big guy?" he says as he gets closer to his son. He grabs Tommy and squeezes him.

"I thought Grandpa might be here," the boy sniffles.

Alan waits for his breath to settle. "He is," he tells Tommy, "in a way. Except we can't see him. I can feel him, though. Can't you?"

He can feel Tommy shaking his head.

He lets the boy go and can't help smiling. Christ, he found him. He's weightless with joy. "Well," he says, "guess what? I was digging behind the house and all of a sudden I heard a voice—it was your grandpa's and the voice said, 'Look what's in your shovel,' and what do you suppose it was?"

Tommy wrinkles his nose. "What was it?"

"It was an arrowhead from old Indian times. And I heard your grandpa say, 'Give that to Tommy. He's going to like it.'"

Tommy blinks. "Do you have it?" he asks.

"I sure do." He reaches into his pocket and pulls out the worn wedge of stone. "Can you believe that an Indian had this on the end of his arrow a long, long time ago? Feel the shape." He hands it to the boy, who turns it around in his hand. "Now we have to get back and let Mommy know you're OK. She was worried you were lost."

"I was only trying to find Grandpa," the boy says.

"I know. But next time you'll tell us before you go looking, won't you?'

"I will, Daddy."

"Good boy."

In a couple of minutes they're back at the house, Alan having shouted the news to Julia before their arrival. "He was just looking for his grandpa," he tells her. "And I told him that his grandpa helped me find an Indian arrowhead for him."

Julia takes the boy into her arms and hugs him fiercely. Alan looks into the forest, determined not to think about what might have happened.

Though they'd planned to eat at the house tonight, he decides that this is a special day and they should go to the Leaping Trout restaurant in nearby Exham. They drive the curving river road that affords spectacular views of the water that glistens in the evening light. The river is dotted with rocks and fly fishermen, around one turn a wooded island looms like a ship of trees. The land rises steeply on the driver's side, and an occasional white rush of water pours out of the rocks. After a few miles, they reach the town and cross the red covered bridge, their tires thrumming on the wooden floor of the enclosed corridor, squares cut into the bridge's wall showing bits of the river like a series of small paintings, silver in the shaded tunnel. The restaurant is only a few feet from the end of the bridge, and in minutes the three of them are sitting at an outdoor table near the river. The adults will dine on trout and share a bottle of wine, while Tommy will be delighted with mac and cheese and a glass of soda. Even before they're served, Tommy takes out the arrowhead several times and turns it over in his hand.

The day, Alan and Julia agree, has been a spectacular one, and as they lift their glasses she tells him how happy she is that she's come back. The panic of earlier in the afternoon is safely buried in the past. "And the best part of the day is yet to come," Julia says with a sly smile, and Alan thinks of the full-sized bed that's waiting for them in the upstairs room. It's certainly an improvement over Richard Mallory's undersized, monastic sleeping arrangements, though the presence of Tommy in the room with them may be an equivalent disincentive to hearty eroticism.

"Hey," Alan says sincerely, "what we've had already is great. But I wouldn't complain about a little gravy."


"So," Julia says the next morning at breakfast, "I suppose you're going to be out there mowing in a couple of minutes." The smell of fresh coffee and toast fills the room, which is cool since the top of the Dutch door is open, though it's not cool enough to warrant a fire in the fireplace.

"I have to wait a bit," he says. The sun hasn't climbed high enough over the back forest to reach the front yard, so the grass out there is still wet with dew. "But you're right: that's the first thing on the agenda."

She shakes her head. "You're a lot more like my father than you'd want to admit."

"Oh?" He looks at her. "That's a surprise."

She smiles over her coffee cup. "You always have to have some kind of project when we're up here. You can never be content to just, well, hang out."

"Hey, I need the exercise," he says. "I can't just lie in the hammock reading and stay slim like you."

"Nah," she counters. "Slim has nothing to do with it. It's a mental thing."

He takes a swallow of orange juice and butters his toast. "OK," he concedes, "maybe it is. But didn't that doctor tell your father he needed some physical activity to keep from going batty? Maybe it's the same with me."

Julia dips her knife into the jar of lingonberry jam and spreads it on her toast. "There's more going on here than staying slim or sane," she says. "Remember, I saw you when you were cutting down all those trees in the clearing. There was something demonic about it. It's a battle, isn't it?" She shakes her head. "You'll never win, you know. The forest is going to swallow all of this up eventually. And all your work," she says in a sing-song voice, "will have been for naught."

He puts down his coffee cup. "Listen to the beautiful witch of the woods. What if I know that and I choose to go ahead anyway, mowing the grass, cutting the trees, clearing the land, holding back Nature for as long as I can? Isn't that heroic?"

"I'm sure that's what those colonials were thinking a couple of hundred years ago when they tried to turn these rocky, tree-covered hills into farmland."

He nods. "Well, their stone walls are still there, in the woods. Those guys left their mark on the forest, didn't they?"

"And Ozymandias left his in the desert. Look what it got him. You men are all such Ahabs."

"Hey," he says, "where's your sense of poetry?"

"I don't have any time for poetry this morning. I'm taking Tommy with me to Rudyard to get some groceries. Anything you need?"

"Could you look for a harpoon?"

Later, after Julia and Tommy have left, a summer quiet falls over the place. It's going to be a warm day but the cicadas haven't started up yet. The sun has already touched the grass and he knows he can start cutting it soon. He remembers the hawk they saw yesterday, soaring above them in a slow, patient spiral, its alert, penetrating eyes fixed on something far below, its wide shadow gliding across the grass and slithering over the stone wall. Even today, the memory brings a shiver of wonder.

There's no hawk this morning, at least none to be seen. The lazy drone of a plane sounds somewhere in the distance; in the silence afterward, Alan can hear a fly buzzing. It strikes him that it's a lazy buzz, that the fly isn't up to anything in particular, just buzzing. Maybe it's recognized the futility of a fly's life and has decided to enjoy itself in the interval before it stumbles into a spider's web or lands on a frog's tongue. Truth to tell, Alan himself doesn't really feel like getting to work right away and maunders into the library, knowing the grass will still be there when he gets around to cutting it.

The contents of the library Richard Mallory assembled over the years are eclectic, the collection including old poetry anthologies as well as insurance company reports, some classic British and American works of fiction and a few novels that were popular thirty years ago and have since sunk into obscurity. Emerson's essays stand cheek by jowl with Thurber's, there are mystery stories and fairy tales, manuals on carpentry and plumbing that were no doubt useful when Julia's father was building this house. Alan has stopped in a corner where a couple of shelves hold books on New England: travel literature, histories, folk tales and a geological survey.

He takes out the WPA guide to Connecticut that was published in 1938. The thick red volume has a pleasing heft and after skimming the pages for a moment, he takes the book back to the breakfast table, where he's poured himself another half-cup of coffee. He turns the pages in an aimless way, stopping here and there to look at some of the black and white photos, which are eerily still, for the most part devoid of people, looking like scenes under glass. You can't help wondering if the occupants of those buildings had any idea of what was in store for them in the next few decades. On the city streets are a few bulbous pre-war cars, invariably dark, artifacts of the Great Depression. There's a hint of the New Deal concerns in pictures of leather-aproned workers, invariably white, in the factories of Waterbury. Alan scans a few of the scenic tour guides, with their meticulous notation of mileages that would be traveled almost exclusively on two-lane roads.

He runs his finger idly across a page and the smell of these old words is suddenly redolent with the mystery of time. Who, opening this book when it was new, could have foreseen that after the war that hadn't happened yet, this little house was going to be built in the Connecticut woods, who could have guessed that Alan would one day be sitting within these walls? It's amazing. On this lazy summer day, he feels blessed.

When the phone rings, Alan goes to pick it up in the library, wondering how Julia could have managed to cover the eight miles to Rudyard already. Possibly she remembered something she wanted to tell him and has stopped somewhere along the road, though he really can't think of any place where there's a pay phone.

"Alan?" There's no hesitation this time. The identity of the caller is unmistakable and the tranquil sense he's had all morning gives way to an abrupt intake of breath.

"Rory?" he answers, his heart pounding. It isn't over then, he finds himself thinking, whatever the hell *it* is.

"Hey." There's Rory's familiar laugh. "I never believed I'd get you at this number, but I guess they were right," he says.

In seconds the floor has gone out from under Alan, he feels as if some sorcerer has snatched his shadow. After all, more than a year has passed since his last meeting with Rory, and he's done a good job of convincing himself that that chapter of his life was finally over. When he'd shaken Rory's hand in the bar in Boston he had the sense he'd dodged a bullet. Now, incredibly, the man has come back, and he's even intruded on Innisfree. "How did you find this number?" Alan asks.

"Hey, dude, it's listed." The voice is all affability. "It wasn't hard."

Alan looks out to the front yard, which he was planning to mow in a little while. The sun has gradually moved up from the clearing, over the stone wall and onto the grass. Soon it will reach the house itself. He feels detached from the scene, as if it were one of those pictured in the WPA book, frozen, silent, gone; and he has to will himself back to the present. He's still trying to get used to the fact that he's talking to Rory, and he reminds himself that he's heard nothing yet that's threatening about this call. "So how are you?" he ventures cautiously.

"Not bad," Rory says, "not bad." After a second, he adds, "Of course, things could always be better, couldn't they?"

If, for a fraction of an instant, Alan might have been able to convince himself that Rory's call might be innocent, whatever that might mean, it's impossible to believe that now: Rory wants something, Alan is sure, and he has the feeling that he isn't going to get off easy this time: this is going to cost him something. "You're not . . . in trouble, are you?" he asks.

"No, no," Rory answers dismissively. "I'm fine."

"That's good," Alan says, engulfed by a sudden desolation. Not that long ago he'd been elated that Julia was beginning to come out of the depression that had dogged her since the death of her father. This morning as he'd looked out at the grass he was going to cut later, he'd felt satisfied with his accomplishments as a man, a husband and father. Now it's all evaporated, and he's on his guard, pursued. "Where are you calling from?" he asks, suddenly alarmed by the possibility that the man might be somewhere nearby.

"I'm in Boston," Rory answers, and Alan relaxes a bit. At least he's not down the road.

Alan is determined to get a hold of himself. "What's up?" he asks with as much casualness as he can muster. "What's the deal?"

He has to wait for the answer. "The deal, yeah." There's a barely audible laugh. "The fact is, I've got a chance at a very good deal," Rory says at last, "but I need some help."

There it is. Alan feels a tightness in his throat. "What kind of help?" he asks warily. "Are we talking about money?"

Rory laughs again. "Sure, we're talking about money. Did you think I was going to ask for your prayers?"

Money, Alan thinks, that was inevitable. He didn't really expect that there wouldn't be a bill for his involvement with the Lyletown business, did he? This is hardly a surprise. Even as he's prayed that his connection to Rory was over, Alan has been aware of the possibility of such a demand. The fact is, money is at least tangible. It all depends on the amount Rory is talking about. Of course, this time it's going to cost something to send him away again.

"Look," Rory says, "I'm just in this area for a little while, but I have a big opportunity and at the moment I just happen to be a little short on capital."

"What kind of opportunity?" Alan asks.

"I'd rather not go into the details, dude. Let's just say it's a pretty big opportunity." He sighs. "But I have a chance to make a bit of money. Like I said, I just need some capital."

"OK . . ." Alan says, a man in the dark wading away from the shore, wondering how deep the water is going to be, "how much capital are we talking about?"

"Five grand," Rory answers.

Alan whistles. "Wow," he says.

Then Rory adds, "But look, it's not like I'm asking for some kind of handout. This would be a loan. Don't worry. You'll get it back. With interest."

Yeah, Alan thinks, and the next time I lose a tooth the tooth fairy's going to drop a little something my way too. All at once he's angry at Rory for the game he's playing. Why not call this business by its real name? If blackmail is too harsh, maybe it's payment for services rendered, for serving time while Alan was free to live a life. In the midst of his anger, though, he feels a sudden spasm of guilt: it's not that hard to understand Rory's position, is it? In fact, after initially being rattled by the amount of money he requested, Alan is relieved by the number, since it's not only a finite sum but one that's in fact manageable, a small price to pay for his continued peace of mind. Given the circumstances, he could even consider himself lucky, since he's already had one visit from Rory that hadn't cost him anything in dollars. All Rory seemed to want then was Alan's presence in that bar in Boston to hear his story, to bear witness. So he ought to count himself ahead at this point: he'd got himself a free year, so to speak. "So you're in Boston again," he says. "For how long?"

"For as short a time as I can manage, dude," Rory says. "I'm not all that fond of this area." After a moment, he says, "Well, what do you say?"

"Look, Rory," Alan tells him, "I'm not as rich as you think I am." He waits for some reaction but when he gets none, he goes on. "I'll admit, I might be able to get my hands on five thou, I might be able to do this to help you out." Business has been good lately, and a couple of years ago Alan established a separate bank account that he's been hoping to use for some special treat, like a trip to Europe for the family. Nothing specific has been planned yet, but he already has close to ten thousand in the account. "Say I can," he says. "Is there somewhere I can send you the money?"

"No, no," Rory says, "this is something that has to get tied up pretty soon or I'll lose my chance. Besides, I'd like to see you face to face." He pauses. "I can even tease you a little," he says, "maybe hold out an inducement."

"What kind of inducement?" Alan asks.

"I have some information about Lily and Serena," Rory says.

That gets his attention. The mention of Lily's name brings back a tangle of feelings from those times and, for the moment 1968 is as real as the present, who he was then, what he thought he wanted; and his being here in the little house in the woods seems like an illusion. Alan Ripley, lawyer, husband and father, homeowner and current occupant of Innisfree—all that is as vaporous as a dream. "I don't suppose you're going to tell me anything over the phone."

"You suppose right, my man," Rory says. "You're going to be back at work Tuesday, right, after the holiday?"

"Yeah," Alan answers, trying to persuade himself that he hasn't made any real commitment yet, though he knows that in the end he's going to give him the money. It's not surprising that he's caved in so quickly, since he can't deny he owes something to Rory, whether or not he'd actually agree with the suggestion that Rory spent time in prison as his surrogate. Still, he has no idea of what to make of Rory's tale about the "business opportunity." Does he really expect Alan to believe he's going to get his money back with interest? That might even be worse than just giving the money away, since whatever "business" Rory would be involved in would likely be questionable at best.

"Can we get together some time then?" Rory presses.

"I suppose," Alan says. "I'm not promising anything, though."

"Well, of course," Rory says. "You'd have to think about it. I have a car. I can come up and see you in your town."

"That wouldn't be a good idea," Alan says, alarmed at this suggestion of Rory's mobility, determined to hold on to whatever advantages he has. The last thing he wants is for Rory to show up at his house. He names a place in Harvard Square that's loud, trendy and spacious, where the two of them can enjoy some privacy in the midst of a crowd. It's far enough from where he lives, a manageable environment—Alan's home turf—unlike the last place where they met. To the extent that he can, he intends to keep the situation under control.

"OK, I'll see you then," Rory says, "at high noon."

When the connection is broken Alan is suddenly awash with relief. It's as if Rory and everything he carries with him have disappeared into the phone line. In fact, Alan feels momentarily safe and secure here in the woods, possibly the way Richard Mallory once did after he'd built his refuge from the world, especially after his terrible war experiences on those islands in the Pacific. Just now Cambridge is a long way away, as is Tuesday. Alan still has time to enjoy being here with his family, if only he can manage it.

The powerful three horsepower mower is heavy and, tilting as Alan pushes it across the sloping lawn, unwieldy as well; but that doesn't keep him from racing double-time over the area, breathing in the mix of exhaust and cut grass as the machine's vibrations throb through his extended arms. Within minutes he's sweating, his breath comes fast, but there's no slackening the pace. *Rory. Rory. Rory.* Those syllables are a thorn in his side. Still, he keeps pushing the heavy machine along the uneven terrain, relishing the effort. His furious mowing isn't enough to quiet his thoughts, though. Why the hell did Rory have to turn up again, carrying a threat in his voice, his laugh, even in his silence? Alan shoves the mower recklessly across the grass as if this kind of speed-cutting will put the genie back into the bottle and somehow Rory will never have happened at all. If only. No, he's going to have to deal with the man, there's no getting around that, and this time it's going to cost him. A loan. Yeah.

A sudden harsh clang brings everything to a halt. Alan jumps back, letting go of the throttle control, the machine's roar abruptly silenced amid a cloud of gray exhaust smelling of oil. Jesus, he hit a rock. He's got to be more careful. When he pulls back the mower, a bone-white scar is visible on the top of a mottled boulder that's probably as big as a bowling ball under the grass. He's lucky the blade didn't break. He stands there a moment, listening to his breathing, to the suddenly audible birds, the leaves rustling in the breeze, and runs a hand across his damp brow. OK, he tells himself, he's going to have to deal with Rory, and racing this way across a sloping terrain that he knows has its share of partially buried rocks isn't going to help anything.

After a couple of seconds he pulls the cord and starts up the mower once more, grateful that it's caught on the first attempt. He begins moving the machine again, making his way more methodically this time, keeping an eye out for rocks. For all his attentiveness, it's not enough to keep him from thinking about Rory. This is going to cost him money, he's already accepted that. But money is tangible, finite. Of course, with something like this, there's always the chance that the five grand will just be the first installment. On the other hand, he doesn't have a lot in the way of alternatives, does he? The point is, if he pays up now, Rory is likely to quiet down for a while. Who knows what will happen later? These thoughts don't exactly satisfy him, but they're enough, combined with the physical effort and the sedating roar of the motor, to calm him; and by the time he sees the car carrying Julia and Tommy up the road, he's managed to cut his way through an impressive swath of the lawn. Good, almost done. It will just take an hour or so to finish the rest of the job.

"My father would have been proud of your efforts," Julia says later as they look from the pergola at the expanse of green that's been trimmed to neat blades of less than an inch. "He would have said you'd just performed a civilizing gesture."

"I agree." Alan takes a sip of iced tea, quietly basking in his achievement. Or he would be if it weren't for an occasional uninvited memory of Rory's call. That's another world, he tells himself, that doesn't touch what's going on here. It's going to be taken care of.

"Now," Julia says, "were you really serious about swimming this afternoon?"

"Oh, yeah, sure thing," he says. "But not in the pond on the property. It's too cold. Let's go to the state park."

She smiles. "I think that's where Tommy would rather go."

"Do I know my own kid or what?" It's going to be just the three of them. Rory doesn't even know about the state park. They're safe up here.

They spend a couple of hours at the lake where the water near the sandy shore is indeed warm, and where small bluegills sometimes come up and nibble on the legs of waders, which at first bothers Tommy, though he soon gets used to it. "Look, look," he whispers, "look how close they come." After a while in the shallow water, Alan decides to swim out to the floating dock. Once he's beyond the beach area, he feels the cooler temperature as the lake's bottom drops away. Out here, he's alone, hearing his own breath and the rhythmic slash of his strokes, his eyes moving as his head turns from the white cloud in the blue sky above to the dark ring of trees around the lake, occasionally glimpsing the shape in the water that's his destination. In a few minutes, he pulls himself up onto the dock, where he lies for a time on its boards drying in the sun, the solitary inhabitant of his own floating island, listening to the water lap against the wood. When he's dry and warm once more he gets up, dives in and heads back toward the beach, and soon he's in the warmer water, the sandy bottom close by. As his limbs move through the thinner medium of air, he's pleasantly exhausted. "I've had it for a while," he says. "Blanket time."

"Look at me," Tommy calls from the shallow water as Alan lies on the blanket beside Julia, who's keeping watch.

"Glad you came?" Face down, he feels the sun on his back.

"Mmm-hmm," she says. "I wouldn't have missed it for the world."

"Even if you had to put up with Ozymandias part of the time."

"Oh, even Ozymandias has his good points."

After swimming they go to the pizzeria at the other end of the lake, where they chew on cheesy wedges flecked with pepperoni, watching the bugs bump up against the screen window. Through the mesh they can see to the beach where they were swimming not long ago. In the deeper water a dark motor boat buzzes, its bright flag rippling against the background of the darkening shore.

"This is nice," Tommy says. His parents nod in agreement.

Back at Innisfree, Alan reads a story to his exhausted son, who falls asleep before he's finished. After he tucks the boy in, he quietly makes his way down the stairs. "Swimming must have done him in," he tells Julia. "He's totally out."

She smiles. "Does that mean we're at the beginning of the adults' hour?" He says nothing but in the silence a sudden gust of kerosene from one of the lamps they've kept from earlier times makes him remember those days. The two of them stand there for a while listening for sounds from above and when they're sure Tommy's asleep for the night, Julia tilts her head in the direction of the downstairs bedroom. Yeah, he nods back, and they make their way there together. Before long they have their clothes off.

"Remember the old beds?" he says, running a hand across her bare shoulder.

She smiles languidly. "Don't knock them," she says. "I think Tommy was conceived on one of those beds."

His hand moves slowly down her body. "The sheer persistence of humans is impressive," he says.

She puts a finger to his lips. "Shh," she says. "Enough talking."

Later, they take a blanket to the terrace in front of the house, where they lie on their backs looking for falling stars. "They don't come until later in the summer," Julia says.

"The Perseids, you mean. But there's always the possibility we might see a lone one."

"A rogue falling star. I like that idea."

"Listen," he says. They hear the long, drawn-out hoot of an owl.

She's silent for a while and he asks, "What are you thinking about?'

"I don't know why, but I was remembering the time the bees were in our roof here. They'd gotten in under the eaves, thousands of them literally, and you could hear them through the ceiling when you were in the upstairs bedroom. The roof was beginning to heave. We'd let the wisteria out front grow and the vine was all over the roof. Between that and the bees we had a big problem. It scared my mother to have all those bees there but my father, for just a little while, got the idea that he was going to sell the honey they produced."

"I don't suppose that lasted long."

"No, but he'd always had this dream that we could be self-sufficient up here, that if there were some apocalyptic crisis and we lost everything, we could live up here."

"The first death from freezing would come in November," Alan says, "given the insulation, or lack thereof."

"Yeah, I think he knew that, but he liked the idea anyway."

Alan smiles. "So how did you finally get the bees out?"

"We had to pull back the wisteria first of all, get it off the roof. That's why we have to keep it cut back so religiously. Then we brought in a professional beekeeper from around here who had one of those outfits like a spaceman, covered from head to toe. He had a can full of something that produced the smoke he needed to get the bees out. I think he had to lead the queen out first. The deal was, he did the work and he kept all the honey he could extract."

"Was there a lot?"

"Seven hundred pounds, was what he told us."

He whistles. "Wow! But I'll bet it was a relief to have all those bees gone."

"Of course. Though," Julia laughs, "my father insisted he missed the sound of all that buzzing in the roof."

"He didn't!"

"It was his little joke," she says. "He said it was like monks chanting."

He shakes his head.

"What?"

"I'm trying to imagine all that honey under the roof and the wisteria vine. Even if you got stung to death by those bees, think of all the sweetness that would surround you."

"Sometimes I think you're as bad as he was."

"Am I supposed to take that as a compliment?"

"Judge for yourself, big boy."

Alan smiles, pleased to be part of this story, pleased to be living under a roof that once held hundreds of pounds of honey. Lord, he thinks, give me honey, give me wisteria, give me my family here. "Hey," he says, "let's not go back. Let's just stay up here."

Julia shakes her head. "What did I say? You're just as bad as my father."

But there's no staying here, he knows. He's got to go back and deal with Rory.


Later that night, Alan awakens from a dream: he was alone in the kitchen of the apartment he'd lived in when he was married to Martha. The kitchen was small but colorful, since a friend of theirs had painted Pennsylvania Dutch hex signs on the cabinets. It was hard to tell what time of day it had been in the dream, but Alan would guess it was morning, that he was getting ready to go to the college for a day of teaching. His stomach was in a knot all that time, it seemed, because he knew he was in the wrong life, the wrong occupation and the wrong marriage. He'd come to realize shortly after that whirlwind weekend when he'd convinced himself they should get married, that getting back together with Martha was an act of penance, a response to the trauma of Lyletown and the close proximity to the utter destruction of his life. Maybe, he must have thought, if he stopped the tape and rewound to some earlier spot, he could travel over the same territory without making terrible mistakes.

Martha was fresh-faced and blonde, an All-American girl who was always up for a bit of fun, though that fun tended to be of the good clean variety. She was smart but not particularly adventurous. In so many ways she was the opposite of Lily and in the terror he felt after Lyletown, Martha seemed a safe harbor. It didn't take him long to recognize that that was no reason to marry someone. Of course, Martha was vaguely aware that he'd hung around with Lily and her crowd, but she knew nothing of Alan's involvement in the Caper. He's sometimes thought that not telling her about it was a mistake but, given what happened, he doesn't see how that would have changed anything.

Those were awful days, hopeless for both of them. Even now, with the prospect of another meeting with Rory, there's at least the possibility of a future, which hadn't been the case in that kitchen.

Breathing in the familiar smells of this room in the house his father-in-law built in the woods, he thinks, whatever sins I committed, if there's somebody up there keeping score, I paid.

As he makes his way along familiar Cambridge streets, Alan is in no hurry to get to O'Reilly's. Dealing with Rory this way is the last thing he wants to be doing. But, then, what choice does he have? He's come here to protect what's most important to him. From the moment Rory resurfaced a couple of days ago, he's made hostages of Alan and his family, not to mention his professional status and his place in the world. That was the threat he sensed when he held the phone to his ear in the little library at Innisfree and heard that voice again. Underneath the talk of a loan and the promise of information about people from their past, there was one simple reality: Rory still has the power to put Alan's whole way of life in jeopardy and they both know it. And for him to have somehow found his way to Innisfree, of all places—talk about the serpent in the garden. Why, Richard Mallory had asked Alan when he first raised the idea of installing a phone, why would you want anyone to find you there? Maybe he had a point. A car's horn jolts Alan back to the present and he pulls up sharply at the curb. Take it easy, he tells himself. There's no point in borrowing trouble. Apocalyptic scenarios are all too easy to imagine, but if this situation is going to be resolved satisfactorily, it's going to take a cool head.

When he steps out of the sunny street at last, it takes him a second or two to adjust to the festive chaos of O'Reilly's, where the manic roar of the patrons overwhelms the Celtic music playing on the sound system. At the glossy mahogany bar, people are nursing carefully poured pints of Guinness or knocking back every variety of cocktail with their lunches, but he can see that Rory isn't one of them. A hurried scan of the booths comes up empty as well before Alan spots him, improbably, at a table near the very center of the room, and his first view of the man gives him a start. Unlike the last time he saw Rory, he's looking tanned and healthy. He's wearing a trim summer weight sports coat and a dazzlingly white shirt that's open at the collar; and from this distance, he seems relaxed as he lounges there, a glass of white wine before him, his long legs stretched out under the table. When he sees Alan, he springs to his feet with a smile, waving him over.

"My man, my man," Rory greets him effusively, patting him on the shoulder, and Alan can't help feeling that, though he's the one who chose the site of their meeting, it's Rory who's acting like the host.

"You're looking good," Alan says, genuinely impressed by the transformation: Rory looks younger, he seems to have recovered a good deal of his old flash. For the moment, the concern Alan has felt about this meeting is overshadowed by a simple sense of wonder: how the hell has Rory managed to retrieve his former self?

"You're looking good yourself," Rory says. "Have you put on a couple of pounds?"

Alan instinctively sucks in his stomach. "I hope not."

Rory gives him a wink. "Just pulling your leg. You look the same. Playing a lot of tennis?"

"Some." Once more Alan is on his guard—he doesn't remember telling Rory that he played tennis. What else does he know about him? He's still trying to take in the changes in the man since their last meeting. "I see you're drinking wine this time, not beer," he observes.

Rory's tan accentuates the whiteness of his teeth when he smiles. "I've spent a bit of time on the coast," he says. "You get into the habit."

Alan is curious about just what Rory's been doing out there, and he hopes he'll find out, though that will probably have to wait for later, when they've got their business settled. Just now, a long-legged waitress with a mane of red hair and an accent straight from Galway is at their table. It's clear from their interplay that Rory has already chatted her up. "Ah, Bridget," he says, "this is my friend Alan, a very important man in legal circles here." Bridget directs a sunny smile toward Alan, who shrugs modestly. "Be sure to tell the kitchen staff," Rory instructs her, "to be particularly attentive."

"I will indeed," Bridget assures him, to all appearances enjoying Rory's game.

"Everything fresh," Rory says, "everything the best. And, of course, a glass of this excellent wine for my friend right away. That OK with you?"

After she's left, Rory turns to Alan. "Nice kid," he says. "But now you and I get our chance to talk." He leans forward conspiratorially. "Let's start with the gossip. I suppose you're hot to find out what I know about Lily."

Alan tries to play down his interest with a casual, "Sure."

Rory's smile is insistent. "Come on, why don't you admit she's still working her charms on you?"

No, he wants to say, it's not her charms I'm thinking about. The fact is, he's fascinated by the idea that Lily is still out in the world somewhere, living a life about which he and just about everyone who knew her back then is completely in the dark. What can that life be like? he wonders. Wouldn't being exiled from everything that once defined her be the equivalent of Rory's prison sentence, except that hers wouldn't have an end point? How could she even be Lily, separated from the aura that was so much a part of her, separated from the scene she'd created for herself? Certainly, whatever she's doing now isn't likely to be anything like her old life, when her local notoriety inspired his friend Zack to call her the Cleopatra of Class Warfare. "Hey," he concedes, "I'm interested. I'm curious."

Rory leans back and is silent for a while, a man who enjoys being the dispenser of information that's so obviously eagerly anticipated. Milking the moment, he lights a cigarette and exhales. "OK," he says at last, "here's what I know. Lily and Serena wound up somewhere in Washington State, just like I thought they would. Where, my source didn't tell me. But Serena died in a car crash not long after they got out there." He takes a drag on his cigarette, exhales and looks through the smoke in the direction of a wall that holds framed photographs of politicians and athletes.

"Jesus," Alan says. "Serena's dead?"

Rory lifts his glass and intones mechanically, "May she rest in peace." After a moment of silence, he goes on. "But you're more interested in Lily, of course. Well, here's a surprise: I was told that Lily, or whatever she's calling herself these days, has become a solid citizen of some little town out there. She married a local schoolteacher a couple of years ago, and the two of them run a bakery and coffee shop." He exhales a cloud of smoke once more. "And get this: the person I talked to said she had a grandmotherly look about her." When he smiles it's with an unmistakable air of smugness.

For the moment the frantic buzz of the faux-Irish pub fades, giving way to a few haunting bars conveyed by fiddle, tin whistle and flute, and Alan tries to reconcile what he's just heard with the memory of the Lily he knew. This latest bit of news about her disturbs him. It certainly makes sense that, spared the punishment of the law, she might have been forced into living the most ordinary of lives. But Lily, with her gold minidress, her cape, the swirl of smoke that accompanied her passionate political pronouncements—is it possible she's serving muffins and coffee to small-town cops and crossing guards in some rainy northwestern town? It seems to him a kind of death.

"But, wait," he interrupts his own musing, "if you know this stuff, how safe, how secure can she be?"

"Don't worry," Rory says. "The info I got was pretty general as far as geography goes. Hell, Washington is a big state. Didn't that airplane hijacker D. B. Cooper parachute into the forest there with scads of money? Nobody's found him, have they?" He shakes his head. "No, there was nothing really traceable in what was told to me. I'd guess that our Lily could stay hidden in that bakery of hers for as long as she wants to." He shrugs. "Of course, there's always the chance that she'll decide on her own to come out of the cold."

Across the room a young guy wearing an expensive suit stands up suddenly and makes a comic bow to the two well-dressed women at the table with him, and all three burst into laughter.

"Well, it's not quite what La Grande Lily envisioned for herself, I'll bet," Rory says. "But then, that's probably true for most of us."

Alan gives a grunt of approbation. He's still trying to digest this new information about Lily.

"Hell," Rory says with a broad smile, "change is what life's all about, isn't it?" He makes a gesture toward Alan. "Look at you: you weren't exactly a Che Guevara back then, but who'd have guessed you'd wind up as a partner in a law firm, with a family, a nice house in the suburbs, a summer place in Connecticut?" It's not clear whether this is meant to be flattering or ironic, and once more Alan feels vaguely threatened. "By the way," Rory asks, "what's that place like? They told me it was in the mountains."

"Who did you talk to about the place?" Alan asks, trying to check the surge of anger that's accompanied his growing uneasiness. Suddenly the room is full of eyes. How does Rory know about all this stuff? Hell, even the FBI wasn't able to find out anything about Serena and Lily.

Rory laughs. "I can't reveal my sources, dude." His expression is suddenly thoughtful. "What's your place like? I can picture some kind of hunting and fishing lodge. Very rustic: moose heads and stuffed fish on the walls. Scratchy blankets, army surplus cots." He takes a sip of his wine and returns his glass to the table.

"No." Alan has calmed a bit. Of course, Rory is just being curious. "It definitely isn't a hunting and fishing lodge," he says. Then, visualizing those shutters and gables, he adds, "It's just a little house in the woods. My father-in-law built it. He called it Innisfree."

Rory brightens. "Like the poem, right?"

"Right." He's surprised Rory's picked up the reference.

"He must have thought it was a kind of retreat, then. 'I will go now . . .'" he begins. "Something like that, isn't it?"

Alan nods, excited by the sudden presence of Yeats's lines here in this room amid carefully chosen images of Ireland: large black-and-white blowups of photos depicting the damaged General Post Office in Dublin just after the Easter Rising, a rocky stretch of Donegal or Connemara, the pale, haunted face of a nineteenth-century teenager preparing to emigrate, all artfully arranged for the delectation of yuppies with lots of discretionary income. "Yeah," he says, "'I will arise and go now, and go to Innisfree/And a small cabin build there, of clay and wattles made.' Well, it isn't a cabin and it isn't made out of clay and wattles, but it is a retreat. Even though it's in Connecticut, it's very remote. We didn't get a phone or electricity till a few years ago."

"Sounds like quite a hideaway," Rory says.

Alan nods. Only a couple of days ago, he, Julia and Tommy were having lunch in the shade of the pergola, watching the hawk's shadow pass over the sunny grass. He wishes he were there now.

"You're a lucky man," Rory says. "Everybody should be able to get away to another world, to his own Innisfree. I envy you." Then he adds, "I'd like to see that place some day."

Over my dead body, Alan thinks. But, then, why are they even talking about Innisfree? That isn't why they've come here, is it? In fact, what's odd is that so far Rory has shown no inclination to bring up the subject of money, the fundamental reason for their getting together. Alan remembers the meeting at Fred's last year: the place was dim and cramped and Rory wore a dark brown shirt, his movements were constricted, as if even in the bar he was remembering the tight spaces of his prison cell. All of the haunted air of that meeting is gone, he seems to take up more space today.

"Did you ever go to Lily's cottage in Moon Lake?" Rory asks out of the blue.

Alan shakes his head. He remembers listening to her talk about the place while he imagined himself there with her, ages ago. He saw the two of them in a boat, himself rowing lazily, going no place in particular. She'd be lying back against the stern, a hand trailing in the water. Just the creak of the oars, a soft splashing as the boat made its loitering way across the lake. He hasn't thought of this in years, and he can hardly believe he's dredged up that sentimental image.

"Me neither," Rory says. Of course, that cottage was to have been Rory's destination if things had gone the way they were supposed to in Lyletown. "Well, that was another world, wasn't it?" he says.

What Lily's lakeside cottage was like, Alan assumes, is one of the many things he's never going to know. Not to mention the bakery and café somewhere in the northwest where she's serving muffins to crossing guards.

Rory's lips curve into a slow smile. "Lily was one fine-looking woman, though," he muses. "I'll give her that." Alan nods, taking this as an invitation to talk further about the woman they both knew; but Bridget arrives just then with their sandwiches, and Rory is distracted, lapsing back into his play-acting with the waitress. Yes, yes, she assures him, the staff has indeed put their orders together with the greatest of care.

"Have they now?" Rory teases.

"And would I be lyin' to you?" she answers with a toss of her head.

"I suppose I'll just have to be trusting you, then." Rory follows her with his eyes when she leaves. "Mmm," he says. "Too bad I'm not staying around here longer. But then, business is business."

"So," Alan says, "things seem to be going better for you." He remembers what Rory told him at Fred's last year. "No more shit jobs?"

Rory grins. "You're damned right." Alan waits for more but that's as far as Rory seems willing to go at the moment. By now, though, Alan is used to facing these closed doors.

Still, as they bite into their sandwiches he feels a rising impatience with what's going on here. Why don't we just cut to the chase, he thinks, and drop the bullshit? Frankly, he'd have been more comfortable with a hungrier Rory, someone who obviously needed money and had no qualms about being up front about it. Things would be simpler then. "What exactly brings you to this coast?" he asks, hoping at least to learn something about what the man's been up to.

"Business," Rory smiles. "What else?" Once again it seems clear that he doesn't intend to say any more than he has to; but then, Alan can hardly expect him to go into details. What kind of business is Rory likely to be involved in, given his recent history? It's a question that might better be left unanswered, even unasked. Here amid the noisy camaraderie of the lunch hour, Alan is apprehensive once more. For all his attempts to reduce this situation to a simple matter of quid pro quo, he has the sense that he's standing at the edge of murky and treacherous swampland where he has to step with special care. He's come here prepared to pay Rory off for his silence about Alan's participation, however peripheral, in the Lyletown operation. He isn't proud to be doing this, but everything about the situation in which he finds himself is a result of his involvement in the Lyletown plot in the first place. He got himself into this mess and he's determined to deal with the consequences. Something is being asked of him, and he'd just as soon get it over with; but it's clear that for Rory, whatever he says, something more is going on here than just a bit of business.

Of course, Alan has assumed that the fiction of a loan is necessary to provide cover and allay Rory's sense of pride. But the man he's having lunch with has nothing of the supplicant about him, and Alan isn't so sure anymore about his earlier assumptions. In fact, in the last few minutes, he's begun to feel that Rory may indeed be thinking of his five thousand dollars as a loan and not a blackmail payment. That should make him feel better; but a loan could be just as problematic as any payoff since, given Rory's apparent circumstances, there's a pretty good chance that the money wouldn't be used for anything legitimate, and Alan's handing it over could put him into an even more compromising relationship with him.

"Business," Rory laughs to himself, "that's what life seems to be all about these days, isn't it?" He shakes his head. "How many people are here today to eat and how many to make deals?"

Alan looks around him. "I wouldn't want to bet against the deal-makers," he says.

Rory smiles. "Including us," he says.

Alan shrugs. "I suppose."

Rory sits there smiling, as opaque as ever. "Are you based on the coast then?" Alan asks.

"I was," Rory answers. "I'm in the process of relocating. But I was in the LA area, mostly."

At least Alan has pried that much information out of him. At the same time, the reference to the coast has unlocked a memory of his own from California. "My wife and I once spent a week in Santa Monica," he tells Rory. "A client lent us his place. It was great there." It was early in their marriage, before Tommy was born, and he remembers fondly the proximity to the Pacific, the lush bougainvillea, the smell of mock-orange in the night, the dry rustling of palms outside their bedroom window on Third Street. "Think you could live out here?" he'd asked Julia as they walked along the beach in the soft night, the ocean hissing at their feet. She'd pulled him closer and whispered, "Don't tempt me; stuff my ears with wax." He couldn't really imagine her leaving the east coast, any more than he was likely to, but at that moment he could understand her feelings exactly. The two of them had been happy in California. It was one of those times when he realized that, in spite of his past experiences, there was good reason to hope he could succeed in this relationship. Now it seems to him that even this memory is threatened by whatever it is that's being negotiated here between him and Rory.

Across the table from him, Rory nods. "Yeah," he says, "Santa Monica's nice." Alan had been hoping for more than that, possibly some clues to what he did out west.

"How'd you wind up working in California?" he persists.

"Through a friend," Rory says simply. A friend from prison? Alan wonders. As Rory reaches for his drink, Alan glimpses a portion of the tattoo on his wrist, not quite as visible this time under his tan. "Hey," he points to the spot, "I noticed that before and I meant to ask you about it."

Rory pulls back his cuff slowly, revealing the purple shape of the spider web, a small, intricate network of lines like a series of ladders converging on a central point.

"Does that mean something?" Alan asks.

Rory laughs dryly. "Yeah," he says. "It means time passes. I got that in the joint, of course." He covers the tattoo. "I thought about having it removed when I got out but, I don't know, it's kind of a reminder of what I don't want to go back to." His eyes take on a distant look. "There wasn't much you could do inside that box but watch old Mister Spider weaving his web. I'm out now, I want to do something more." Once again, with the reference to prison, Alan feels the encroachment of something dark, and he isn't prepared when Rory asks him, "What about you?" Alan is confused. Is he asking him what he feels about tattoos, spider webs, or prison? "What's it like to be married," Rory clarifies, "to have a family?" He looks at Alan intently. "I mean, I'd like to hear it from the horse's mouth, so to speak."

"Oh," he says, "being married is great. Well, I can only speak for myself, I guess, but, yeah, it's great." Having answered honestly, he's on his guard once again: he's determined to keep Julia and Tommy separate from Rory and all he brings with him. At the same time, he's aware of the blandness of the declaration he's just made. If he'd really wanted to convey the complex texture of his married life, he'd have to try to explain the mysterious flow of closeness and distance between himself and Julia, the alignments and disjunctions of their separate rhythms that can bring surprising gifts and inexplicable sorrows; he'd have to talk about how his own history has been joined with hers, the way her past, or at least as much of it as he's had access to, has been fed into his psychological bloodstream, so that her father, her sister, her own girlhood aspirations are part of him too. None of this, of course, would begin to suggest anything about his and Julia's connections to their community, their friends and colleagues, special people like Sam, a presence even after his death. And certainly there's no way to express how Tommy has brought an element of unforeseen joy and dread into their lives. You couldn't possibly know, he wants to tell him. Instead, he says, "I was married before. That didn't turn out well at all, so I have some basis for comparison." He looks at Rory. "What about you?"

Rory eases back in his chair. "I don't think I'm the marrying kind," he says with what looks like the faintest trace of a smirk. "Maybe I'll just have to be content with the vicarious experience."

Alan can't help looking at the part of the tattoo that's visible, and he's struck again by just how little he really knows about this man. "I know not everybody gets married these days," he says. "But what about serious relationships?"

He shrugs. "What do you call serious? Spending the night with her?"

Alan smiles, conceding that, for whatever reasons, Rory may feel compelled to adopt a tough guy persona. Of course, there was all the time he spent in prison. Maybe that would make it difficult to commit yourself to anyone or anything once you got out.

As if he's read Alan's mind, Rory says, "I don't know. Maybe I got off on the wrong foot. Maybe if I'd have started out differ-ently . . ." He takes a sip of wine. "That's one of the things my little tattoo reminds me of," he says, "the lost chapters of my life, you might say." He shrugs. "In the end, though, you can't really do anything about what's already happened, can you? You can just try to make the most of what you've got." His eyes meet Alan's and he holds his gaze for a couple of seconds, as if to underline what he's just said.

Alan nods. "That's what I've tried to do," he says, thinking that if Rory believes his own words, he wouldn't be interested in black-mailing him, would he? He can feel his shoulders lift just a bit.

Rory taps the table gently with two fingers. "Like they say, you are what you do. In the end, my friend, we have to make ourselves."

Alan lifts his glass. "I'll drink to that," he says, and all at once he's swept up in an uninvited sense of solidarity with those young plotters of more than twenty years ago, Lily, Serena, Rory and himself. Yes, he'd been there, he'd been one of them, he'd once believed strongly that there was no other way to fight the perva-sive injustice around him than by committing himself to a criminal act. Jesus.

Rory clears his throat. "Well," he declares, "Like I said, I try to put all that stuff behind me. It's over. So," he pulls himself straight, suddenly all business, "what about today, what about our little transaction? Do we have a deal?"

Alan yanks himself back to the present. This is the time to be alert, now that they're getting close to the payoff. "You didn't say much over the phone. You kept it pretty vague."

Rory nods. "There's a lot about this business that's iffy. With this kind of speculation, sometimes it's best not to go into too many details." He leans forward amiably. "Finally, it's all a matter of trust, isn't it?"

Alan smiles. "So you're asking me to trust you, right?"

"Right," Rory says. "Just like I trust you. Nothing gets signed, nothing's on record. Just two friends doing a little business together." He laughs. "The way they used to do it in the good old days."

Whatever is going on here, it's certainly true that this transaction comes down to a matter of trust: Rory trusts that Alan's check isn't going to bounce and Alan trusts that Rory won't make any trouble raising the ghosts of Lyletown. "So," Alan says, "we keep it simple. That's fine with me." The truth is, he has no interest in keeping track of where his money's going. Better, in fact, not to leave a trail. "I have the money," he says, relieved that they've come to this point at last. "I can give it to you as a cashier's check."

Rory smiles thinly. "Excellent. I assure you, you're not going to regret this."

Alan extracts the check from his jacket pocket and hands it to him. After giving it the briefest of glances, Rory slips it into the inside pocket of his own jacket. Alan watches the green rectangle of paper disappear. "If we're really doing this the old-fashioned way," Rory extends his hand, "we've got to shake on it." After they've performed that final ritual, Rory lifts his glass. "I believe this little deal is going to make both of us richer, my friend," he says. When he's taken his drink, he settles back into his chair and sighs, as if he too is relieved that the financial details have been attended to. "Partners again," he smiles. "Let's hope this goes better than our last venture."

Alan isn't entirely comfortable with the idea of their being partners. Still, he says, "I certainly hope so." In the last couple of seconds he's become convinced that the money he's just given Rory is indeed a loan, and it makes him feel easier about the whole situation.

Once again there's a burst of laughter from the table with the man and two women. "Ah, youth," Rory says. "Enjoy it while you can." He looks in the direction of the happy group. "How old do you think they are? Early twenties?"

Alan nods, guessing what Rory's thinking: that this trio of kids who are dressed for success inhabit a very different world from the one the two of them knew when they were a similar age. Who could have predicted it? Masters of the universe, he thinks. In a different time, would they have marched on the Pentagon? Planned Lyletown? For the briefest of instants, Alan feels like Rip Van Winkle.

Meanwhile, across the table, Rory appears to be lost in thought. When he's come back after a few moments, he's frowning. "Do you know what the odds were against the Caper getting fucked up the way it did?"

Alan looks at him. How did we get back here so quickly? he wonders. Didn't Rory just say he put all that stuff into the past? Apparently, that doesn't keep it from bobbing up anyway.

"Luck sure as hell was running against us that night," Rory goes on. "There's no reason why that job shouldn't have gone off without a hitch." He shakes his head. "Because you run that thing ten times and nine of them are going to work—hell, make that nineteen out of twenty." He's silent for a while. Then he says, "We just happened to get stuck with the odd one."

Alan takes another sip of his wine, recognizing that he's already feeling a bit of a buzz. Maybe part of it is the relief he feels with his recent conviction that the transaction he's just been part of was really a loan and not blackmail. At the same time, Rory's inclination to return to those days has stirred him to a surprising degree. Alan had come here hoping to keep things strictly business and not to get dragged back into the past; but now he's beset by powerful, contradictory feelings. "I've got to tell you," he says, "there are times when it's hard for me to believe that I was actually part of that,

that any of us were, that it happened at all, the insane hopes we had for the good that could be accomplished by what we were planning. I mean," he gropes, "it just seems unreal sometimes. Maybe surreal." Glamorous Lily and earnest Serena, the ex-cons Ben and Bobby, Rory and himself, all of them seriously planning a robbery of hundreds of weapons. And at least some of them doing it to help save the world.

"It sure as hell is real for me," Rory says.

"Well, yeah, for me too, obviously," Alan goes on, pursuing the thought. "But I guess one of the things I'm trying to say is that in the end, though, it's only going to be real as long as there are people who remember it. And now, if Serena's dead, at least two of the people who were in on it are gone. Who knows about Ben?"

Rory lets out a breath. "Like those old Indians I saw on TV," he says. "The last ones alive that speak their language. When they die, the language is gone." He pauses a moment. "As for old Ben, I'd be surprised if he's still walking the earth. And if I'm right about that, besides Lily, there's only you and me to remember it from our side of the fence. The last three Indians." He falls into a silence that's broken only when he catches another waitress's eye, a raven-haired one this time, and signals to her. "Hey, you'll have another glass, won't you? Lunch is on me, by the way."

Alan has to get back to work this afternoon and he's already a bit lightheaded, but he knows he isn't going to refuse this second drink. The fact is, in the last few minutes his earlier uneasiness about this whole situation has dissipated, and he's excited to be talking to Rory about those times. "Sure," he says. "Why not?"

Both of them are silent for a while. "Jesus," Alan says, suddenly wondering how many people within a hundred mile radius would have the faintest idea of what they've been talking about, "when I think of Bobby . . ." Skinny, with thinning hair and big eyes, Bobby would hunch over when he talked, he'd cup his hand over a cigarette, protecting it from the wind even when he was indoors. His voice would go shrill when he'd get caught up in whatever he was talking about, he'd sometimes spoil his own jokes by laughing too soon. "Who knew," Alan says, "that he'd be packing heat and that he'd panic when that cop came in?"

Rory's voice is flat. "That was a wild card, all right: Bobby the Gunslinger."

Alan shakes his head. "I mean, he was a loudmouth, a bullshitter and all that, but to have that happen to him. . . . Jesus, the poor bastard."

Across the table from him, Rory makes no response for a few seconds, though his face has darkened. "Fucking Bobby," he says after a while. At first Alan thinks Rory is simply sharing his own wonder that Bobby, of all people, should have been the reason Lyletown turned violent. But when he speaks again, there's no mistaking the naked anger in his voice—the amiable Rory of minutes ago is entirely gone. "That fucking little shit," he spits out. "I used to think about him when I was in there, and you know what? I was glad he died the way he did. I hoped he'd suffered the whole time." Rory's eyes are cold, and the word "murderous" comes involuntarily to Alan. "Hell," Rory says, "as far as I'm concerned, that little bastard got off too easy. All those years I had to spend in there. An hour's pain in dying wasn't enough." He looks into his glass. "Who's going to pay me for what I lost?"

The sudden transformation is unsettling. This is the guy, Alan thinks, who said a couple of minutes ago that he'd put the past behind him. What happens when he really starts remembering things? It's a genuinely scary moment.

Just then the waitress arrives with their drinks. In a flash, Rory brightens, and within seconds he's fallen into the same kind of banter he'd engaged in with Bridget. It's hard to believe that just moments ago his eyes were as cold as a wolf's. When the waitress leaves, he takes a sip of wine and smiles thinly to himself. Alan watchfully brings his own glass to his mouth, wondering which Rory he's looking at now.

The noise around them has grown louder, an oceanic roar, drowning the musical lament for a lost home. Still smiling to himself, Rory shakes his head. "Ben and Bobby," he says. "What a pair."

There's nothing left of the fury of his earlier declaration. "How dumb did we have to be to follow those two?"

Alan is relieved by this shift in tone. "I guess they had their own agendas from the beginning," he says, feeling that it's all right to return to the topic. "Ben, for sure. Lily might have thought she was running the show, when all along it was them. Sometimes it seems as if the rest of us were just along for the ride."

Rory has lit up again and takes a fierce drag on his cigarette. "I don't see it quite that way," he says emphatically, almost aggressively. "Sure, some people had their own plans and motives, but remember, we all played our parts. And we didn't have to be there, did we? I mean, it was my choice to get in on the Caper. Whatever my motives might have been, however desperate the plan might have been, nobody dragged me into it."

"True," Alan says, impressed by the force with which Rory's insisting on his responsibility for his choices. As he remembers his own experience, things weren't quite so clear-cut. "But we were all so young," he says. "There was so much about that whole business that we didn't want to see. Hell, neither of us would go for something like that today, would we?"

Rory shakes his head. "You can't pick the times when you have to make choices. What I know is that once I made that choice I couldn't pretend to be innocent anymore." There's a sudden lull in the ambient sound around them, for the moment even the music has stopped. Angels walking across your grave, Alan's grandmother used to say, and he feels a chill at the memory.

"OK," he ventures warily, "but you'd certainly agree that your choices afterward were limited by what happened that night, right?"

"Of course," Rory says. "But the important thing is that, even after that, I did have choices. Even in prison I had choices." Once again, there's no way to miss the urgency of his insistence on his freedom. Hadn't he said something earlier about how we have to make ourselves? Apparently, this is something he has to believe.

Alan takes another swallow of his wine. He isn't sipping it anymore, he's drinking it as if it were beer. Slow down, he tells himself, recognizing that he's being pulled along by a powerful current he doesn't understand. But Rory is the only person on the planet with whom he can talk about this stuff. The recent mention of prison has made him aware once more of the vast barrier between his experience and Rory's, it reminds him of how close he came to sharing that experience. But, damn it, however scary Rory's momentary transformation may have been, he seems to have survived, even prevailed; he does seem to have created himself, at least the version who's here today. "Listen," Alan says, "you sure have come a long way from when I saw you last time. I mean, I'm impressed."

Rory makes a dismissive gesture. "Well, we can't just stay in the same place forever, can we?"

"So it would seem," Alan says. He glimpses an opening to learn something more about Rory's recent activities. "You said you're not working in California anymore?" He makes it a question, hoping for an answer.

"I'm going down to New Orleans for a while," Rory says. "If certain things work out," he adds.

Well, there's some real information at last, apparently. New Orleans. The name evokes a sense of tropical heat and languid movements, of balconies with wrought-iron railings, beards of Spanish moss hanging from the twisting branches of live oaks, the bluesy wail of a saxophone. He wonders whether this trip of Rory's has anything to do with the five thousand dollars he's just handed over. Once more he appreciates the other man's vagueness about the transaction they've concluded. Buoyed by the wine, Alan has been tempted more than once to come straight out and ask him, but he's been able to keep his curiosity in check. In the end, though, he's judged that it might be best for everyone to leave things where they are. It amuses him that, even a little buzzed, he's still thinking like a lawyer.

A young guy who's just walked in with a couple of others does a couple of steps of an Irish jig as the party makes its way toward the bar, and once more Alan is struck by the essential theatricality of this restaurant in Cambridge that, he's certain, no inhabitant of Cork or Limerick would be likely to confuse with an actual

Irish pub, in spite of the imported waitresses and bartenders. What must it look like to Rory, who spent a dozen years behind gray concrete walls?

Just now his attention is directed toward the bar as if he's studying the photos there that depict Ireland's beauty and its troubled past. Alan has no clue to what Rory might be thinking about. Once more his own thoughts have drifted toward Lily. He imagines a small shop with a bell on the door, a counter and a few empty tables, the smell of freshly baked bread, maybe cinnamon and apples, rain spattering the windows, gray skies outside. What he wouldn't give to find out what the schoolteacher's wife thinks about her earlier actions. Does she regret them, does she feel that, having been duped by Ben Fraley, she's responsible for what happened to all the participants of the Caper; or, even as she pours the cop his coffee, is she unrepentant? He feels a surge of emotion. If he were somehow to meet her today, what would he and Lily say to each other? That life has turned out to be stranger and more surprising than they'd dreamed it to be?

"Hell," he says aloud, "I don't have to tell you I used to have very complicated feelings toward Lily . . ." Sure, she was melodramatic, even pretentious, and yes, in the end she was naïve, but she believed strongly in justice and she stood by her commitments. If she's happy these days making coffee and rolls, there's nothing wrong with that. He remembers what Sam said about forgiving your earlier selves. "Now," he says, "I guess, whatever she's doing, I just wish her luck."

"Hey, we're all trying to make our way in the world," Rory says. "We need all the luck we can get. Well," he taps the pocket where he put Alan's check, "like I said, I think you and I are going to do OK on this deal." Alan just nods. In truth, he's not sure exactly what his hopes are for whatever deal the two of them have just made.

In a few minutes they're on the street amid the bustle and glare of the Cambridge afternoon and Alan feels a sense of lightness, of shadows at least temporarily chased away. He allows himself to take delight in the scene: shoppers, joggers, tourists and students push past them in all directions, a cop and a cabbie are yelling at each other while a silver-haired man in a tweed jacket looks on, a green book bag slung over his shoulder; the smell of curry is on the air, mixing with the exhaust of a bus.

"Which way you going?" Rory asks. When Alan tells him, he says, "My car's in the other direction. So I guess it's goodbye for now."

Alan remembers their last parting. "Hey," he says, "last time you said it was going to be my turn to pay when we got together again."

"Did I?" Rory smiles. "I guess you owe me again then, right?"

Alan shakes his head. "You're a hard man to figure, you know that?" he says.

"Hey," Rory says, "let's just hope our deal turns out well."

After they shake hands once more, he moves off into the crowd. Alan watches for a while until he's out of sight. Looking at the bobbing heads of strangers, he remembers the cold fury that came into Rory's eyes for a few seconds as he talked about Bobby Pelham. He remembers his question, "Who's going to pay me for what I lost?" What the hell have I gotten myself into? he thinks, even as he takes the first steps in the direction of the car that will take him back to what he hopes will be his normal life.


A little more than a month later, he's going through his mail at the office when he finds an envelope with a New Orleans return address. That gets his attention. He glances quickly toward the door to confirm that nobody's nearby, then he opens the envelope. Inside is a cashier's check for six thousand dollars. He whistles involuntarily when he sees the sum written out, then looks at it again to assure himself he's read it correctly, though the numerals to the right are clear enough. "We did OK, partner," is all Rory's note says. Jesus, Alan thinks, he really meant it when he said I'd get my money back with interest: twenty per cent! And yet, that doesn't make him feel better. No tracks, he thinks, no trails. Just a couple of friends doing business.

Somewhere close but out of sight, Sally is talking to Karla about the upcoming session in the Boston Housing Court, and for a few seconds Alan lets himself be soothed by the pedestrian details of their conversation. Still, there's the check on the desk. He quickly folds it and slips it into his shirt pocket. Six thousand. Where did it come from? Well, nothing will be official until he banks it. "OK," he hears Karla say, "I've got all that." In a few seconds Sally's typewriter is clattering furiously, and Alan tries to resume his inspection of the mail but all the while he's aware of what's in his pocket.

For a few days afterward he's uncertain about what he's going to do with the check. No, he tells himself, if I don't accept the money I didn't have any part in whatever was done to make it. But that's sophistry: he'd already made that decision when he handed his own check to Rory at O'Reilly's. It only makes things worse that he can't say anything to Julia about his quandary. In the end, he decides to cash Rory's check and replace the five thousand in his special fund, a simple enough decision. The other thousand he donates to the American Cancer Society, as Sam's widow Annie had requested Sam's mourners to do in lieu of flowers. At least this way he's not the one who's profiting from whatever business his money helped Rory to conduct. This doesn't keep him from feeling that Rory has somehow got the better of him.

~ 1991 ~

For a time, the business with Rory bothers Alan. Everything was settled at O'Reilly's, he keeps telling himself, it's over and that's that, the check has been cashed and the money accounted for. And yet he can't help feeling uneasy. Just the fact that Rory is floating around somewhere on the fringes of his life again is disturbing. In the days immediately following Rory's visit, whatever he sees in the papers or on TV about New Orleans excites his curiosity. Is Rory there? If so, what's he up to? It's easy to imagine his old friend looking down from a balcony into the French Quarter, eating in one of the city's great restaurants or watching a toy-like streetcar ply its course down a palm-lined avenue. Yet even as he conjures these images, Alan tells himself: this doesn't have anything to do with me. Well, yes and no, he has to admit.

In the end, the steady passage of time buries these concerns. World events astound everyone: the Russians are driven out of Afghanistan, the Berlin Wall comes down, the Soviet Union unravels and eastern European countries break free. People can begin to believe in a different kind of world now. Reagan is gone, as is Thatcher, even Gorbachev is soon an ex-ruler. And yet, it isn't long before the U.S. is leading a coalition in a Middle Eastern war. How much has changed, after all?

For Alan too, the succession of days brings shifts: between his putting his head to the pillow and his awakening the next morning, old habits and old preoccupations reassert themselves, his present life and concerns take on sharper definition; and one day he realizes that it's been almost two years since he's seen Rory, and that meeting at O'Reilly's seems part of another world.

"A crisis a day keeps boredom away," Alan's friend Charlie Winchell likes to say. Today's crisis, though, is more than just an antidote to boredom. On this warm summer Thursday, Mrs. Sadowska's case has reached the point of no return and the process of evicting her has finally, irrevocably, been put into motion. Not that there's any surprise to this development. Pretty much from the time he'd been appointed by the court to represent the woman and had actually spoken to her, Alan suspected that she wasn't the kind who was likely to bend or adapt, and that eventually he was going to run out of ways to prevent the inevitable. He'd been down this road before, of course. This time, though, he's made the mistake of taking a case too personally, which is why it isn't easy to sit in the office this morning and just wait for things to take their course. After an hour or so of trying to convince himself that he's working, he decides that he can't just wash his hands of the Sadowska affair without seeing her one more time—he owes her that much.

"I'm going to be out of the office for about an hour," he tells Sally. "I'm going to see Mrs. Sadowska."

Sally, who knows all about the old woman's case, gives him a sympathetic nod.


Halina Sadowska came from Poland, though there was no such country at the time of her birth. "I am born subject of Czar of Russia," she declared with a full appreciation for the drama of the statement that linked her to the age of eastern autocrats, a time of bearded holy men and saber-wielding hussars. In the course of her life in Poland she experienced not only two world wars, but the brief independent existence of the restored Polish nation. It was at the university that she met her future husband, Roman Sadowski, whom Alan knows only as a plump, mustached man wearing a tweed suit as he stands under an arch and squints in the direction of the camera, a pipe in one hand, the other jauntily stuffed into his trousers' pocket.

The couple were schoolteachers in their native town, progressive in their views, Halina Sadowska assured Alan. From her accounts of life in inter-war Poland, he's been able to construct a picture of a bright young couple whose childless house was the lively center of a group of small-town intellectuals who talked, drank and smoked French cigarettes as they danced and flirted during a brief interval of freedom before the storm that was to engulf all of Europe. "We have literary evenings," she told him. "Somebody read his poems. Then we will roll back rug and play Victrola. There is dancing." Even as she described this idyll of provincial intellectuals, she seemed aware of its comic aspects. "It is not Warsaw," she said, "but we try very hard to make it so." Did they sense even then, those amateur poets, those flirtatious dancers, what was coming? Knowing what he knows, it's easy for Alan to imagine that some of them must have smoked their Gauloises more hungrily because they could guess that all too soon even those simple pleasures would become a luxury. It's possible that as they held ice-cold glasses of vodka between their fingers, they could already foresee that before long their only recently independent country would become a vast graveyard. Or did they think the literary evenings would go on forever?

Most of what Alan knows about Mrs. Sadowska's war-time experiences he learned in his first meeting with her. She didn't go into detail, but she told him enough. He knows, for instance that in the depths of the Nazi occupation, her husband Roman was recruited for a raid on the town police station. The hope was that the raiders would be able to overwhelm the guards and spirit a cache of weapons to the resistance fighters in the nearby forest. "Roman is not brave, he is not hero," Halina Sadowska told Alan. "I am no hero, none of us are. But in this time, you must do."

Roman and his comrades were unlucky, as it turned out. "They are betrayed," Mrs. Sadowska told him with no obvious emotion, and the plotters were executed in the town square the next day. Of her own solitary life after that, she said little. Alan could only guess at the horrors, the trials and privations she experienced trying to stay alive in her ravaged country. She dismissed those times simply with, "What happens to me happens to everybody." What Alan does know is that, having survived the war and having lived in displaced persons camps, she made her way to America at last in the late nineteen-forties.

"I lose everything," she told him that first time he'd come to see her. "My husband, my family, my position, my country." What struck him from the beginning was that this small, bird-like woman wasn't complaining, she was just stating the facts. "That I should live—there is no reason, but it seems I want to keep living. Only I do not know why, I cannot . . ." She searched for the word. "I cannot justify it."

She'd worked cleaning houses, she'd been employed in a school cafeteria, she'd managed to make ends meet, eking out a bare, glamourless existence in her long, anticlimactic life of exile. She may have felt despair, but she persisted. "Why I am living? I do not know. There is no reason." Alan had noticed, to his surprise, the absence of religious symbols in her apartment. That may have been part of what she meant when she called herself and her husband "progressives." At any rate, when she crossed the ocean she'd apparently done so without the consolations of religion. Alan imagined her living among the Americans, invisible, looking on as the forties gave way to the fifties, then the sixties, the decades accelerating, America changing around Mrs. Sadowska as she continued to grapple with questions: why had she been spared, and what was she going to do with the life she'd been given?

Of course, he'd gotten involved in her case because she'd become a problem. Her apartment had fallen into noncompliance, the management complained. "She's a hoarder," Ed Graziano said darkly, and Alan knew that these were among the most intractable cases. When he went to visit her for the first time, he got a glimpse of what Ed was talking about: not only were tables and chairs covered with books and sheets of paper, but areas of the floor as well. A closet door bulged open, unable to keep back whatever was stored there. There was little evidence of housekeeping. Dishes were piled in the sink, and from what could be seen of the other rooms there was a similar disarray. He could imagine dead roaches lying like fallen angels on the dirty linoleum. All of this had happened recently, he had to assume. After all, the woman had been living here for decades.

She'd fixed him a cup of tea. Just a Salada teabag and hot water. The cup was reasonably clean and there was space for him to sit, though barely enough for him to set down the cup and saucer. In response to his questions about her life, Mrs. Sadowska had given him the bare details that constituted the sum of his knowledge of her. She stopped abruptly in mid-narrative. "Why I am allowed to live," she said in her strongly accented English. "This is great mystery." She sat there looking at him. "Not no more."

Her eyes were suddenly ablaze. "I have dream," she told him. "I see Roman. I see our friends." She gave a satisfied smile. "I know I must tell story. My story. People I know." She showed him a handful of sheets that were covered with Polish words, set down in a cursive script he could only think of as a schoolteacher's. He nodded at the incomprehensible sentences with their clusters of consonants and odd accent markings. He could respect her desire to tell her story. It was an intelligent, a rational response to her situation to try to put it into words. But there was an unnatural intensity to her commitment to this project. Did the writing of a memoir require her to constrict her world into this tiny space, as if she'd chosen to strand herself on a desert island? And why did she have to keep every scrap of paper she'd collected for the last few months? Well, he thought, artists aren't housekeepers, are they? Maybe there was such a thing as creative disorder. But surely, coming at this late date, her project was a fantasy. Of course, maybe it was just therapy, and didn't need to be completed. Oddly, thinking about the proposed memoir, Alan remembered Rory's formulation, "the lost chapters of my life." Was that what Mrs. Sadowska was trying to write?

But things hadn't yet arrived at the worst stage in those early days. There was clutter, the smell in the apartment was stale, the smell of an old person's unwashed flesh. There was dust, a faint trace of leftover food gone bad, no doubt countless discarded flakes of skin. But if there was a sanitation problem, it was still minor.

"You can understand," he ventured gently, "why the company would have a problem, why in their terms this apartment isn't in compliance."

She shrugged. "I have things to do."

He told her he'd try to help her, that he'd present her position in the best possible light, but he wanted her to understand that the company wasn't likely to be very flexible, that there were instruments they could bring into play that might result in her being evicted. "You certainly don't want that to happen," he suggested.

She looked back at him, clear-eyed. What's happened to me, she seemed to say, has had little to do with what I wanted.

There were various legal stratagems yet to be tried, he told her, that could buy her some time. They might send in a social worker, Mrs. Sadowska might be encouraged to have someone come in to clean the apartment regularly. "I'll be in touch," he told her. "I'll let you know how things are going."

As he bade her goodbye at the door, he tried to be hopeful about the situation. "There's a way of working out things like this," he said. But the steely gaze with which she regarded him made it clear that the only way she thought things could work out was on her terms.

The next time he visited her, he could see that things were worse. The housekeeping had gone from negligent to unsanitary and a thin reek greeted him at the door. He could understand why the neighbors had begun complaining more energetically. He told her once more what the company was demanding, he explained what legal measures could still be invoked. She listened and nodded, her eyes afire with the need to get back to her writing. She was only half-listening, pulled back toward that quicksand of Polish sentences. The social worker paid a visit and found her uncooperative. "This is one sick lady," she averred. Mrs. Sadowska was offered cleaning help. "No, thank you," she said. She didn't want her papers disturbed. As dedicated as she was to her project, she was equally determined to refuse assistance. When Alan saw her again she seemed to have shrunken. Always small, she looked smaller, yet there was no diminution of the intensity in her eyes. How was the project going? he asked her. It was going to be difficult, she conveyed to him. If she was going to do the subject justice, it wasn't going to be easy, it was going to take a long time. Time, though, was something she had very little of, having long since tried the patience of the management company. "You know . . ." Alan wanted to warn her.

Beneath the wildness that lit her gray eyes, he sensed that she was aware of what was in store for her, that it had all happened to her before and that she wasn't afraid of it. She was herself, she was telling him, and she was going to continue to be herself. She wasn't asking for pity. In the end, he was just going to have to accept that he couldn't help her.

Atwood Gardens is one of the city's oldest projects. There's not much grass left, but the few trees are ample and the squat, utilitarian buildings are for the most part well-maintained. Not much, but at least it's a decent roof over your head.

"I like her too," Ed Graziano, the building manager said about the Polish woman, "but there's nothing more we can do for her. There are all the other tenants to think of. It's their home too, you know."

"Mrs. Sadowska," Alan says as he stands before her apartment.

The woman eyes him warily behind the half-open door. It's me, he wants to say, Alan Ripley. I'm on your side. He's not sure, though, that she recognizes him anymore. Her posture is tense, defensive. From what Alan can glimpse, the disarray and accumulation behind her may have reached entropic proportions. Even here in the hallway, he can tell that the smell has grown stronger, nothing has been done to fight the encroaching decay.

"Mrs. Sadowska," he repeats, and gives his name. Her eyes are glazed, her mouth is held firmly, she's guarding the door. Alan knows he isn't going to be invited in for tea this time. "I suppose you've heard the news," he says, though she gives no hint of understanding. "I'm sorry. We tried everything we could."

The woman continues to stand at the door, her hand on the knob. She hasn't relented at all.

"I hope your project goes well," he says. Then once more, "I'm sorry." Her eyes give back no recognition, only the fierce determination to hold her ground, to fight back and face the world to the extent that she can on her terms.

"Goodbye," he says. He'd intended to have a word with Ed Graziano after his visit, but the encounter has shaken him and he makes his way out of Atwood Gardens, back to his office in the suburbs.

Later that afternoon when he gets a call from Laura Wicklow, who's with Legal Services, he can't keep himself from bringing up the subject of Mrs. Sadowska, whose case Laura knows about. "I've tried," he says, "but there's no way I can be objective about her."

Laura says nothing for a few seconds. "That woman has problems," she suggests at last. "Major problems."

"Don't we all," Alan says reflexively.

"Thank God, though," Laura says, "most of us are able to control our problems a little better. We own the problems, the problems don't own us."

Alan knows he's obsessing about the old woman, and getting a more detached view from someone like Laura is healthy. "I'll accept all that about her," he says. But he remembers his last encounter with her, her tense guardianship at the door. True, she seemed further gone than ever into realms beyond rationality, but there was a quality of unflinchingness about her that he couldn't help admiring. "OK," he says, "she's slipping away from reality. Still, there's something very strong about her, very clear-sighted. And on some level what she's trying to do is understandable enough to me. After all, she knows she doesn't have long. Wouldn't she want to put her life in order in some way? Wouldn't any of us? Especially with all that she's been through."

There's a change in Laura's tone. "Yeah," she says. "I suppose you have to try to put yourself in her shoes. It takes someone special to recognize what the world probably looks like to her." After a pause, she says, "She was lucky to have you as her advocate."

He lets out a sigh. "Not that I've been able to do much for her. From the start I knew there was nothing more that I could do for her legally but delay the final outcome. I guess somewhere in the back of my mind I thought I could convince her to relent just a little, to pay some attention to the place." He shakes his head. "I should have known better. Talk about hubris."

"Don't beat yourself up that way," Laura says. "From what you've told me, I'd say she recognized that you understood her."

He wonders about that. In their last encounter at the door, when she faced him as if he were the adversary, as if he represented everything in the world that she's had to battle all her life, might she at least for one brief instant have recognized that he'd been trying to help her? "Well," he says, "if I performed even that for her, I'm glad. Otherwise, I'd feel completely powerless in all this."

"I think you've been very important to her," Laura tells him. "If she ever finishes that memoir, you ought to get a page or two in it."

For a moment, he allows himself to believe she might. But that's a fantasy. Still, he appreciates Laura's sentiment. "That's very generous of you," he says.

When Laura responds after an interval, it's in a brighter and more cheerful tone. "Hey, maybe some time you'll be generous enough to play tennis with me after all."

It's a relief, after talking about Mrs. Sadowska, to think about tennis. God, he wishes he were on the court right now. "OK," he says, "you've worn me down." He appreciates Laura's sympathy. "Let's do it."

"I'm warning you, though," she says, "I'm not very generous with a tennis racket in my hand."

The image makes him smile. "I'll bet," he says.


Once he's committed himself to playing tennis with Laura, Alan can't help wondering why, after all her previous overtures, he chose to accept her offer this time. There are plenty of obvious answers to that question, of course. Laura is attractive, about a dozen years younger than he is, smart and sexy, someone who causes heads to turn when she enters a room. Whatever her motives, it's certainly flattering to know that she's been so hot to bat the ball around with him. An older male finding some kind of rejuvenation in the attentions of a younger woman, whether in the bedroom or on the tennis court, is a familiar enough story, and Alan can't completely dismiss that element from his decision.

There's something else, though, he knows, and it has to do with Mrs. Sadowska. It bothers him more than it ought to that he wasn't able to resolve the old woman's situation and keep her from being evicted. Of course he's cared about other people he's dealt with in similar situations—he doesn't have to go any further than Zelda Laval, someone who had so much going for her when she was clean, and who, in fact, had in the past shown an ability to kick the habit, at least for a time. Watching her slide back into her addiction was a blow he took personally, and it had left him feeling betrayed. You could beat yourself over the head asking why she'd choose to return to that kind of bondage, rejecting a life that, though it couldn't offer her the illusory solace of the drug, at least gave her the opportunity to achieve small victories on her own that were real. It doesn't make it any easier to tell yourself that everybody knows how junkies wind up. Sometimes they make it.

Halina Sadowska's case is different. Unlike Zelda, the Polish woman had no previous history of backsliding. To all appearances she'd been able for decades to deal stoically with the hideously unfair hand life had dealt her. Why should she, in her later years, when her situation was objectively better, be shaken into a fervent, all-consuming passion to record her life to the exclusion of even the most minimal obligations to the daily decencies? It was a break as radical as that of some early Christian ascetic who chose to retreat to the desert and live in a cave, an act that in effect dismissed as irrelevant the preoccupations of most of his fellow humans, making him incomprehensible to them. Not only does it sting that Alan was powerless to help Mrs. Sadowska with her living situation; it seems a cosmic joke that, however long she may have clung to the possibility that she could weave some modest pattern of meaning out of the small, repeated gestures of daily life, she should be unsettled at the last moment, sent off on a lonely mission that disconnected her from the familiar world, making her indifferent to its demands while she searched for some significance that might lie beyond what the rest of us can see.

Whatever his complex feelings about the Sadowska case, the fact is, he's talked to Laura about them, she's actually seen the woman and she has some understanding of Alan's emotional investment in the case. Maybe it's gratitude that lies behind his agreement to play tennis with her. Does he think that, between games, he'll be able to talk to her about what he feels for the old woman?

Though it doesn't make much rational sense, this rendezvous on the courts is tinged with guilt. It's not sexual, though it has to do with intimacy. Alan has told Julia about the old woman as well, but he hasn't gone into his feelings about her in as much detail as he has with Laura. Julia, for her part, is wrapped up in her efforts to become a dean at the college where she teaches and, for her, Mrs. Sadowska is just one more name from Alan's work. At the moment, other names, like Roger Wexelblatt, the outgoing dean, are more important to her. She isn't likely to grasp the full texture of Alan's feelings on the subject because he hasn't pushed them on her. Given her present situation, she shouldn't have to. So if there's guilt, it's minor.

In truth, though he finds Laura sexy and attractive, Alan doesn't really expect to be seduced by her charms. At another time, maybe, but the moment has passed. Just now, his concern is with how good a tennis partner she's likely to be. Because the fact is, he misses those games with Sam. Their playing styles were complementary, Alan being more impulsive and erratic, inclined to take chances, while Sam, who moved with a sandpiper's quick, furtive steps while his upper body remained taut, played a patient, dink and dunk game; but their skills were about equal. Laura certainly talks a good game, but he has no way of knowing what she's like on the other side of the net.

Alan arrives early at the high school, where the courts are surprisingly empty, and he starts at the practice wall. It's a perfect day for tennis, bright, clear, with no wind to speak of, and he experiences a mysterious sense of well-being. He hits a few soft drives into the wall just above the painted white line, sets himself for the easy return and sends the ball back, quickly establishing a comfortable rhythm. Once he gets a little warm, he picks up the pace, slamming the ball into the green barrier, placing his shots in a way that forces him to alternate his returns from the forehand to backhand sides.

"I can see you're going to be a tough one," Laura calls to him when she gets there. She's wearing white shorts and a dark-blue hooded sweatshirt, a Red Sox cap and big sunglasses. She carries a very professional-looking tennis bag.

He catches the ball off the wall with his hand. "No, no," he tells her. "I'm one of those guys who's good in practice but folds in the game."

"I'll bet," she says, clearly enjoying the gamesmanship.

It doesn't take him long, once they're on the court, to realize that she's for real. Their practice rallying shows that she has a strong, smooth ground stroke and her backhand is at least adequate. She's a good athlete, quick on her feet, though she seems inclined to stay back and hit from the base line like someone who has a fairly conservative game plan. After the first couple of exchanges, Alan makes an adjustment for the surprising speed with which her ball crosses the net so he has more control over his returns. His spirits are roused. It's clear she'll be a good, even a challenging partner.

"You must have been playing for quite a while," he says.

"We all had to as kids," she says from across the court, bouncing a ball idly with her racquet. "Want to practice some lobs and smashes?"

"Sure thing." She comes from a suburb north of Chicago and he can well imagine a youth in which tennis played an important social role. She moves with long, easy strides, gracefully and efficiently covering ground, her shots are true. They spend a couple more minutes at practice, then Laura says she's ready. She takes off her sweatshirt and her long tan arms are dark against the white tee-shirt.

"OK," she says with a grin, spinning the racquet idly, her knees bent in readiness.

Once they start to play in earnest, with Laura serving, Alan is able to see more of her game. Her serve itself is sound, accurate, but not particularly tough to handle, which he counts as an advantage to himself. Still, she doesn't make any unforced errors and her strong forehands keep him backed up against his own base line, limiting his opportunities to charge the net. When he tests her backhand she responds well, better than he would have expected from what he'd seen in practice. And when she has to, she can move like a jungle cat. They play fairly evenly, going to deuce a couple of times. In the end he manages to take the first game, breaking her serve, but it hasn't been easy. Once again he wonders whether someone like himself who picked up the game as an adult will always have a harder time than someone who learned tennis as a kid.

"Hey," he says after the first game, "this is good." He's managed to work up a decent sweat.

Her shots come across the net a bit more swiftly in the next game, the yellow ball blurring, and he has to be quick fending them off. Thwack! Thwack! The two of them drive the ball back and forth. He realizes that she's controlling the game, keeping him on the defensive. Could she have been holding back in the first game, trying to see what he had before making her move? Her challenge brings out a response in him. OK, he says to himself, you're good, you're going to make me work. That's fine with me. They battle back and forth in a long rally that sends the two of them from one side of the base line to the other. Gradually, Laura works him into the far left corner, where he realizes that he's a sitting duck, and she fires a passing shot that comes flying across the net. As the ball dips toward the asphalt, his only chance is to lunge in its direction, and he leaves his feet, making a desperate forehand swipe as he sails through the air. His extended racquet manages to reach the ball with enough force to send his shot into the tape at the top of the net, where it seems to hang suspended for a moment before dropping to the asphalt on Laura's side.

"Good thing we're not playing for money," she says, "or I'd say you're trying to hustle me."

"Lucky shot," he says, panting. But he feels proud of himself. A damn great shot, he knows. Bouncing the ball energetically on the asphalt before his serve, he feels the sun on his arms, inhales the smell of grass just beyond the courts, and he's happy. Nothing from his job, nothing from anywhere outside this court is in his mind. There's just the game. This was a good idea: Laura's turning out to be a good tennis partner.

Once they've started up again, he gets more aggressive, charging the net, then recovering quickly when she returns his shot, and he gets off a lucky backhand to win the point. But she easily takes the next one. They've established a rhythm, then gradually accelerated that rhythm, and both have been equal to that demand. Running, stopping suddenly, swinging at the ball, moving this way and that, getting into position, he's arrived at the point where there's no thinking, only reacting. Sneakers squeak on asphalt, he grunts as he moves toward the place where Laura's shot lands with a plop, he's already lining himself up, bending his knees, pulling back the racquet and swinging through the ball, following through. He and Laura split the next couple of games so that Alan is leading 2–1. He realizes that this is the most fun he's had playing since the days of Sam.

In the middle of the next game, he sends a hard forehand toward the corner and rushes the net, winding up slightly to the right of center, which leaves Laura in a great position to send the ball back into the acres of open space to his left. He's aware of it all happening in slow motion, his sudden sense of exposure and vulnerability, his instinctive pivoting to the left to protect his flank even as he watches Laura bend her knees, pull back her racquet and coolly drive the ball toward the open area. The ball makes a soft sound coming off the strings and his brain is already sending an alert that jolts his body into an urgent twist in the direction of the shot's anticipated trajectory. As he and the ball move, he's sure he'll never get to it in time, then he feels there's a chance, a real chance, then comes the realization that he's actually going to be able to reach it; but all that gives way to the sudden sharp pain in his left knee that brings him down abruptly, the sound of his racquet clattering against the asphalt, followed by silence.

A couple of seconds later, Laura calls from across the net, "Are you OK?"

"Yeah," he nods, though the pain is brutal. "I have to wait a second or two."

Soon she's beside him. "You going to need any help?"

He takes a deep breath. "Let me try to put some weight on it," he says.

She gives him an arm and he pulls himself up with the good leg, then ventures a tentative step. "Oww," he yelps involuntarily. "I guess I have to wait a bit longer."

"Is it your ankle?" she asks. He can smell her hair, feel the sweat on her arm.

He shakes his head. "It's my knee."

She says nothing, probably thinking what he's thinking: how bad is this going to be? Knees, they both know, can be big trouble. Arcane words like meniscus and initials like ACL and MCL drift through his consciousness. After a little more rest, he tries to walk again. He can manage only relatively better, keeping the pain somewhat in check, but there's no way they can continue the game. The fact is, it's going to be hard enough to walk more than a few steps. "I'm done," he says. "Shit."

"I'm sorry," Laura says.

"You didn't do anything," he says.

"I'm sorry it had to stop. We were doing OK."

"Yeah," he says. "Me too."

"Maybe all you'll need is some ice," she suggests.

He nods. He knows the formula R-I-C-E: rest, ice, compression and elevation. Moving the knee a bit without putting any weight on it, he can only hope it's as easy as that. But a painful attempt to actually take a step makes it clear that walking isn't a very good idea just now.

"You're going to need some help getting to your car," Laura says. "Want me to help get your things together?" He tries a stiff-legged step that emphatically discourages any further notions about walking for the moment. "Shit," he says again under his breath. Laura gathers up his things. "Look," she says, "are you sure you can drive? Do you want me to take you to the emergency room?"

He stands there, all of his weight on one leg, aware that the left knee is hanging there, damaged in some way. Julia is at the college and it seems as if the emergency room is what he needs at the moment. "Actually," he says, "if you could, that would be great."

He sighs and stands there listening to the sounds of other players on nearby courts on this bright, windless day, aware that he's been separated from the world of the able. Jesus, he thinks, just like that, out of the blue.

In a curtained-off area near where he's waiting to be transported to the operating room for arthroscopic surgery on his knee, Alan reclines on his slightly raised gurney, feeling diminished. They've taken away his clothes, his watch, his keys and his wallet; all he's wearing is a hospital johnny that ties in the back. With his name and birth date on the plastic bracelet around his wrist, he's become just another patient. He takes some solace in the fact that most of the other johnny-clad citizens of this nation of the sick are a lot worse off than he is. It occurs to him that the hospital ought to issue color-coded badges that differentiate people like himself from the serious cases. The operation he's anticipating has become routine, after all. Recuperation should be quick enough, Doctor Leslie has promised him, but there's no way he can think about more tennis this summer, and the loss of that opportunity grieves him more than it ought to, because it certainly looked as if he'd found a good tennis partner in Laura.

"You shouldn't have much trouble getting back to work right away," Doctor Leslie said. "Lucky you're not in some more physically active occupation." She herself, he'd learned in talking to her, was a dedicated tennis player. "Take it slow getting back and you'll have a lot more years charging the net," she said.

"I used to play with Sam Wasson," he told her. "He used to be a patient of yours."

She nodded. "A sad story," she said. "I liked Sam. He could be very funny."

"Sam always spoke highly of your work," Alan said. "That's why I came here."

When they looked at the x-rays her long finger indicated the impaired area on the ghostly picture. "This is a pretty common injury," she told him. "It's easy enough to fix. It's a blessing that these days we can scope it." She worked on college and professional athletes and had some interesting anecdotes about them. Though he'd like to have thought he was above it, this association with the famously hale and fit lifted his spirits about his ultimate recovery. "You can watch the whole procedure on TV," she said. He was all for that. "A minimal cast," she said, "a few weeks of physical therapy and you should be as good as new." He calculated the weeks in his head, wondering if there'd be a chance to get back on the courts before the snow started falling. He knew that it was best to be conservative about the healing, that rushing back into intense physical activity would be tempting fate. Still, he didn't want to close out the possibility entirely.

Now, remembering that conference, Alan is impatient to get the whole thing over with, the operation, the recuperation, the restoration of his old self. He's happy to see Julia when she comes back into the curtained space. "Are you cold?" she asks. "You look like you're freezing."

"Actually," he admits, "it is cold here."

"Let me get a nurse," she says, and steps out beyond the curtains, returning soon with a short, middle-aged woman in green scrubs. "Has the doctor been in yet?" she asks. No, not yet, Alan tells her. "They're running late this morning," the nurse says. "She should be by soon, though, to paint your knee."

She glances from the monitor to Alan. "Your wife says you're cold. Do you want a blanket?"

"Yeah," he nods. "That would be great."

"No problem." The nurse, who exudes an air of friendly competence, disappears for a few seconds, returning with a clean white blanket that's blessedly been heated.

"Ah," he says, "this is more like it. Deluxe service."

"I'll check back in a couple of minutes," the nurse says.

When they're alone again, Julia looks at her watch. "I hate to leave you like this," she says. She has an important meeting at the college.

"Hey," he assures her, "this is a routine procedure. There's nothing to worry about." Nevertheless, he appreciates her wanting to be around.

"I know," she says. "Still . . ."

"It looks like I won't be going in for at least another half-hour," he says. "Leslie said the operation is supposed to take about forty-five minutes and I'll have to stay in the recovery room for an hour after that."

"I gave the hospital my number at the college," Julia says. "And I'll call in about an hour. God, I hope that meeting is over by then."

When Julia is gone, Alan is the sole occupant of his curtained retreat. He's already surveyed his surroundings, which consist of a monitor, some tubes with gauges whose purpose is a mystery to him, a dark green canister, presumably for oxygen, a yellow plastic container labeled "Biohazard Waste" and a shelf that contains, among other items, a box of purple latex gloves and a container of hand wipes. All of them are bathed in the fluorescent light coming from the ceiling. Through the closed curtains he's aware of people moving by, and he hears snatches of a half-dozen conversations. "She shouldn't have done that," a male voice says. "She knew better," a female voice agrees. Are they talking about a doctor who botched an operation or a roommate who brought a friend to spend the night? "Terry's worked a couple of shifts already," another voice announces. "She looks it," someone else pipes in. A few seconds later: "He's in OR One with His Majesty David Sturges." "Did you read what Tom Selleck said?" an older woman asks. "He's competitive. So am I," a man asserts belligerently.

The curtain is pulled open suddenly. It's Doctor Leslie in green scrubs, her head capped, looking like someone who's running late.

"I have to paint the knee," she says with a formal smile. "Just to make sure we do the right one."

"It's the left one," he says.

"Right," she acknowledges, making her mark. "The correct one."

"Do they do the wrong ones often?" he asks. "Just out of curiosity."

"Only a couple of times a week," she deadpans. Then, just in case he didn't get the joke, "Actually, we're very careful about these things. Don't worry," she gives his knee a tap. "I'll be seeing you pretty soon."

Shortly thereafter the stocky anesthesiologist with sideburns looks in on him and tells him he's going to administer an intravenous sedative.

"Running late this morning?" Alan asks, trying to break through the man's businesslike air, but his only response is a curt nod. "This is just to calm you down a bit," he explains after he's set things up. As he leaves, he assures Alan that it will only be a few minutes now. Alone again, he watches the yellowish fluid make its way slowly in the IV tube. The heated blanket has long since cooled and he's aware of the faint ripple of a returning chill. It could be the temperature, he thinks, though it might be a bit of nervousness.

Soon the curtain is pulled back with a sharp screech and a couple of linebacker types are there to transport the gurney to the operating room. "Show time," one of them says. After they get him into a recumbent position and disengage the brakes, they maneuver the gurney out of his sanctuary and through the busy room just outside. From his prone position he catches sight of the cabinet where the blankets are heated, he gets a look at some of the people in scrubs, wondering whose conversations he was overhearing in the waiting area. In seconds, though, he's left that place behind and is moving down a long sloped corridor where the ceiling is a different color. People hurry past him, on their way to a dozen destinations. Abruptly, he feels the gurney slowing. One of the aides pushes a button and a set of doors swings open before him. Not long after that he's in the operating room, his attention drawn to the large lights on the ceiling. Doctor Leslie and her team are visible, but as he's being pushed to the center of the room voices buzz concernedly around him. Sedated as he is, Alan's curiosity is aroused. Something is up, he knows, but what?

Now Doctor Leslie is talking. "We don't like what we're seeing on your heart monitor," she explains very carefully, as if she's not sure he speaks English. "It's showing that your heartbeat's irregular. We're sending you to the cardiac unit to stabilize it." What does this mean? He's never had any trouble with his heart before; but now, through the mild fog of the sedative, he feels a twinge of anxiety.

"What is it?" he asks her, trying to sound calm.

"It could be a lot of things," she says. "There's a good chance it's nothing at all. We can't ignore it, though. We have to do this."

Soon he's being moved with obvious urgency along other corridors. Doors fly open in front of him. In another room a different team is waiting for him. Who are these people? he wonders. A nurse comes up to him with a hypodermic needle. Behind her, others are engaged in preparations around some kind of machine that's been wheeled in on a trolley. "You're experiencing atrial fibrillation," the nurse explains in an accent Alan can't place, though her voice is soft and reassuring. "I'm going to inject you with an amnesiac drug now," she says, indicating the needle. He notices that she has a faint mustache, her brown eyes are kind. "Then we're going to perform cardioversion, we're going to give you a shock."

"Electric shock?" he asks.

She nods. "Don't worry. After the injection, you won't remember anything. Hold still now. It's going to be over in a moment."

He's still awake when another nurse begins shaving his chest.

When Julia gets to see him in the recovery room she's frantic. "I'd just left thinking it was going to be routine, and when I called they said you were in the cardiac unit. Doctor Leslie explained it, but it still was quite a jolt."

"I'm going to be OK," he says, still feeling a little distant from things. "That's what they've told me. Look, you can see from the monitor that my heartbeat is stable." She doesn't look reassured.

"They wouldn't be sending me home if they thought there was a problem, would they?" Actually, after his heart's surprising misbehavior, he feels safer here in the hospital, with doctors and nurses near at hand, but that's not the kind of thing he's going to tell Julia. "Doctor Leslie said most likely it's nothing at all."

Julia nods, though she's not hiding her worry. "It could have been tension," she says.

"Most likely," he says. It's possible, he supposes, though he doesn't remember feeling all that tense.

"You were cold," she reminds him. "Maybe that triggered something."

He nods. The fact is, he has no idea what this episode means. All he knows is that he came to the hospital this morning as an inpatient expecting to undergo a routine procedure, and the sudden delinquency of his heartbeat triggered a medical emergency. He tries to picture his inert body on the table, the metallic plates attached to his chest connected by cables to some machine that can deliver a powerful surge of electrical current to his heart. It's a Frankenstein image, more than a bit scary. Did his shaved chest heave under the force of the charge, did he spasm? What did his face look like when the bolt of man-made lightning passed through his rib cage? None of this information is available to him. Whatever happened lies buried under the amnesiac drug.

What he does remember is the rushing gurney, the hastily assembled cardiac team, the nurse with the mustache and the soothing voice. He wants to believe Doctor Leslie when she says that this episode may mean nothing at all. She's asked him to schedule an EKG with Doctor Henshaw, his primary care physician. "If you get a clean one, we'll scope you a couple of days later," she told him encouragingly. "It happens every now and then." Still, he never expected, when the day began, to be lying on a table having his heart's rhythm corrected by an administered jolt of electricity. How could he have known that before the day was over his heart would turn out to be an untrustworthy organ?

He's wheeled to the hospital entrance and Julia drives him home, but the familiar setting is transformed by what happened earlier in the day. Does he miss the ever-present nurses and the beeping of the vigilant machines? "I think I'd just like to sit out on the back porch," he says, though when he's there the scene before him, the sloping green sweep of the yard, the picket of shadow on the Perlmans' fence, is tinged with poignancy.

"You OK?" Julia says, checking in on him.

"Yeah," he answers, "just a little tired. Actually, more than a little." Already he feels himself succumbing to a great heaviness. "The drug is going to affect you after you get home," the nurse with the mustache told him, and here on the back porch he feels himself being pulled under.

"I think you should lie down," Julia says.

"I think you're right," he responds, already yearning for oblivion.


In the days that follow, Alan is ostensibly blithe about what happened, entertaining people at the office with colorful accounts of his medical adventure. "But what caused it?" Sally asks.

He shrugs. "As the Brits say, it was a one-off. That's the best I can do. The phases of the moon, maybe."

He's happy for the distraction of the Boston Housing Court, where, like a returning hero, he manages to get the sympathy of his colleagues as he makes his limping way among them. All the while, though, he's thinking about his appointment with Doctor Henshaw. He's elated when his EKG turns out to be clean, a fact which he immediately reports to Doctor Leslie. "Good," the woman in the office says. "She cleared a space for next Friday on the assumption that things were going to be fine."

He calls Julia. "I'm booked for next week."

"Great," she says. "This time I'm not leaving the hospital."

In a couple of days he's back in the hospital and this time he makes it to the OR with no detours. "How was it?" Julia asks him when she comes into the recovery room.

"A piece of cake," he says. "I watched the whole thing on TV. It was terrific."

She lets out a sigh. "I'm glad this is over at last."

"Me too," he says. It was a tense moment when he'd left her in the waiting area and was being wheeled toward the operating room. "How's the heartbeat?" he kept wanting to ask the people who could see the monitor, but they just went about their business without any comment, so it was clear that the heart wasn't going to be a problem. Still, though the operation is over, some kind of uncertainty and wariness lingers. Maybe not everything was banished from his memory by that amnesiac drug.


Alan is busy at the office when Julia calls. "I didn't get it," she says abruptly, and he knows without having to hear any more that she's talking about the deanship at the college. "They picked Claire Doucette," she hurls the words at him.

"Damn." He pushes aside the papers he's been working on. "I'm so sorry." He knows how much she wanted that job. "Those dumb bastards are going to regret it," he says. After a moment, he asks, "When are you getting home?"

"I'll be home by six," she says. "That's when Tommy gets back from his play date with Jonah. Janet and I are going to have a drink at Dooley's."

"Good idea," he says. Janet has been, in effect, her campaign manager for the deanship, and they probably both need to commiserate. "I'll see you at home, then. Meanwhile, just try to hang in there." Already he's thinking: flowers, a good bottle of wine. This is a big loss for Julia and it requires some kind of response.

His sympathy is genuine, but it's complicated by his knowledge that in these last few crucial weeks he probably hasn't provided the support he might have because he'd been caught up in his own recuperation, approaching his recently completed physical therapy as if it were some kind of Olympic competition. "Good job," Carlo, his therapist would tell him after he'd done the sequence of leg lifts with ten pound weights, then pushed his leg up and back against the pressure of Carlo's hands, performed his squats against the wall with the exercise ball, and put in some time on the stationary bike, finishing up with a brief stint on the stair step platform. Those PT sessions that began with applications of heat and ultrasound to his knee constituted a soothing ritual, and Alan hoarded all the compliments he'd gotten from Carlo and Ellen, the other therapist, though neither of them could have guessed what lay behind his fierce dedication to the therapy. How could they possibly know that what he was trying to recover from wasn't just the injury to his knee, but the interior shock caused by the surprising revolt of his heart in the hospital a few weeks ago? It didn't make any sense, but he'd come to feel that as long as the knee was healing well, as long as he kept regaining more range of motion all the time, it meant that he'd eventually get back to normal in other ways as well, that he was putting further behind him that singular, upsetting episode, that one-off, and he'd eventually be able to breathe more easily, leaving his heart to its own routine and dependable devices.

There's no question that this subterranean preoccupation has kept him from being the help to Julia that he could have been during this important time for her, and he's going to try to make up for it tonight. Already he's asked Sally to call the flower people. "Roses," he tells her. "Say a dozen. Nice, nothing cheap. It's for a celebration."

"They're wonderful," Julia says when she sees the flowers. She goes to the sideboard, where he's put them into a vase, she leans over to smell them, then bursts into tears. In seconds, he's by her side. "We're not going to mourn," he says, putting an arm around her. "We're going to celebrate your great qualities, which are too numerous to cite. I got us some Australian chardonnay because the Aussies wouldn't just sit back and mope. You know, Waltzing Matilda and all that."

She laughs at his mangled attempt at an Australian accent, her eyes still wet.

"I should lose out on a dean's job every day," she says. She touches his forearm. "Don't move," she says. "Let me get Tommy his mac and cheese." When she returns, he hands her a glass of wine. "I guess Claire Doucette wanted that job more than I did," she says.

It's the kind of statement that requires a careful response and Alan waits a moment before answering. "That may be. Still, you'd have been the better choice."

"I don't know," she says. "When I first heard the news I was mad. And hurt. Yes, definitely hurt. It was a rejection, of course. There's no way to deny that." He waits for her to say more and watches her mouth curve into a lazy half-smile. "But the truth is," she says, "and I'm not just making this up after the fact, the truth is that when I heard about it I felt a sense of relief as well. Like, OK, that's out of the way, now you can get serious." He nods, acknowledging her statement, but he doesn't interrupt. "And that's pretty scary," she goes on. "I mean, all along I was pretty ambivalent about that deanship, wouldn't you say?"

He nods once more, though in fact it wasn't all that evident to him. What he doesn't deny is that he was certainly ambivalent about it. There's no question that Julia's pursuit of the job had caused a strain between them in the last couple of months, and possibly her having won it might have made things worse. But that's no longer a live issue.

"I mean," she says, "when you first met me, did you think 'Now there's a woman that's going to be a dean one day?' "

He laughs. "No, absolutely not. I was thinking a lot of things, but I can assure you that wasn't one of them."

She takes a sip of wine. When she looks directly at him, her eyes are quietly blazing. "I mean, I went into teaching because I loved literature, especially those nineteenth-century English novels."

"That you certainly did. I'll vouch for that." He remembers their first summer at Innisfree, when she'd read aloud passages that moved her. The memory calls up the particular smell of the house Richard Mallory built in the woods of Connecticut, the lazy warmth of summer there, the distant drone of an insect by now long dead, the soft light of a kerosene lamp.

She laughs. "How in hell did I manage to convince myself that what I wanted to be was a dean, of all things?"

Though he's inclined to be careful, he doesn't take this as merely a rhetorical question. "Well, from what you've said, you thought you could influence the college's policy, the curriculum."

"Yeah," she says, smiling. "It's kind of, if you can't beat the administrators, join them."

He nods. "The perks are better than they are for mere teachers, that's for sure."

"True," she says, "and you have some kind of spurious authority." She sighs. "But at the end of the day, you're still the creature of the administration, aren't you?" After a moment, she adds, "Like Orwell, in Burma, you're the civil servant who represents the colonial power."

"The little man carrying the elephant gun," he says. She's taught Orwell's essay plenty of times and he knows it well.

"So what's all this telling me?" Julia goes on, her brow knit. "Where do I go from here?" Knowing she has an answer, he waits. "It's telling me this: somehow I convinced myself that, in spite of my doubts, being a dean was a big enough deal, it was worth taking a shot at, that if I got the job I could be the kind of civil servant who'd work to subvert the colonial power and help the natives find their own authority." She pauses for a moment. "Could I have made that happen? I don't know. It might have wound up being a very frustrating experience. But I saw myself wielding some sort of power, and using it for the good. Now that's gone and what am I left with?"

He could tell her she has a home, a family, friends and a community, but he knows that she's aware of that and that she's talking about something else.

She takes a sip of her wine. "Well," she says, "I'm left with what I had at the beginning. I still love those nineteenth-century British novels and I still think I have some smart things to say about them. But it's a lot harder to write a decent book about literature than it is to become a dean." She shakes her head. "You know what I think? I think I tried to distract myself from that hard truth with those fantasies about the deanship. The whole thing might just have been an elaborate bit of evasion." After a while, she says, "The book is still there, damn it. The book is still there, waiting to be written." Then she falls silent.

It's his turn to say something, to react to what she's just said. He's cheered and heartened by her attitude. Still, he knows that, given his own feelings about her pursuit of the deanship, it's hard for him to appreciate fully how much she feels she's lost, how much she may be trying to rationalize. "I don't know," he begins, "maybe at this stage you're throwing around a lot of ideas, maybe you're testing your responses." She looks at him unblinkingly. "But if," he goes on, "if what you've just said is true, then losing that deanship was a big favor to you." She keeps looking at him. "And it means that what you've decided on for the next step is going to require you to be pretty brave."

"Thanks for being honest," she says. "It's certainly true that the idea of going back to my book project is pretty scary."

He leans toward her. "But I'll bet it's exciting too, isn't it?"

She laughs. "That it is." It's clear that the prospect of returning to her book has fired her imagination.

"Well, I'll back you a hundred percent on that plan," he says. "Really, we're making enough money nowadays that we can afford to buy you some time to work on that book." He tries to gauge her reaction before continuing. "Hell," he says, "you could even take a semester or two off from teaching, you know."

She takes another sip of her wine and puts down her glass. "Wow," she says, "that is scary." As she contemplates the possibility, though, her mouth slowly curves into a smile. "But you're right. It's exciting too." The smile is quickly replaced by a frown. "Are you sure we can afford that?"

"Absolutely," he says, thinking of his secret stash of money. "We can absolutely afford it." He lifts his wine glass. "To a long and distinguished career for Dean Doucette."

"She's welcome to it," Julia declares. They touch glasses and drink. He's glad he can offer her the assurance of time off from her work to pursue something that, really, he's convinced, she's much more passionate about than being a dean. To be able to give her this gift is a way of making up for his recent inattention while he devoted himself to rehabilitating his knee, and he wants to prolong this moment. "Look," he says, suddenly inspired, "what do you say we go up to Ogunquit this weekend? Just me and you. Ellie's been talking for months about having Tommy spend the weekend with Josh. Let's see if she's up to it. I know Tommy's been pushing it."

He can see that she's interested. "But isn't it supposed to rain this weekend?"

He shrugs. "The weathermen could be wrong. And if it does rain, we can stay inside and strategize about your grand plans. You can bring along a nineteenth-century novel or two."

A smile slowly emerges. "Now that is an appealing thought."

"Remember," he says, "this is Day One of your renewed book project."

"OK," she says, "you've convinced me." She raises an admonitory finger. "But maybe we shouldn't be too rigid about strategizing. It would be all right, wouldn't it, just to eat lobster and walk under leaden skies along the rocky cliffs? Let's bring our slickers and just enjoy ourselves in the rain."

"If the weather's too awful," he says, "we can always spend some quality time in a jacuzzi."

She smiles to herself.

"What are you thinking about?" he asks.

"Poor Claire Doucette," she says. "Better her than me."


Their motel is a rambling, capacious set of connected buildings, more comfortable than luxurious, not on the ocean, but a walkable distance away. Once they've gotten themselves settled, they venture into the damp air, heading directly for the Marginal Way, a paved path along the rocky coast that rises and dips along the edge where the Atlantic meets the North American shore. The narrow road twists frequently, providing suddenly changing views of the shoreline: in places the rocks are worn smooth, covered with lichen; elsewhere, huge striated blocks resemble the ruins of some gigantic prehistoric building project. A constant wind whips off the white-capped Atlantic as the incoming surf booms off of the rocks and sends up spray; tidal pools fill with rushing saltwater that retreats with a sigh, bringing hungry, shrieking sea birds to prey on the marine creatures trapped there. Beyond, the gray vistas carry the eye all the way to the blurred eastern horizon where some long dark shape makes its way across the open ocean.

The mile and a quarter path isn't particularly arduous—Sam, who was a serious hiker, used to call it a walk for old ladies—but in places the footing can be tricky for Alan's still recovering knee and he's pleased to find that he's up to the effort. Anyway, if he overdoes the walking, he knows, he can always pop into the soothing jacuzzi later. Picking his way among the timeworn rocks to get a better view, he's sure he can feel his strength and stamina returning. If he lived in a place with a warmer climate, he might already be thinking about returning to tennis by the end of the year.

Before they go out to dinner, they call their friend Ellie to check up on Tommy. "How's the guy doing?" Alan asks when Julia gets off the phone.

"We may not be able to get him back," she says, putting on a comic long face. "He couldn't wait to get back to pigging out on popcorn and watching *E.T.*"

"*E.T.* again?" he asks.

"A great work of art is a new experience each time."

Alan shakes his head. "Our little boy's growing up. Remember when we used to read him *Make Way for Ducklings?*"

"And *Goodnight, Moon,*" she says.

"Stop it," he says. "You're making me feel old."

Later, in the restaurant, he asks her, "Remember that time we had in California?"

"Sure," she says. Just outside the window the heaving ocean surges against the dark rocks, throwing up a cloud of white spume. Gulls coast on the wind currents overhead, ever vigilant for the flash of something moving in the water below.

"Ever think of going back there for a year or so?" he asks. "The West Coast?"

"Mmm," she closes her eyes, "I remember Santa Monica." Then she blinks them open. "But what about Tommy's school?"

"He's still young enough to adapt to things," he tells her.

Now her expression changes. "Are you serious?"

He shrugs. "I don't know. I'm just tossing out ideas. We don't want to get stuck in the mud, do we? I just think we should keep an open mind about things."

"Did you just win the lottery or something?" she asks.

"No, but I do have a little secret that I'm going to tell you about."

"Aha." She leans closer. "You're really a nobleman in disguise."

He laughs. "Better. A few years ago I realized I was making a fair amount of money and I decided to keep setting a bit of it aside for something special, like maybe a trip to Europe. I was going to announce it when I had a sizeable bundle. Well, it just kept growing. That's why we have enough to bankroll a year off of teaching for you." He smiles. "The fact is, you don't have any excuse not to write that book now." He looks out at the white surf slamming into the dark rocks. The moving ocean excites him. Ever since the episode with his heart this summer he's felt the presence of a shadow. Now he feels that life is opening up for the two of them. Julia's going to write that book, after all. She isn't going to have to settle for just being a dean. And soon his knee will be back to normal.

"What other secrets are you keeping from me?" she asks.

He laughs. "Think I'd tell you?"

The next day the weather is foul, the rain is constant, and, at times, under the persistent battering of the wind, almost horizontal; but Alan and Julia, in their GORE-TEX slickers, are up for it. During a breakfast of fresh-baked muffins and coffee they decide to go to Kennebunkport, where, Alan vaguely remembers, there's a Franciscan monastery run by Lithuanian monks. "If we find it, good," Julia says. "If not, we'll run into something interesting, I'm sure." They set out shortly after breakfast and manage to get themselves lost several times, only to be delightfully surprised by the discovery of a fantastic out-of-the-way Victorian house looming in the murk.

"Didn't we see this place before?" he asks.

"Who cares? It's just as wonderful the second time around. I love it."

Eventually, quite by chance, they stumble upon the monastery, whose spacious grounds contain pieces of sculpture that range from the tritely pious to the interestingly avant-garde; but it's not an ideal day for viewing outdoor art, and they decide that the thing to do is to visit the chapel. The place is small and deserted, like the sculpture a mix of modern and traditional elements; but the ground they stand on is charged with mystery to Alan, for whom the very notion of a Lithuanian monastery in Maine is surreal enough. After they leave the chapel, he lingers in the vestibule area, where there's some literature on the monks and their observances. He's intrigued by the nearby corridor that leads to other rooms, including apparently a dining room, to judge from the smell of coffee and the distant clatter of cutlery.

"Listen," he says, and they hear voices coming from the corridor. As the speakers approach, it's clear they're not talking English. Two bearded men, wearing raincoats over their robes, their feet in sandals, smile briefly at the visitors before returning to their conversation and leaving the building for the rain outside. Alan wants to hang around this place, beguiled by the notion of a stout Lithuanian cook in the kitchen breaking eggs for a recipe that might have originated somewhere near the Baltic, amid birch forests where peasant girls wearing kerchiefs crossed themselves before setting out to hunt for mushrooms. "We've passed over into another world," he tells Julia, and she nods, "Amen," but it's clear she wants to move on, eager to continue their explorations.

In town, where they stop for coffee, the waitress tells them that as long as they're here they should try to get at least a glimpse of the Bush compound at Walker's Point, even though the president is in the capital just now. "It's not far away," she says, "but don't expect to get too close, with the security and all. Still, it would be a shame if you didn't see it, having come up all this way."

Outside, Julia says, "Do you think she spotted us for liberals? Think this is some kind of trap?"

"She did seem kind of insistent, didn't she?"

"We'll just have to stay on the alert." But all fantasies dissipate when they've left the confines of the village and are headed north, since the real world is fantastic enough. Only a few feet away on the right is the most turbulent ocean either of them has ever seen, a pulsing mass of sea whose titanic swells roll heavily far from shore, the incoming surf pounding against the rocks, sending up a spray of saltwater that sometimes overleaps the stone wall and pours onto the road itself.

"Looks like Neptune is angry," Alan says. "Very angry."

"Isn't it wonderful?" Julia exclaims. The whole world, it seems, is in motion.

It doesn't take them long to get to where they can make out Walker Point in the mist, a spit of land thrust like a slender ship into an ocean raging with whitecaps. I'd hate to be out in a boat in this, Alan thinks.

"Wow!" Julia rolls down her window, turning her face toward the pelting spray. "This isn't something you forget," she says. "And I don't mean seeing the Bush compound."

When they return to town, they stop at a small local museum the waitress told them about. As was true in the monastery, they're the only visitors to the place and there's an eerie quiet as they make their way across wide-planked floors through the half-dozen rooms filled with local artifacts. On the walls hang portraits of long-dead sea captains and some of their wives, as well as watercolors of their spanking new ships making their way across stylized, two-dimensional oceans. Weird as their being the only visitors may be, the museum is a tranquil eddy in the midst of the raging weather outside, audible here as a faint windy sigh and a spattering against the windows. Alan stops before a picture and reads the accompanying plaque that identifies the subject as one of those captains who died at sea before he reached forty. The man, formally attired and with mild eyes and rosy cheeks, has the air of a benevolent schoolteacher rather than some blood-and-thunder sea dog used to shouting into the storm as he urged his men to batten down the hatches. Alan is still looking at the picture when he feels Julia take hold of his hand.

"That guy was younger than I am when he died," he says.

She squeezes his hand. "You've got a lot more seas to sail, old salt."

When they return to the motel, the woman at the desk informs Alan that there's a phone message and both of them are alarmed. When they had checked up on Tommy a few hours ago, he was still eating popcorn and watching *E.T.* It turns out, though, that the message was from Sally, Alan's secretary. He'd asked her to find out about Mrs. Sadowska, he remembers. If anything important turned up, she was to call him at the motel.

"Let me find out what this is all about," he tells Julia. "Why don't you have a hot chocolate here? This shouldn't take more than ten minutes." Back in their room, he calls Sally. "Mrs. Sadowska is dead," she tells him.

His stomach lurches. He sees the old woman hanging from the ceiling, her head tilted toward the clutter of her accumulated papers, her black shoes dangling. The image doesn't make any sense, since she would no longer be living in that apartment. He waits a few seconds before asking, "How did she die?"

"I couldn't find out," Sally says. "All they told me was that she's dead."

"It wasn't anything violent?" he ventures.

"No, no. She was in the shelter and they said it was from natural causes. Sorry I couldn't find out any more."

"No, no, that's OK. You did a good job." Possibly Mrs. Sadowska died in her sleep. Leaving a life that had known so many troubles would have been a blessing, wouldn't it? Still, not being able to set down all the names, dates and places, to die with her task uncompleted—it would be just one more loss for her. Alan's recognition that all of us leave things unfinished does little to assuage the feeling. What's surprising is how the old woman's death has cast a heaviness over everything when he'd felt so great all day. It makes no sense, he knows, there's no reason for him to feel guilty. Still, why does Mrs. Sadowska's death upset him so?

He's determined not to spoil Julia's stay here by moping, though. "Just routine business," he tells her when he returns. "How's the hot chocolate?"

"Good," she says. "Actually, while you were gone, I checked up on Tommy on the pay phone here. He's fine."

"Still watching *E.T.* and eating popcorn, I suppose."

"Something like that." She smiles to herself, sadly, it seems to Alan. "Look," she says, "the rain's stopped at last. Want to take another crack at the Marginal Way?" In fact, the idea isn't very appealing just now. His knee hasn't held up as well as he'd hoped. "Come on," she persists. "We can drive to the entrance and just do a bit of it."

"OK," he agrees. But this time the uphill and downhill climbing take more of a toll, and soon his knee is aching. He finds himself dragging his left leg along, and finally at one point he suggests that they stop at a memorial bench that looks out over the rocks to the ocean.

"I wonder where you'd wind up in Europe if you went straight east?" Julia asks.

"All I know," he says, "is that it's always further south than you think." His knee is throbbing a bit, but he's hopeful it will get better. Maybe some ice from the machine at the motel will help. He looks out over the huge, dark Atlantic, which is still turbulent, and he remembers the savage pounding of the ocean a few miles north of here. How puny you'd feel out there in the middle of the buckling sea, far from any place where you could glimpse the shore. He's caught up in a dizzying sense of vastness, the way he'd sometimes felt when he was a kid and the nuns would talk about eternity and other mysteries of the church. Trying to grasp that concept could bring about a kind of vertigo in which it seemed possible to lose the very notion of your self. He remembers the story of St. Augustine watching a boy spooning water from the ocean into a hole in the ground. When the saint asked the boy what he was doing, he replied: "I'm going to empty the whole ocean into this hole." To Augustine, Sister Romuald would declare with her hand raised, a knowing smile on her candle-pale face, human beings who attempted to fathom God's mysteries were doing the same thing, trying to empty the ocean with a spoon.

How the nuns loved those grand metaphysical panoramas. Sister Romuald had a special passion for All Souls' Day. The dead, she liked to proclaim, are far more numerous than the living. She wanted her charges to remember that, however much the living might think they were alone and unobserved in this world, count-less souls had been here before them, and they weren't gone; she wanted her students to recognize that at every moment as they walked the familiar streets of their neighborhood they were sur-rounded by these departed multitudes.

Once more he thinks of Mrs. Sadowska. In her book she wanted to set the names down, names of those who'd done good things and those who'd done evil. All had been part of her life and all were gone now, lost to everyone, remembered only by her. And now, she's gone too. Looking at the ocean, Alan wonders who would people a book of his, if he were to write one? His own dead, though not nearly as numerous as the Polish woman's, would still constitute a sizeable group. There were his parents, of course, countless aunts and uncles, a cousin named Charley Sweet whose bike got hit by a drunk driver when he was ten, Rodney Some-thing-or-Other from his history class in college who killed himself by jumping off the roof of South Quad, others whose names he's forgotten. Richard Mallory, who'd built Innisfree, was there among them too, wasn't he? And it didn't stop. More recently, those dead had been joined by Sam and now Mrs. Sadowska. Of course, you couldn't forget Bobby Pelham and Serena Beltin.

"What are you thinking?" Julia asks.

There on the windy northern shore facing the open sea, Alan leans over and their slickers crinkle as he kisses his wife long and passionately.

"Whew!" Julia says when he pulls back. "That's some thought." She's silent for a long time, looking at the ocean.

"There's something on your mind," he says. "I can tell."

She turns toward him. "What would you say to our getting back early?" she asks.

Alan smiles. "You miss our popcorn eater?"

"Maybe." She nods. "Still, I'm feeling so much better. Really. But I'm ready to go home, I guess."

"I guess I am too." At the moment, he's just as happy to be heading inland.

I t's the picture he sees first, grainy, black-and-white, Lily, looking as she did when he knew her: the cloud of dark hair, the small, perfect features, the slightly aloof expression—in an instant his pulse is racing. Why is he seeing this in the paper? Then he becomes aware of the words alongside the image: "Sixties Radical Comes In From the Cold." The dateline identifies a town in Washington he's never heard of. His eyes jump to the quote: "I intend to cooperate fully with the authorities." His breath is pulled out of him. Does it mean she's going to tell them about him?

No, Lily.

Even before the words can be formed, he's freeing himself from the dream, and after a few beats of his heart he assures himself that he's awake, lying beside Julia here in his house west of Boston. Relief washes over him. Then he wonders, could it actually happen that way?

"How's the old knee?" Barney O'Shea asks later that day when Alan returns to the office after lunch.

"Fine, fine," he answers, though he wonders if he's moving with a noticeable limp after walking up the flight of stairs. More likely, Barney is just being politely solicitous.

"You ought to look into golf," Barney says with a smile. "It's a lot easier on the body than tennis."

"Yeah, I know," Alan waves his comment away. "But I'm afraid that riding around in a cart all day would give me one hell of a case of hemorrhoids." It's an old argument, a pleasant enough ritual.

"I'll get you out on the links yet," Barney retorts. "I guarantee, you'll like it."

"Only after I've played a set with you at the high school courts," Alan fires back. Both of them know there's not the slightest possibility of either fantasy being realized.

"Well, go easy on that knee," Barney says with a note of genuine concern before ducking into his office.

The truth is, Alan's knee hasn't been all that good since he came back from Ogunquit a couple of weeks ago, and the disappointment of its slow healing weighs on him. He's wearing an Ace bandage that gives him a bit more stability, but every now and then an unwary turn will bring a sharp twinge and he'll remember his accident. "Don't worry about it," Doctor Leslie has told him. "Every knee heals according to its own timetable. You may have sprained it up in Maine. Take it easy. Take a couple of ibuprofens if you think you need them. Ice should help too." So it isn't as if he believes there's anything permanent in his present condition; still, the delay in healing continues to cast a shadow. In his imagination, he used to move like a twenty-year-old before that unlucky step on the courts with Laura.

Work, as usual, is the best distraction. At the top of the afternoon's agenda is the case of Mary Hollis, who's almost $850 behind in her rent payments at the Reese projects. Alan is representing the housing authority, which, given the state of Mary's affairs, has been compelled to begin the process that could culminate in her eviction. She's fought the authority every step of the way, fortified by her belief that her delinquency is justified, since it was caused by a hospital stay that drained her slim resources. A hearing has been scheduled for next week in the Housing Court where she's prepared to make her plea, but the fact is, legally, the landlord holds all the cards. On the other hand, the housing authority has no great desire to evict her and it would be in the best interests of both parties if she were to waive the hearing and accept the terms of a settlement that she and the authority could live with. Alan's challenge will be to persuade her that, while he understands her position and sympathizes with her, even acknowledges the justice of her moral claim, as the law is written, she really doesn't have a case; and it would be better for her to promise that she'll punctually pay her rent of $200 on the fifteenth of each month as well as something on what she owes—Alan has come up with the figure of $70—until she's paid it all off. If she agrees in writing to do this and actually keeps abreast of her rent payments for six months after the old debt is settled, the landlord will remove the order for execution and she'll have a clean slate with the authority.

Alan knows it's not going to be easy. People for whom justice is most elusive can be very stubborn about pursuing it. A solidly built, deeply religious woman in her thirties who distantly resembles the Dodgers' Hall of Fame catcher Roy Campanella, Mary will want Alan, or someone, to hear her side of things—again—before she'll even consider making a deal. Still, he's fairly confident that in the end he can get her to see the wisdom of a pragmatic settlement before she risks going before a judge.

He's dotting the final i's of the agreement when the phone rings. "Alan Ripley," he answers.

"Alan." It's a voice he hasn't heard in more than two years. Something about it is different, though. Even in the two syllables of his name he can hear the note of appeal, but today there's something more demanding, even desperate about it. A vertiginous sense of the uncanny comes over him as he recognizes once more that a part of his life he thought he'd buried has returned. He holds the molded plastic receiver to his ear, listening to the silence on the other end, thinking that it just keeps coming back, doesn't it, and there's nothing he can do about it.

"Rory?" he asks into the phone, suddenly remembering this morning's dream. Could it have been a foreshadowing? He takes a deep breath. "What's up?" he asks, trying for a casual note.

"Look, dude," the voice comes over the wires. "I need your help."

With those words, Mary Hollis is forgotten, as is the Housing Court, even this office, and once again Alan is suspended between what he's come to think of as his real life and whatever it is that Rory brings with him. "Where are you?" he asks, praying that he's at least a couple thousand miles away.

"I'm at Logan airport," Rory answers. "I just got in from New Orleans." Of course, Alan thinks, he'd have to be here. "I need a ride into town."

Alan's shoulders sag. Showing up like this out of the blue isn't fair, he wants to shout, it's not just. "Can't you take a cab?" he asks. "I mean, I'm working."

"Listen," Rory's response is quick, peremptory. "I've got to see you. Now. This is important, this isn't a game I'm playing."

This barrage catches Alan off guard, and it's a moment before he answers. "Are you in some kind of trouble?" he asks. Instinctively, he's keeping his voice down.

"That's for me to tell you when I see you," Rory says. The pencil Alan's been holding snaps in two. His hands are trembling with anger, but he keeps his eyes resolutely on the wall, which is painted an exotic shade of blue that verges on gray, but whose name he can't remember. Here we go again, he thinks. From the sound of Rory's voice, he hasn't come here to offer him a business opportunity this time. Whatever the deal, it's going to cost Alan, he knows; he's already calculating sums. "Look," he begins, "I'm pretty busy . . ."

Rory doesn't let him finish. "I said I've got to see you now."

Keep things under control, Alan instructs himself, get some distance on the situation. "OK, you know I'm at work." He's unable to keep the irritation out of his voice. "I can't just leave like that."

"Don't give me that shit," Rory says. "Aren't you a partner? You can do whatever the hell you want. I told you once already, this is important. Like life-and-death important." After a pause, he adds, "And you owe me big-time, buddy. Don't try to deny that."

There it is, the hammer Rory's always held, the one he's never really had to put out there on the table. Well, it's out there now, all right, lethal, menacing. Alan remembers the last time he saw the man, when he seemed flush and it looked as if all his troubles might be behind him, and behind Alan as well. If only.

"I mean it," Rory says. "I'm in some pretty deep shit and I need your help. I can't go back there." Underneath the harshness of the man's voice, he can hear the plea of someone at the end of his rope and he can't help feeling a measure of sympathy. At the same time, he wishes he were somewhere else. Or maybe somebody else. For a few seconds he listens to the comforting sound of Sally's typing, but that comfort is fleeting. The fact is, on this chilly Wednesday afternoon in early October, Rory Dekker has reentered his life, there's no denying that. Once again it's Rory who's calling the shots and Alan is obligated to respond. However much he may wish this weren't happening, he knows he isn't going to be able to ignore Rory's plea; he's going to wind up getting involved one way or another, but that doesn't mean he has to like it. "OK," he says, trying to keep down the resentment, "let me make some arrangements here. Give me a ring in fifteen minutes and we can make plans where to meet." So he needs a chauffeur from the airport. What else does he want?

It isn't hard to spot Rory at the agreed-upon rendezvous point outside the terminal at Logan: amid the hurrying crowds of travelers lugging their suitcases, Rory is a fixed point, standing there smoking beside his brown duffel bag like a castaway on a desert island. That castaway bears little resemblance to the Rory Dekker who came by two years ago with a business proposition that paid off so handsomely for Alan. For that matter, he doesn't much resemble the man who'd called him from Fred's a year before that, not to mention the Rory of Lyletown. Could he really have lost an inch or so of height? Even standing stock-still, he has the unfixed quality of a shapeshifter.

When Alan sounds his horn and signals to him, Rory flings the stub of his cigarette to the pavement and grinds it out under his shoe as if it were a deadly viper. He picks up his bag and walks deliberately toward the car. As he approaches, his gaze seems turned inward, or backward, and whatever he's seeing isn't making him happy. He's traveling light, to judge from the duffel bag he's carrying, and the thin gray windbreaker he's wearing over a black knit shirt can't offer him much protection against the chilly October weather. Everything about him says he's a man who's left in a hurry.

"So you showed up," Rory says when he pulls open the door. "Score one for the home team." He tosses the duffel into the backseat, drops into the car beside Alan and lets out a long sigh. Hello to you too, Alan thinks. "Jesus, I'm beat," Rory says without looking at him. "I need a place to stay for the night. After that, I have to make more long-range plans."

Alan has the sense of coming into the story without the benefit of sufficient exposition. "So you've left New Orleans for good?" he asks, waiting for the cab in front of him to move before he can pull away.

Rory nods, still looking straight ahead. "That place is finished for me," he says. He pulls his lips together for a moment before going on. "I blew that gig. I blew it big-time." On his face is the sullen expression of a man who knows he's done something stupid and irreversible. At the same time, there's an air of defiance about him, as though he'd do the same thing over again if he had a chance.

Alan negotiates a tricky lane change and is soon on his way to the airport exit. When it's clear Rory isn't going to say anything more, he ventures, "You said you were in trouble. Maybe life-and-death trouble."

Rory lights up a cigarette and exhales, frowning. Alan, who doesn't smoke, feels like frowning too. Maybe the smell won't linger, he thinks. "Yeah," Rory says at last. "I pissed somebody off real bad, a guy I worked for down there. That's why I had to get out of town."

Alan waits for more. When nothing more is forthcoming, he offers, "We all piss people off." How is he supposed to help if he doesn't know the story?

"Not this guy," Rory says with an air of truculence. "This guy's got major juice down there. And, I assure you, he doesn't like being pissed off." It sounds like a boast. He looks out at the traffic around them and lets out a long exhalation. "Fuck," he says. Rory's gloom is palpable, it fills the car like the accumulating smoke from his cigarette.

"So you can't go back to New Orleans then," Alan says.

Rory gives him a quizzical look. "Go back?" He laughs mirthlessly. "I'm not crazy. Under the circumstances, I'd settle for not being able to go back there." He takes a quick hit of his cigarette. "In my worst nightmares this guy is going to have people tracking me down the way they used to for runaway slaves."

The melodramatic language is a bit much for Alan, but he reminds himself to keep an open mind about what he's hearing. Possibly Rory believes this stuff. Or wants to. Maybe has to. "Are you serious?" he asks.

"I'm dead serious," Rory says. "This guy I'm talking about, one of the things they say about him is that he has short arms but a long reach."

For some reason, the image is chilling to Alan, and all at once the question of whether or not Rory's exaggerating seems beside the point. The fact is, something has driven him out of New Orleans with only a duffel bag, something has caused him to make a radical change in his life, and, whatever it is, it's become Alan's business as well. From the moment he heard Rory's voice on the phone, he should have known that: Rory's problems have become his problems, and it has nothing to do anymore with the threat of blackmail, or at least the kind of blackmail that involves money. By now it's become clear to him that when Rory took his place as a lookout at Lyletown, some kind of bond was forged between the two of them, a bond that's not going to be broken, no matter how much Alan might wish it. Just now he feels the tightening pressure of that bond. "What are you going to do then?" he asks carefully.

Rory shakes his head. "I don't know. I have to figure something out. I've got an idea or two. The main thing is, I have to have some quiet place where I can think about things."

Alan has a flash vision of the Lithuanian monastery he and Julia visited in Maine. Remote, hidden away in a lost corner of a rainy, windswept universe, that place certainly had the air of a sanctuary. Wouldn't it make a perfect hideaway? The hushed, ritualized world of the monks is far away from the noisy, exhaust-filled Sumner Tunnel through which they're traveling. Alan catches a glimpse of Rory out of the corner of his eye: he looks tired, harried, and pursued, and yet even in the way he's smoking his cigarette there's a kind of stubborn pugnacity. "This guy," Alan ventures, "this guy that you crossed, did he have anything to do with that business venture you were involved in last time I saw you?"

Rory looks vaguely ahead for a few seconds. "I had it made down there and it was my own fault," he says at last. "I threw it all away." He draws on his cigarette. "Like always," he adds. "Yeah," he says, finally responding to Alan's question, "Leo set me up, he put me onto a few things and I made out OK." A furtive smile flickers across his face. "You did too, as I recall."

"I did," Alan admits, not particularly relishing his own connection, however indirect, with this short-armed man with a long reach. "Yeah, that turned out well." Meanwhile, Rory has fallen into silence again, and Alan pursues, "So this guy's name is Leo?"

"Yeah. Leo Guerard."

"And he's a big man in New Orleans?"

Rory nods. "Leo's got his fingers into all sorts of things down there." His voice is even, expository, but tired. "Some of them are even legit, but a lot of what he's into you don't want to examine too closely." He makes a short, snuffling sound. "There are a lot of people who owe something to Leo," he goes on, "and they're not all down in New Orleans." He sinks back against the seat. "That's why I have to keep on my toes, even here."

OK, Alan reminds himself, even if it sounds like something from a B-movie, you can't dismiss it out of hand. "And you said you worked for him?" he pursues, hoping to prise out of him some specific details.

"There were contacts I made in prison," Rory says. "There were connections." He draws on his cigarette. "Hell, I tried playing it straight for a while, but there was nothing." He sighs. "In the end the only way for me to get anywhere was working the other side of the street, so what choice did I have? I got lucky with Leo: he took a liking to me and I got to do a lot of things for him." His voice turns suddenly sharp. "I know that might make it sound like I was some kind of flunky, but it wasn't that." He shrugs. "Sure, if you're in that kind of position you have to eat a certain amount of shit, but I'm no dummy, I know which side my bread's buttered on, I can play the game. It's not pretty a hundred percent of the time but then, what is? I mean, like the song says, I once was lost and now I was found, so it would be stupid not to go along."

As a lawyer, Alan is grateful for the vagueness of Rory's account thus far: what he doesn't know can't be used against him. But he can't help wondering about the kind of things Rory might have done for this Leo Guerard. It's hard to envision the man sitting beside him as an enforcer, even if he were younger, but Rory's always had an easy, ingratiating manner and Alan can imagine him being anything from a chauffeur to a gopher to this hazy Louisiana warlord.

"But you did something to this guy? Something that pissed him off." If the shadowy Leo Guerard is so powerful and dangerous, what could have moved Rory to cross him? He had it made, he said, and he blew it. Was it because he'd become greedy, or desperate? And how did he piss Leo off? Did he steal some money? Drugs?

Rory just nods. Apparently he isn't ready to open up about whatever grave insult he inflicted on his former boss.

Alan accepts that Rory's recent past is going to remain shrouded until he himself decides to clear it up. But he still has no idea of what kind of help Rory expects from him. "Why did you come to me?" he asks.

Rory turns toward him. "Simple, man. I couldn't think of any-one else."

Alan is thunderstruck by that admission, which suddenly makes Rory seem like the loneliest man in the universe. That notion is punctuated by the momentary silence that follows his declaration, during which Alan can do nothing more than to contemplate the sluggish traffic on the Central Artery. How the hell, he wonders, did I become Rory's refuge in a storm? "OK," he asks after a while, "what is it you want from me?"

"Look," Rory says, "I just need a place to hole up for a bit. Right now my life is all tangled up and I have to figure out a way to straighten things out. I thought you might let me stay at your place, out of sight for a while."

The alarm Alan feels is instant and visceral. No, he can't come to Wildwood Street, not Rory, bringing in his wake Leo Guerard and God knows what else, not Rory on the back porch looking toward the Perlmans' fence. Those two parts of his life have got to be kept apart. The man may have a hammer, but there's no way he's going to use it to knock down the door and come into Alan's house. Distantly, he remembers how he'd felt when Rory first reentered his life three years ago, like some creature from a fairy tale come to exact a payment for a debt incurred long ago in another place. The troll from the forest can't be allowed to pass through the front door. "No," he says emphatically. "I couldn't do that. Not my house."

Rory laughs suddenly, a couple of curt syllables that sound like a bark, a look of incredulity on his face. "Hey, man," he says, "that's not what I meant. I wasn't asking to stay at your house." He shakes his head. "I can understand how you'd feel about me being there. Especially if you have a kid. You don't want to have your family tied up with all this." He lights another cigarette. The snap of his match is followed by the sharp tang of sulphur, then burning tobacco.

Alan feels a surge of relief at Rory's being so reasonable about this, as well as a tinge of embarrassment at having apparently wildly misinterpreted his request. But if that's not what he meant, what did he mean? The answer isn't long in coming. "No," Rory says, "I was thinking about that place in Connecticut. That place in the woods. It's a summer house, isn't it? Nobody would be using it right now, I suppose." His words come quickly. "That would be perfect. All I'd need is about a week by myself. Just some place where I could figure out my next move." He smiles. "You said it was a refuge, didn't you?"

Rory's idea has blindsided him completely. "Jesus," he says, surprisingly unsettled by this request, "that place isn't even insulated. We don't usually stay there past Labor Day. It can get pretty cold there at night this time of the year." He realizes he's just stalling for time. Sure, it can get cold up there, but nobody's going to freeze to death in October. They haven't even turned off the water and closed the place down for the winter yet. How can he refuse him? It's not Wildwood Street, after all, where, a moment ago, he'd thought Rory was seeking refuge. He thought then that he'd dodged another bullet. Still, the very idea of Rory at Innisfree carries a threat that feels just as dangerous as if he'd asked to bring his duffel bag into the guest bedroom on Wildwood. If he goes to Innisfree, it's going to cost me, Alan thinks, it could wind up costing me plenty.

"I don't mind the cold," Rory says.

"Well . . ." Alan continues to play for time. The fact is, he has no rational defense against Rory's request. He's right: no one else is using the summer place just now. Still, there's an instinctive resistance to yielding to Rory on this point, and this time it's more than just a gut feeling. For one thing, he can't give Rory any immediate assurances about Innisfree because, though legally it belongs as much to him as to Julia, he couldn't possibly agree to Rory's proposal without talking to her about it.

That's what's so threatening about Rory's request: talking to Julia about that scenario would necessarily involve telling her about Lyletown, it would require bringing things to light that he's kept hidden from her all these years. All at once Alan feels a sense of entrapment. He can't help thinking that Rory has boxed him into a corner. Still, he can't just refuse him outright. "Innisfree," he says aloud, "well, that's a complicated situation. I'll tell you honestly, I'd want to clear it with my wife first. I think I told you, her father built the place."

"I understand. You'd certainly want to do that." He doesn't say any more. He doesn't say that he holds a hammer over Alan, as he always has. He doesn't have to.

"Yeah, sure," Alan says, "I'll have to talk to Julia about it tonight." Just now that seems a long way away. They've finally pulled off the Artery near Back Bay and they have to deal with immediate questions. "Now let's find you some place where you can stay till then," he says. "I can get back to you later tonight."

Rory nods. "I'd appreciate that." The glint in his eye might be hope, though it could also be smug satisfaction; and for the first time Alan wonders when exactly Rory hatched his plan to stay at the house in the Connecticut woods. "Thanks, bro'," Rory says, "I appreciate what you're doing for me."

In deference to Rory's concerns, real or imagined, about possible pursuers from New Orleans, they find him a modest hotel off the beaten path. As Rory goes through the registration process, Alan tries to fight the simmering anxiety and discontent he feels with an appeal to the past: after all, he's dealt with Rory before and managed to emerge unscathed. When Rory suggests a drink at the hotel bar, he tries to beg off, but Rory insists. "Look, I still haven't told you what happened down there." The implication is that his presence is obligatory.

"A half-hour," Alan concedes, and accompanies Rory to the bar where he orders a ginger ale. "So tell me," he says, aware of the clock, "about Leo, about how you pissed him off."

"OK," Rory says, "Leo is a short, burly guy in his sixties, he's got a wrestler's build. Like I said, he's not a guy you mess with. With Leo, if you even think about crossing him, you start remembering stories about people who wind up face down in the Mississippi or become alligator food in Lake Ponchartrain."

"And you managed to get on the bad side of this guy?" Given this picture of the man, Alan is intrigued once again by what could have caused Rory to cross him.

"No." Rory lights up a cigarette and blows out the match. "It's more complicated than that," he says. "Leo I always knew how to deal with. His son Bo is the reason I'm here and not in New Orleans." Rory's mouth twists into a scowl, as if he's just swallowed something unpleasant. "Bo's in his thirties," he tells Alan. "Unlike his old man, who learned everything he knows on the streets, Bo went to decent schools, he's a lawyer now, though he doesn't practice much. He's a pretty boy with a lot of blonde hair that he keeps brushing back with a sly little smile, as if it's some kind of performance and you're supposed to applaud. You know the type.

"Well, Bo's one of those guys who expects everyone to like him. And of course, a lot of people do, or at least say they do, because everyone figures that sooner or later Leo is going to give him the push he needs to make it in politics, and who knows how far he can go?" When he makes a gesture with his cigarette Alan catches a brief glimpse of his tattoo. "The problem is," Rory goes on, "the guy's got a mean streak a mile wide and, for some reason, I seem to set it off. Hey, to each his own, I say. Some people are just going to be like that." He shakes his head, he's quiet for a while and Alan assumes he's thinking about Louisiana. When he resumes, it's with an air of wonder and incomprehension. "But I swear, from the get-go, Bo had his eye on me, and for no reason at all, he hated me. No reason at all," he repeats. "The minute I saw this kid I knew he was going to be trouble."

Alan listens, trying to visualize these characters, short-armed Leo who could have been a wrestler, pretty boy Bo flashing his golden locks. It's as though Rory feels I have to see them for them to become real, he thinks.

"Mostly I was able to let Bo's nasty stuff slide by," Rory says. "But you can't just let everything go, can you?" He pauses a moment as if it's a genuine question to which he expects an answer. "OK," he says, "I know you're waiting for an example of how Bo operates. Here it is. He's there one day at his father's place when Leo discovers he's out of Collins mix and asks me to run down to the store and get some more. Hell, what's the big deal about that?" he asks. "But that bastard Bo has to chime in, 'Yeah, you do that, Uncle Ben,' just loud enough for me to hear, and you could tell he thinks it's the funniest thing anyone's ever said since the Nixon administration." Rory frowns, his face darkens, it's clear he still feels the sting. "So from then on he starts referring to me as Unc; and one afternoon not that long ago when he's on his father's boat with one of his bimbos he asks me, 'Can you get the little lady a Coke, Unc?' and she says, 'I didn't know he was your uncle.' 'No, no,' he says, 'it's just a little joke between us. See, he's like Uncle Ben on the box of rice. You know, the faithful butler. Only he don't have as nice a smile.' And then he starts laughing that heh-heh-heh, that irritating forced laugh of his, showing his perfect teeth, the hand going through the hair, real slow, like it's something sexual. Well, that's the one that got to me. I know, sticks and stones and all that. But you just can't keep taking it forever."

Rory drives the stub of his cigarette into the ashtray and twists it. For a moment he's silent no doubt remembering the incident. On the TV that's too far away to hear, Judge Wapner is listening to a plaintiff's claim. When Rory speaks again, it's as if to himself. "Sometimes," he says, "you just want to kick yourself."

Alan feels the need to say something. "Well, I think I understand . . ."

Rory's already lit another cigarette. "Now, I knew better," he says. "I knew that, given my history, I didn't have all the choices I might have and it was important to keep my cool. I understood that. And mostly I'd learned how to deal with things, to stay within myself, like the jocks say." He smiles sourly. "I knew that, for all Leo's setting the kid up, Bo hated being his father's son, he felt that Leo sat on him too hard, but that Bo would never dare lash out at his dad, so I figured that's why he was going after me. I knew all that and I damned well knew I should just keep looking the other way when he pulled that kind of shit. But I don't know, maybe it was the laugh, you know what I mean?" He shakes his head. "I just couldn't stand it anymore. And I guess I let my guard down. Because I let him get to me so bad I knew I had to get back at him. And I knew exactly how I could."

Rory takes another sip of beer and puts down his glass, a man catching his breath. Alan can imagine him in some bar in New Orleans doing the same thing, nursing his grievance against Bo, wondering how he could strike back against him.

"There's this small-time thug named Herm Guillorey, nasty as a rattlesnake," Rory says, "and he hates Bo's guts. I happened to know that Bo was banging Guillorey's old girlfriend and I knew where. Bo's married, of course. Did I tell you that? Anyway, after the kid had called me Unc in front of the bimbo and laughed that laugh, somehow for me that was the last straw. I made sure a couple nights later that I was in a bar where Guillorey was drinking—and you know how sometimes when you want to for whatever reasons, you can pretend to be drunker than you are—I let it slip that Bo was with Lucy St. James at the Crescent Motel, and I knew that Guillorey would go crazy at the news and he'd sure as hell want to do something about it. I guess I was feeling real clever for a little while. But when I found out his goons had beat Bo within an inch of his life, and Herm had arranged for the papers to get the story of the 'tryst' in that motel so that any plans Bo had for a political career were going to get severely detoured, I knew I'd gone too far, and that Leo would start his hounds searching for whoever had done this to the golden boy. Right away I knew I was finished there. And it was my fault, just like when I thought I had to go to that alley in Lyletown to see what was happening and I jumped off that fucking dumpster." He drives his half-smoked cigarette into the ashtray, snapping it in two.

Alan puts up a hand as if to protest, but it's doubtful Rory even sees him. He shakes his head and when he starts speaking again, he's very quiet. "I was in the French Quarter when I heard what happened to Bo and I realized I was finished down there. I went to the foot of Canal Street, by the river near where the Algiers ferry comes in, and I looked out at all that water, wide as a lake, that had come from way up in Minnesota and everywhere in between, and was sliding into the Gulf. All that force, all that flow, never stopping. There was a horn from a boat somewhere on the river, a bunch of birds came flying by, beating their wings, and I smelled the water and I realized how much I'd come to like it down there. At the same time it was clear to me that I'd fucking incinerated all the bridges that were behind me." He stops abruptly and in the silence Alan can sense the desolation Rory must have felt looking at that river. When Rory looks up, though, he shows no signs of desolation. "You know what's funny, though?" he says. "I knew I couldn't keep doing things like that, I knew I had to change things; but I swear, even when I felt that dryness in my mouth thinking about what I'd done to myself, still I was glad I'd been able to give little Bo his comeuppance, to, as they say in the books, deliver him into the hands of his enemies."

He falls silent once more. After a while, Alan feels the need to say something. "I can see . . ." he begins.

"No, you can't fucking see," Rory cuts him off, suddenly angry. "You can't see at all. You can't see what it's like to have your life taken away from you." He holds him with his gaze for a few seconds and Alan wonders who he's seeing. Then Rory turns away. He shakes his head and laughs to himself. "That fucking little twerp Bo," he says. "I wonder how he's going to feel when he finally finds out it was old Uncle Ben who was responsible for him getting his ass kicked big-time." His smile is for himself alone.

As the images from Rory's account of his departure from New Orleans swirl around in Alan's consciousness, he can't help thinking that the man has a special talent for the self-destructive act. He's a real artist. In the continuing silence that follows Rory's latest declaration, Alan becomes aware of the harsh tang of the dead, bent cigarettes in the ashtray. He tries to imagine Rory standing beside the Mississippi, contemplating the latest turn of his life. Was this when he got the idea of coming to the woods of Connecticut?


However much Alan might want to keep the Rory business bottled up until he can deal with it later tonight, his reappearance colors the rest of the day at work; and he can't help feeling that he's somewhere close by, huddled behind the door of the tiny supply room, say, his elbow resting on a ream of copy paper. Superficially, he's able to go through the motions at the office: swapping anecdotes with Barney O'Shea about bad motels the two of them have known; holding his ground on the phone with Ed Graziano, who wants him to delay an upcoming visit to Atwood Gardens; or, once he's got more time to himself, jotting down, crossing out and rearranging on his legal pad the numbered elements of a compromise that might just keep Ellen Boyce in her apartment in spite of a troublesome neighbor's insistence that the woman is too old to take care of herself and is therefore a danger to the other tenants. But, hovering on the fringes, there's always Rory.

Alan has generally found satisfaction in the pedestrian details of his work, he enjoys being an agent in a complicated system that, however imperfect, makes a kind of sense and provides genuine opportunities to achieve something purposeful; but today, these familiar actions are played out against the background of a muffled, discordant music. Throughout the afternoon, he keeps coming back to the image of Rory holed up in his hotel room in Boston, no doubt surrounded by a cloud of cigarette smoke, likely staring at some generic landscape painting on the wall and thinking about New Orleans, which now lies on the other side of a burned bridge. At a time like this, how could he not think about Lyletown, the place where everything started to go bad for him?

But in the end, that's Rory's problem and not his, he tries to persuade himself. And still, he feels he owes something to the man who went to Lyletown when he didn't, the man who refused to give the cops Alan's name. How can he turn away?

It's not a vengeful Leo Guerard that Rory's fleeing, Alan has pretty much concluded. It's just too hard to believe in that wrathful pursuer. Alan has no problem accepting Rory's picture of the man: undoubtedly he's tough, even ruthless in his own domain. But would he really bother to chase his former employee to the ends of the earth? The idea strains credibility. The fact is, by his own admission Rory seems to have pretty much gratuitously wrecked things for himself down there, and that's left him at loose ends, desperate. Having made New Orleans impossible for himself, he's now facing the problem of inventing the next step. For some reason he's decided he has to do that inventing at Innisfree.

"I'm going out to get some coffee." Sally's voice breaks his reverie. "Can I get you anything?"

It takes him a moment to respond. "Thanks," he says. "I'm good." When she's gone he looks at the words he's set down on the legal pad and in the bottom corner he writes "Innisfree," then below it a capital R; he encloses both within a rectangle. That doesn't make it any easier to imagine the fugitive Rory, on the run from whatever demons are chasing him, hidden away in the little house that Richard Mallory so improbably thrust upon those

Connecticut hills whose woods are threaded by the lichen-covered stone walls of departed colonists. And yet, that's exactly what he's going to have to talk to Julia about in a few hours, and when he does, a pack of sleeping dogs is going to be roused at last.

There's a rap on the door, and Barney pops his head into the office. "I forgot about this motel in Newark," he says, smiling in anticipation of what's going to follow. "They had a sign that said, 'Love Your Neighbor—Here.' "

"An unimpeachable sentiment," Alan says. "I like it." And for a moment the world seems lighter, less fraught, a place where the furtive trysts of cheating lovers are simply part of the human comedy, a world of punch lines and no dark shadows. "You didn't actually stay there, did you?" he asks.

Barney puts a finger to his lips. "I'll never tell."

"Begone, Satan," Alan waves him away. If he could only stay at the office.


At home, Julia picks up on his preoccupied mood right away. "What's the matter?" she asks when he comes into the dining room with a couple of ice cubes in his glass.

"What do you mean?" he counters disingenuously.

Her smile invites confidences. "You look tense. Tough day at work?"

Alan pours bourbon into his glass and listens to the crackling of the ice, savoring the rich, dark smell of the liquor for a second or two before taking a sip. "Actually, it's more than that," he says. "There's something we've got to talk about. But later."

Sensing her sudden stiffness, he immediately wishes he hadn't put it that way. "Hey, it's not anything big," he tries to reassure her, though of course it is. "There's something I have to ask you about Innisfree. But we have to talk about that later, after Tommy's in bed."

Her relief is evident, as is her curiosity. "Aha," she ventures, "you've got some elaborate building plans for the place? A tower, maybe. A wing?"

He shakes his head. "Not a jacuzzi in the library either."

She tilts her head inquisitively, obviously enjoying the game. "Come on," she says, "can't you at least give me a hint?"

"I think it's best if we wait till later," he says. "But I can tell you that it has nothing to do with building. And I'm not thinking we should sell the place either, if you were worried about that."

She throws up her hands. "Well, you've certainly piqued my curiosity. No hints, really?"

"No hints."

"OK, Mr. Tough Guy," she smiles. "This better be good."

Alan says nothing.

Later that night after dinner, when Tommy's settled in bed, they're alone in the living room. He hands Julia a glass of wine. "OK," he says, cheerfully, even as he senses that he's pushing off from some safe shore. "About Innisfree." He waits a moment. "Somebody I know wants to stay there for a week and I told him I couldn't give him an answer until I talked to you."

Her frown betrays her disappointment: this isn't very interesting news. "At this time of the year?" she says. "He knows you can't do any hunting on the property, right?"

Alan shakes his head. "He's not going there to hunt, I can assure you of that."

Julia looks over her wine glass. "Well, that's a relief. For the deer, at least."

Alan smiles. If only this were about hunting. "Here's where it gets complicated," he says. "This guy wants to use the place basically as a retreat."

Julia pulls herself erect. "Are we talking spiritual here?" she asks. "Like meditation?"

"Not exactly," Alan admits, wishing it were otherwise. He isn't eager to tell this story—after all, he and Julia have had a wonderful relationship, haven't they, without any need to bring Lyletown into their lives; but as he approaches the outer edges of this thing, he feels the burden of all those years of silence and he doesn't want to add to it with a lie—lying would just make things worse. "No," he says, "what this guy wants to do is . . ." He doesn't know how else to put it. "Well, he kind of needs to hide out." Julia's surprise is evident, she's about to say something but he holds up his hand. "Look, he's someone who's got himself into some trouble. According to him, people might be after him."

Julia leans forward, intent and curious. "Is this something political?" she asks. "Are the cops looking for him? The FBI?"

Once more Alan shakes his head, even as he realizes that in a sense his connection with Rory is certainly political. At least it started out that way, however far the two of them have strayed from that starting point. "No," he says, trying to choose his words with care, "this is somebody who seems to have got tied up with shady characters and . . . well, he's in trouble." He's out over deeper water now and he feels a growing sense of apprehension. He's upped the ante considerably with what he's just told Julia and he has no idea of how she'll respond.

She's silent for a few seconds, taking in this new information. "Is this someone from the housing projects?" she asks.

"No." Alan pauses a moment, aware that his palms are sweating. "He's just come up from New Orleans," he goes on. "The . . . the bad guys he says he's running from are from down there. He says he crossed one of them and now he's afraid they might come after him."

Julia looks at him incredulously. "You're not pulling my leg with this, are you? I mean, this sounds like something from TV."

"No," Alan says. "I'm basically telling you what he told me."

"But why would you want to let someone stay at Innisfree if there's a real danger of . . . of gangsters showing up there?"

"Honestly," he says, "I don't think there's much of a chance of that. What am I saying? Actually, I'm sure there's not the slightest chance that any gangster is going to turn up at Innisfree."

She shakes her head. "I guess I don't understand."

"OK," Alan says, aware of how foolish he's been to think there was even the remotest possibility he could pass this off as something casual, "this guy is someone I've known for a long time.

It's . . . an involved story. It goes a long way back." He takes a quick sip of wine, feeling a shiver of panic now that the time for explanations is finally at hand. "This guy's name is Rory Dekker," he says slowly, trying to make his voice sound calm and reasonable. "He's someone I knew a long time ago, when I was in grad school." Julia looks at him expectantly, her brow furrowed as if she's encountered some puzzling formulation on a student paper and is trying to make sense of it. Having finally uttered Rory's name aloud, Alan is relieved, but momentarily he's run out of words and he takes another sip of his wine. "Actually," he says after a breath, "this is where it gets really complicated." A few feet away, Julia nods helpfully, and he goes on. "This all started in the late sixties when . . . when everything in the country seemed to be coming apart." The words come in a rush. "The Vietnam War just kept going on until it seemed as if it would never end. There were assassinations, riots, marches and demonstrations all the time. Hell," he says, "you remember how weird things were then." In fact, Julia is five years younger and likely has a somewhat different take on things. "Anyway . . ." He drains his glass and quickly pours himself some more wine. "Look," he says, "things were so crazy then, you could believe that a revolution was just around the corner—I know I did."

"You mean like when you were part of the march on the Pentagon?" Julia asks. He doesn't remember telling her about that episode, but he must have, and momentarily he's grateful that at least the two of them have shared that memory.

"Yeah," he says, "that was part of it, exactly." He shakes his head. "But the fact is, the march on the Pentagon, huge as it was, didn't really change much." She looks at him, making it clear she isn't going to interrupt him, probably wondering how this is going to connect with gangsters in New Orleans. "A lot of us were desperate," he goes on, "we were ready to try anything. I . . ." He's careful about how he wants to present this. "I got mixed up in something political . . . well, it was more than just a demonstration this time." Julia nods slowly, urging him on, her expression unfathomable. "This is tough to explain," he says. "Again, though, you have to remember the times. There was a small group of us that started talking about doing something, some people from the university and a couple of ex-cons." Julia's brows lift at the mention of the ex-cons, and Alan is silent for a while, gathering strength for the next hurdle. "OK," he says, "we were actually planning . . . well, an action, we would have called it then, a political action." The phrase brings with it the fevered temperature of those desperate days of rage and non-negotiable demands, a time when apocalypse was always around the corner. He shakes his head. "The plan we came up with called for robbing a gun store and giving the weapons to black activists."

There, he's said it. He feels as if he's sprinted up a steep hill carrying a heavy load. At least now he can lay down the load and catch his breath. Across from him, Julia's look is still hard to read, but it's clear this latest revelation has made an impact. She says nothing, though, and he takes it as a signal to continue. "Well, it got beyond the talking stage, that plan," he says. "The ex-cons were going to provide the know-how and . . ." He breaks off with an attempt at a dismissive laugh. "I know it must sound crazy. We were going to be revolutionary Robin Hoods. We were going to take the guns from the oppressors and give them to the oppressed, something like that." He looks into his wine glass. "We were stupid, maybe," he says, "we were dreamers who got conned by a pair of ex-cons, but in the end I got lucky." Julia continues to lean forward, listening intently, still conveying nothing of her response. "The thing is," he says, "I was never a hundred percent behind the idea, I was ambivalent about the whole thing, as you might imagine." He pauses again. "Not ambivalent enough to back out of it completely, I guess," he admits. "Still, ambivalent." He looks at his wife, who's clearly trying to relate the man she knows to the protagonist of this fantastic tale. "Like I said," he tells her, "I got lucky—actually, I got sick." He laughs nervously. "I had an attack of appendicitis and I landed in the hospital. I never did go to Lyletown—that's the name of the place where the gun store was." He stops as if this were the end of the story—it would certainly be a happy ending—and for a moment neither of them says anything. The house on Wildwood Street is quiet.

"So what happened to the plan?" Julia asks at last, and Alan is pulled back into his interrupted narrative. "Well," he says, "the others went through with the job, they went to Lyletown, and it was a disaster. By chance an off-duty cop showed up, there was shooting and one of the ex-cons was killed, three of the others got away—nobody knows what happened to them—but Rory was captured and went to prison." Julia's eyes grow large at the mention of the death, she shakes her head in disbelief. "You can imagine," Alan goes on, "how I felt in the hospital, following the reports on TV and in the papers. It was awful enough, what happened to the others. But how did I know the cops weren't going to come for me any minute?"

Julia is silent for long seconds, taking it all in. "But you didn't do anything," she says after a while. It sounds like a question.

"No," Alan says softly. He takes a quick sip of his wine. "The problem is, legally, that wouldn't have mattered." He pauses and plunges on. "After all, I took part in the planning, I didn't make any effort to stop it; so, you know, in the eyes of the law, I'd be as guilty as the others." He's silent a while and the two of them ponder the implications of what he's just said. "So I was in big trouble, even in the hospital. But when the cops questioned Rory, he didn't tell them anything about me." After a pause he says, "He did me one hell of a favor."

Julia leans back against the chair for a moment. All at once she looks exhausted. When she speaks her voice is flat and distant. "And this is the man who's in trouble now? He's come back and he wants you to return the favor?"

Alan nods. "Sort of. Yeah, I do owe him."

"Well," Julia says, pulling herself erect once more, "this is cer-tainly a lot to take in all at once." She looks at him as if she's no longer quite sure who he is. "And this is the first time you've seen him since those days?"

The question unsettles him, but of course, he should have expected it. "Actually," he admits, "I've seen him three times in the past couple of years," and again he sees his wife stiffen. "Rory called me in '88. It was the first time I'd heard his voice since those days and I didn't know what to make of his showing up like that, asking me to meet him in Boston. When he called that first time I felt I had no choice, I had to see him. You know, because of Bobby Pelham—he was the ex-con—because of his death, the statute of limitations doesn't run out on something like what happened in Lyletown. Here Rory was, showing up after all those years. I didn't know if he was going to try to blackmail me. Even at that late date, he could have done serious damage to my career . . . to everything." As he speaks, he feels the weight of it, as he had when he'd heard Rory's voice over the phone three years ago, and the hairs on the back of his neck tingle. "But he didn't, that's the important thing. He didn't."

Across from him, Julia is silent, like someone listening to a story about complete strangers, her own husband among them. "I can see why he'd be a threat." Her voice is dry, noncommital. "But did he ask for money then? Did he try to blackmail you?"

"No," Alan says, "I don't think Rory was ever interested in blackmail. But you can see why I'd be . . . concerned. Believe me, when I went to meet him after all those years I wasn't sure what to expect. He'd been in prison and all." He stops, remembering that meeting. "Our situations could easily have been reversed. But he didn't tell the cops anything then, and he wasn't interested in telling them anything now."

The silence around them thickens, increasing Alan's discomfort. At last Julia shakes her head. "The thing I don't get," she says, her voice low and tight, "is that when this all started up a couple of years ago, you didn't feel there was any reason to tell me anything about it." When she continues, her words are tinged with accusation. "About this possible threat to us, to our family."

For a time neither of them says anything. The air in the room has become charged and heavy. "Look," Alan says after a while, "once I survived that Lyletown business I wanted to put it behind me for good. We didn't need that in our life, yours and mine. I mean, we each had our own histories when we met, right? There

was no reason to drag everything from my past into the present."
Julia continues looking at him but her eyes are expressionless. "I
mean," he says, "when I met you I felt as if I had nothing to do
with that kid who got involved in the Lyletown business, no way."
He lets out a long exhalation. "And when Rory showed up again
like that I just didn't want to bring all that back. I mean, OK, it
was my trouble in the first place and now it was coming back. I
was hoping to deal with it without involving you, or Tommy."

She shakes her head, her disappointment evident. "But if this
Rory had decided to try to squeeze you it certainly would have
affected me and Tommy, wouldn't it?" she asks. "If he brought you
down, he'd have brought all of us down, right?"

He nods. After a moment, he says, "I thought I could handle it
alone. I did handle it alone."

Julia's voice rises suddenly. "But you weren't alone anymore.
Did that ever occur to you?" She pounds her fist into the arm of the
chair. "I mean, why didn't you see that? You just said you weren't
that kid who got mixed up with a couple of ex-cons. That might
have been true, but you were with me, with our family. Didn't that
mean anything to you?" Abruptly, she pulls in her lips and stops
talking. Her ensuing silence is stony. She sits there with her glass
of wine but doesn't drink from it.

"Look," Alan pursues, "I wanted to bury that Lyletown business. I didn't want any of it to touch our lives, ever. And for a
long time it worked out that way." When she says nothing, he
continues, "OK, OK, it was my judgment and I realize now that if
I were doing it again I'm sure I'd do a lot of things differently. I'm
sorry," he says at last.

Julia gets to her feet and takes a couple of quick steps, as if
she's about to leave the room; but, just as suddenly, she stops, her
arms folded tightly before her, "Alan," she says, "you just don't get
it, do you?" She lets out a long exhalation. "OK," she says, "you
got mixed up with that robbery that maybe you shouldn't have. You
weren't the first one to do something like that, and besides, as you
said, those were desperate times. Didn't you think I'd have been
able to understand if you'd have told me about it? Getting mixed

up with those people, awful as the consequences were—that's not an unforgivable sin. Not for me it isn't." Her voice drops. "But this other thing. When did you say this Rory first showed up here?"

"Three years ago," Alan says. "In '88."

"Three years ago," she repeats almost inaudibly. She continues to stand there, a few paces away from him. Her voice is louder when she speaks again. "You recognized that our family was in danger of losing everything we had, but you decided you'd rather be the lone cowboy and handle things by yourself." The accusation cuts deep: the last thing he'd think about himself is that he's a lone cowboy. Meanwhile, Julia says nothing more. When she speaks again, she's looking away from him. "I'm sorry," she says wearily, "I guess that intellectually I might be able to come around to understanding all of this," she says. "Maybe." She turns toward him. "Still, at some gut level it feels as if you shut me out, and, damn it, that hurts."

He feels unjustly accused. She's seeing all this from the outside, he knows. He wasn't trying to shut her out, he was trying to protect his family. "I'm sorry," he says again.

"No," she insists, "don't keep saying that. That doesn't help at all." She expels her breath harshly and comes back to the chair where she was sitting, but she isn't looking at him. "You did what you did and it's done," she says before taking a sip of wine. "Being sorry doesn't change anything." She puts down her glass. "It's just . . ." she says. "It's just . . . ah," she makes a dismissive gesture with her hand. "Just don't expect me to accept all this all at once. I'm going to have to catch up a little first."

Not that long ago the two of them were in Maine, marveling together at the furious sea, walking through the hushed spaces of the Lithuanian monastery while the rain raged outside. Alan leans toward her and touches her hand. "But we're in this together, aren't we?" he ventures.

She pulls her hand away. "Don't do this," she says irritably. "Don't try to force things." Then after a few seconds she says, "Oh, of course, of course we're in this together. We have no choice, do we?" She shakes her head. "Only, I wish you'd felt that way earlier. Still . . ." Her voice trails off and for a time all that can be heard are random indistinct household sounds. "I suppose what's been done can't be undone," she says when she continues, "and certainly from what you've told me about this Rory guy, you do owe him something." She gives him a skeptical look. "But these people who are after him, like I said, it sounds like something from TV. Do you think he's really in that kind of danger?"

Alan shrugs. "I don't really think so, and I'm not sure he does either. I think he may need to believe that because he seems to have messed up his life and . . . Well," he acknowledges, "he was in prison. Of course, he knows some pretty rough characters." He pulls himself up short. "But, I don't know, there's something more going on here. I mean, as I said, he's not interested in blackmail."

"How does he know about Innisfree?" she asks.

Not for the first time tonight, Alan feels the weight of betrayal. "He found out from someone in the office," he says. "He called me in Connecticut once, the second time he came back."

Julia looks away.

"He says he wants a place to stay, for no longer than a week. I think he just wants to try to get his life together. He said he'd be able to figure something out by then, and he'll be gone."

"But why there?" she asks. "Why Innisfree? Why can't he just straighten out his life somewhere else?" Once more, the anger breaks through. "I guess it wasn't enough," she says, "that you kept a whole part of your life secret from me; now you've decided to bring part of that world into a place I thought was special to us." She shakes her head. "I mean, guns, ex-cons, New Orleans gangsters—all that at Innisfree. I don't know . . ."

"I don't really think . . ." Alan begins, then stops himself. "I can say no to him," he says quietly. "That's why I wanted to ask you first."

Her smile is scornful. "I'd say the asking has come a little late. No, you obviously owe something to this man and it's got to be paid." She shakes her head. "Let's just get this thing over with," she says. "I still think it's strange that he should want to go to Innisfree, of all places. Don't you find it strange?"

Alan nods. "I know it doesn't seem to make much sense. I've thought about it and all I can come up with is that he feels he and I are connected because of Lyletown." He laughs to himself. "The thing is, we really weren't all that close back in the old days."

"You're connected now, all right." Julia sighs. "Do you think he'll actually be able to come up with some kind of plan after a week up there?" she asks. "And leave?"

"Honestly," he says, "I don't know what he's going to do, but, yeah, I think he'll go away when he says he will. I mean, he may be exaggerating about the danger he's in from this New Orleans business, but I'd say he's basically honest. Then too, it's probably going to be cold up there at night and I doubt that he'll find it very comfortable." When she says nothing, he pushes on, but it's like walking through knee-deep water. "Look, this whole thing can be wrapped up pretty quickly. He came up from New Orleans and he doesn't have a car. If we agree to this, I'd have to drive him up there tomorrow. By next week, though, he should be gone, it should be over. I'll leave him a sleeping bag, some food and supplies. Of course, I'll tell him to be careful with the place."

Julia takes a long, slow sip of wine. At last she says, "If we're going to have to do this, let's get it over with as soon as we can." For the moment a silence falls over them. It's then that Alan thinks of Julia's father and his idea of a refuge in the woods. Richard Mallory certainly never had anything like this in mind. Alan can't help feeling the need for some refuge himself. At least, he knows, he and Julia are in agreement about one thing: they just want this to be over soon. At the moment the idea of short-armed Leo Guerard pursuing Rory with an insatiable lust for revenge seems like the most farfetched of fantasies, which only makes Rory's desire to go to Innisfree more mysterious. Just now, though, Alan's concerns are closer to home: the more quickly Rory's situation is resolved, the sooner Alan can start to repair the damage this intrusion has brought to his marriage. "A week," he says to Julia, "and then this whole thing will be over."

She looks at him. "You probably thought this was over long ago, didn't you?"

He turns up his hands. "That's true enough."

She speaks softly, as if to herself. "Lyletown. I wish I'd never heard of that place."

You're not the only one, he wants to say.

Later, he phones Rory at the place where he's staying for the night. "OK," he says, "we can do it. I can drive you out there tomorrow just after noon."

"Sure," Rory answers, "I'll be ready." Alan is stung by the man's seeming ingratitude. Christ, he thinks, this guy has caused me all kinds of grief already and tomorrow I'm going to be his chauffeur and all he can say is "Sure." Once again, though, he realizes that he isn't going to turn away from Rory. He remembers how painful it was to tell Julia about Lyletown, the way it must have sounded to her: that a group of which Alan had been a part had planned the robbery and everyone else had to pay a heavy price, with himself escaping through pure luck. Telling about it, he couldn't help feeling . . . what had it been? Guilty? Unworthy? After all these years, after all he's done since. It isn't fair, he wanted to say to Julia, it isn't just. But, he tries to reassure himself, it will all be over soon.

"I'll be here," Rory says.

"OK. See you then." He wishes it were already tomorrow.

Rory tosses his duffel into the backseat before getting into the car with a curt, mumbled greeting. He looks as if he didn't get much sleep last night, and Alan fears this could be a long ride. Seated beside him, his withdrawn passenger appears content to look out dully at the passing street scene, inviting no conversation. His eyes are glazed and there's an air of touchy sluggishness about him, like a reptile in winter that hasn't quite slipped into hibernation. Alan can't help remembering a younger Rory, dressed in jeans and a buckskin jacket, a cowboy hat tilted back on his head, his golden hair spilling out over his shoulders as he lounges on a sofa, completely relaxed but ready to spring to his feet in an instant. Today's Rory has none of his predecessor's lightness of step; instead, he sits there in a funk, a petulant Napoleon contemplating his self-imposed exile. But then, it wouldn't be at all surprising if he'd spent the night having second thoughts about the rash action that cost him a soft life in New Orleans.

In the uncomfortable atmosphere caused by his passenger's gloomy silence, Alan feels snookered. It's bad enough that Rory has got the better of him by appropriating Innisfree, not to mention getting Alan to chauffeur him there. Now he's laying the burden of providing even minimal sociability on Alan as well. But maybe he just hasn't had his morning's quota of caffeine. "Want to pick up some coffee on the way?" he suggests.

Rory responds with a shake of his head.

"The weather's good, anyway," Alan offers after a while.

Rory grunts something that sounds like apathetic agreement.

You think I want to be here any more than you do? Alan wants to tell him. Rory's air of morose self-absorption feeds Alan's own simmering anger: at Rory for all the trouble he's given him, at himself for letting himself be used this way, for the way he handled the situation last night with Julia, for his involvement in the Lyletown business in the first place. It's not as if he can really believe he's helping Rory in a time of imminent danger. The idea of a vengeful Leo Guerard unleashing an army of thugs, no doubt complete with bloodhounds, to inflict rough justice on the transgressor, wherever he may be—as Julia said, it's like something from a bad TV movie. Though it does raise the legitimate question of just who it is that Rory's intending to hide from at Innisfree.

At Copley Square, they dive into the tunnel under the Prudential. When they leave its dark echoing confines, they're under blue skies again, headed westward on the trench of the Mass Pike that cuts a swath through the densely packed city jammed against its sides—Fenway Park, BU, the red brick apartments of Brookline—until the roadway rises and the view opens out, with the low skyline of Cambridge visible across the loitering Charles. In minutes they're beyond the city and its inner suburbs, amid brilliant fall foliage, bright leaves jittering in the wind. They're moving west—all of America is west of here—and in spite of the burden of Rory's glum presence Alan can't help feeling a slight irrational lifting of his spirits.

"Sure about that coffee?" he asks. "There's a service area coming up soon."

Rory shakes his head, not even turning toward Alan. Whatever arguments he's been having with himself don't seem to have been settled yet. This is the guy who kept quiet about you when he could have squealed, Alan reminds himself, you owe him. It doesn't make Rory's behavior any easier to take, though.

After a couple more minutes of silence, Alan decides he has to take the initiative. If Rory's going to continue this Garbo act, Alan is never going to satisfy his curiosity about certain aspects of his passenger's story; and as long as he's providing transportation as well as lodging, he's owed a few things too, like an account of what's really going on here. "Look," he says, determined to rouse Rory to some response, "I've got to tell you, it's hard for me to believe that this Leo Guerard would be quite so relentless in hunting you down, wherever you might be."

That gets his attention. He turns toward Alan, his eyes narrowed. "Are you saying I'm lying?"

Alan doesn't flinch. "I'm saying I don't think I'm a complete idiot, and it's pretty hard for me to believe, given what you've told me, that he'd drop everything and come after you, like," he gropes for a comparison, "like the Hound of Heaven. After all," he adds, "from what you said, Leo must be a pretty busy guy."

Rory doesn't respond for a while. "You're saying I just made the whole thing up then?" he counters.

Alan shakes his head. "No, I don't think you made it up, not Leo, not Bo, not whatever the hell was the name of the guy who beat Bo up. I'm just saying, well, you might have been exaggerating Leo's thirst for revenge."

Once again it's a while before Rory answers. "OK," he says. "Let's say for the sake of argument you're right. Why in the hell would I do something like that?"

"I don't know," Alan says. "If I try to put myself in your shoes, I . . . I guess maybe I might think, I have to leave this place anyway, it looks like for good. Maybe I'd want to believe that the reason I'm on the run is that Leo is after me, rather than . . ." He breaks off abruptly.

For a while there's an uneasy silence. At last Rory says, "Rather than admitting I fucked it up myself, are you saying?"

"I'm not saying anything, I'm kind of thinking out loud," Alan is quick to respond.

Rory takes a long time lighting a cigarette, then inhales deeply and lets out the smoke with a brief metallic laugh. "Let me see if I've got this straight. You're saying that for me to claim that Leo would have his musclemen trail me all the way to Boston, this Hound of Heaven stuff, as you put it, it isn't just jive, it's a kind of self-motivational myth."

That's it exactly, Alan wants to say, I couldn't have put it better. More cautiously, though, he offers, "You're putting words into my mouth."

"You don't know anything about Leo," Rory spits back.

"I won't dispute you there," Alan says. "Hey, I'm just guessing."

The silence that follows that exchange is less charged, though, and Alan is glad the ice has been broken. Rory hasn't really denied Alan's speculations, even as he challenged them. At least he's been roused into human contact. Now he seems to be pondering things rather than just seething. Meanwhile, the green mile markers on the Turnpike go by without either man saying anything. Not for the first time, Alan thinks of Rory as someone who's lost, someone whose life broke in two at Lyletown and who's been trying to put it back together ever since. There's a very real possibility that he has no idea of what he's going to do next, at Innisfree or afterwards, he just knows he has to do something, and this flight to Connecticut is the ultimate Hail Mary pass. After all, for a while now he's had to make things up as he goes along. Maybe in New Orleans at the moment when everything went bust for him, he just happened to remember the place Alan had told him about in the Connecticut woods; and he gratefully wove it into a story, a plausible next chapter of his life, believing that a retreat to this sylvan refuge he'd never laid eyes on would somehow redeem his expulsion from New Orleans, turning this phase of his life into a story of loss and redemption. Now, having had some details of his story questioned by Alan, could he be dealing with the possibility that there might be no story at all? What would it be like to have to contemplate that kind of open-endedness? Isn't it at least possible to imagine him deciding that the option of blackmail wasn't such a bad idea, after all? It's a line of thought Alan has no inclination to pursue.

His curiosity about Rory's motives can't nullify the presence of the world outside the car, though. "Look at that," he says as a grove of fiery red maples comes into view. Glazed with rain, the trees could be part of a glass forest. "That scene could be on a postcard."

Rory looks on without responding. He keeps his eyes on the road for a time before saying, "I had a calendar in prison."

Alan can't see the connection to anything he's said, but he's on the alert. "Yeah?" he pursues. "A calendar?"

Rory nods. "That was early on," he says. "When I just got there. The calendar was from an outdoor store and there were the usual kinds of scenes from the seasons: a cabin in the snow, geese flying south, a lake in the mountains—what we passed a little while ago could have been on that calendar." As he speaks, Alan tries to imagine the bare prison cell, adorned only by this tiny window on an idyllic set of landscapes. "Those pictures were important to me," Rory muses distantly. "I'd look at them for a long time, memorizing every detail until I could see them with my eyes closed." After a moment, he continues. "It was a way to keep from going crazy, I guess. Especially in those early days. Freedom, I told myself. Someday I was going to be out there, by that lake, in that cabin."

He takes a long drag and exhales a cloud of smoke. He says nothing more for a while, as if he's determined to hang on to this memory by himself, not inviting Alan in. But Rory must have brought it up for some reason and Alan is determined to pursue whatever leads he's given him. "It seems to have worked, that calendar," he says. "You obviously didn't go crazy."

When Rory answers, he speaks quietly, and Alan has to strain to hear him. "Yeah. Just barely, though," he says. "But things were pretty dicey in the beginning." After a pause, his voice is stronger. "When I got past that first year, I didn't need the calendar anymore. All those pictures were in my head by then. I was lucky."

"Lucky?" Alan asks, feeling again the incursion of that dark planet, Rory's prison experience, that separates the two of them so profoundly.

"Yeah," Rory says, "I got some good advice from an old-timer. It helped me get through the hard part and find what strength I had."

When he falls silent again, Alan can see that he's withdrawn into himself once more. He's reluctant to break into the man's memories, but he's curious. How close did he come to not making it? Who gave him the good advice? "I guess not everybody had the strength?" he suggests at last.

Rory nods absently. After a while, he says, "There was this dude named Raoul that everybody thought was so tough." There's a pause during which Rory might be summoning up the lost Raoul. "He was a big guy with arms like telephone poles," he goes on, "and he was strong, all right. You'd hear him grunting with the weights, you'd hear the metal clang—it sounded like he was flinging those weights around like toothpicks. Hell, he looked like he could lift the Statue of Liberty. He was a mean mother, too. He kind of strutted and swaggered, like he was always looking for a fight." Rory's voice drops. "First time I saw him, I'll admit, he scared the shit out of me. He wasn't the kind of guy you wanted to make prolonged eye contact with."

Seconds pass, and Alan can only assume that Rory's seeing the eyes of this former nemesis. "What happened to Raoul?" he asks at last, knowing it can't have been anything good.

"He killed himself," Rory says with obvious satisfaction. "After a year and a half in the can he hanged himself in the laundry room." He shakes his head. "He was looking at a life sentence, no possibility of parole, and in the end he just couldn't take that."

"I guess I can understand," Alan ventures after a moment. "If he had no chance of getting out."

"Hey," Rory says belligerently, as if he suspects Alan of taking Raoul's side, "you know how many people are in there without a chance of getting out, and yet they somehow manage? And I'm talking about all sorts of guys. I mean sometimes it's some little pencil-necked professor type with glasses, sometimes it's a guy who reminds you of your aunt Alice. But one way or another, they hold up, when our tough friend Raoul just couldn't take it." Rory is silent a while before going on. "When you're inside," he says, "you've got very little control over anything, but that's one thing you do have control over: you can choose to wake up the next morning." The last words have the air of a challenge.

"OK," Alan says carefully. "I'll buy that." For a while Rory sinks back into himself again and Alan is reduced to filling the conversational gap with observations about the scenery, politics, even TV, to which Rory seems mostly content to listen. Soon they're off the Pike and are headed south on 84, toward Hartford. Though Rory's part in the talk is limited, he no longer seems surly, as if his spirits have been lifted by his memories of prison days. Alan is talking about changes to Boston since he's been there, when Rory says, a propos of nothing, "Old Raoul—who'd have thought it?"

How did we get back to Raoul? Alan thinks.

"When somebody decides to cash it in like that," Rory says, "people always try to find reasons. I call them excuses. Whatever spin you want to put on it, checking out like that is just giving up, that's all." Alan can only assume that he's been thinking about this ever since he brought up the subject of Raoul. "I mean," he goes on, "we only get one chance, right? What's the point of throwing it away? Hell, no matter what kind of cards I have, I figure it's always better to stay in the game." It's a sentiment Alan has no wish to challenge, but he can't help thinking that while Rory may not be suicidal, his actions in New Orleans seem to have been pretty self-destructive.

"I mean," Rory says, with quiet insistence, "who wants the show to stop, right?"

"I'm certainly with you there," Alan responds.

"Staying in the game," Rory says, "that's the only way to see things, isn't it? And I've seen lots of things, man, good and bad." There's excitement in his voice now. "Hell, one night on Santa Monica Boulevard I was looking down the barrel of a loaded .357 Magnum that was being held by a two-bit Guatemalan drug dealer. This guy was so shaky that, I swear, if a leaf had fallen off a tree and hit the sidewalk a half-block behind him, he'd have blown me away. I knew his ugly horse-face might be the last thing I saw on earth, but I tell you, I was wide awake every second of that time. I mean, sure, I was scared and, sure, I didn't know how things were going to turn out, but I was alive, like totally alive. There were haloes around the street lights from the fog, I could feel the dampness on my skin." He laughs quietly. "The funny thing is, I was doing a friend a favor. Otherwise, I wouldn't have had to be there at all." He shakes his head. "The memory of that time comes to me every now and then and I always feel as if I'm experiencing it all over again. And when that happens, you know what I think?" he says, a wondering quality entering his voice. "I ask myself, when I'm gone, who's going to know about that?"

I guess I do now, Alan thinks.

"Of course," Rory smiles to himself, "there were other times, sweeter times . . ." He's silent a while. "Things I wouldn't have wanted to miss for anything. There was a night under the stars in a hot tub in Mendocino. You ever been to Mendocino?"

Alan shakes his head. He has the sense that Rory, whose confidence must have been challenged severely by his ignominious flight from New Orleans, is trying to shore it up with his memories of earlier feats of survival as well as memories of other, as he called them, sweeter experiences. Once more Alan is aware of an opacity in Rory that he'll never get past.

"You're right about Leo," Rory says suddenly, almost dismissively. "He's got more important things on his mind than tracking me down." After a moment, he adds, "I had to get out of there, that's the point." Alan waits for more, but all at once Rory moves in another direction. "You know what's really strange," he says, "one of the best moments I ever had happened on the way to Lyletown."

"That's a surprise," Alan says.

Rory lights a cigarette, a sour smile playing about his lips. "Yeah, Lyletown," he says. "I mean, it's easy for everybody now to say that the whole thing was such a fiasco," he goes on. "The Radical Cadre That Couldn't Shoot Straight, that kind of stuff." He expels a cloud of smoke. "And all that's true enough, I suppose, if you're sitting in front of a typewriter pecking words onto a page and passing judgment on people you don't know from shit. What can you know if you're just looking at it from the outside? But let me tell you, my friend, for a few minutes that night I was in a zone all by myself. I mean, for one thing, I was seeing everything super-clear. On the drive up there in the van, old Ben, who was in the front seat with Serena, kept bobbing his head like some sub quarterback sitting on the bench reciting the plays to himself, hoping the coach calls on him and at the same time scared shitless that he's going to fuck up when he gets his chance." His smile widens. "Imagine, the great Ben Fraley. Of course, next to me in the backseat, Bobby was chewing gum a mile a minute and talking nonstop about all sorts of shit—some kid in high school named Sharpie who used to give everybody blow jobs, an uncle up in Michigan who built a log cabin—until Ben had to tell him to cool it. Serena didn't say ten words but I never smelled sweat so strong."

Alan is surprised by the excitement that grips him as he listens to Rory's account of that night. This glimpse from the inside has brought him back to those times. It must have been something to have been in that van, all those hearts beating separately and together as they headed toward the unknown. "And you?" he asks at last.

Rory looks out at the road. "What surprised me," he says, "is how calm I was on the way to that job. I'll say this, during that time when we were still on our way toward Lyletown I wasn't thinking about anything political, like stolen guns going to arm the blacks, or revolution, none of that. I was just pumped and ready for something, and at the same time I was as cool as can be. I knew there might be trouble, of course, but I accepted that. Time just stopped for a while, and I was happy. Yeah, happy—ain't that a bitch? I remember feeling as if I'd passed some kind of test," he goes on. "It was like going into combat. I felt I was handling things better than any of the others."

This is a surprise to Alan. Did it really happen that way, he wonders, or has Rory reshaped the event in his memory? There's no way he'll ever know. "Of course, the way things turned out . . ." he ventures.

"I know," Rory cuts in impatiently, "I know things didn't go so well once the job started coming apart and I'll admit I made some dumb moves then, but that still didn't change the fact that, going into it, when everything was up in the air, I knew I could do it, I was ready for it, I wasn't afraid." He nods to himself. "It's something I'll always have." The pride comes through in his voice.

In the ensuing silence, Alan is remembering that time, his own peripheral role in those events. He remembers the days when he still expected to be part of the operation. In his basement apartment he tried to imagine what it was going to be like. When the time came, was he going to be up to it? But he hadn't taken part, and that makes all the difference, or it should.

"Lyletown, shit." Rory shakes his head. "We were such amateurs. Who knew how really nasty things were going to get later? The Weathermen and their bombs. The Panthers. The SLA. Automatic weapons, bandoliers, shootouts with SWAT teams. Hell, we were like a warm-up act, only we had no idea what the main act was going to be like."

"Lyletown scared the shit out of me," Alan hears himself saying. "I mean, I came so close to having everything blow up in my face." He laughs. "And I wasn't even there. Christ, I remember when I got out of the hospital. I was weak from the operation, I felt like a rag doll—maybe that had something to do with it. They told me not to lift anything heavy, and I just hung around my apartment feeling as if everything had been sucked out of me. But I was worried all the time, waiting for a knock on the door, like in some black-and-white movie from the forties. Of course I was wondering what was happening to you, what happened to the others, but mostly, I've got to tell the truth, I was thinking about myself, how I'd managed to let myself get so close to screwing up my life, and I wasn't so sure I hadn't. At the same time, I was still feeling the anger that got me into the Caper in the first place, I felt the bad guys were winning all over the world. The fact that Lyletown turned out the way it did was just another example of that. But I guess what I was thinking was that if I was lucky enough to dodge that bullet, what I wanted most of all was to be able to make a separate peace, to go under cover, in a way. I can tell you, I didn't necessarily feel good about that, but it seemed like what I had to do just then." Having delivered himself of this memory, he feels depleted, and for a while they drive on in silence.

"You know," he says at last, "about the first thing I did after things quieted down was to get married—for the first time—as if I

thought that was going to solve all my problems. It was a disaster."
It's hard for him to think of that episode without remorse. Trying
to use Martha that way was more than just stupid, it was cruel to
punish her for his own inadequacies. He could see from the beginning what a mistake he'd made marrying her, but he couldn't bring
himself to do anything about it, even though the marriage was
suffocating both of them. It was Martha finally who had the guts
to say that the whole thing was wrong, that they had to end it. It
must have hurt like hell for her to have said that, but, damn it, she
was right and she was brave enough to say it out loud.

Looking back at his life at that time, all he can see is a series
of wrecks and failures, and yet he'd been able to get past them. He
still finds it amazing that things have turned out the way they have
for him. "I guess some of us have to travel twisting paths to get to
where we are," he says. He can't help thinking of Julia, her long
arms and quick stride, her crooked smile, the soft fall of her hair,
the way that, within seconds, she can lose herself in a book; and he
feels a sudden rush of tenderness for his wife. He knows it's likely
that when he gets back home there will still be tension between
them because of what he told her about himself last night, but he
really can't believe it's going to last. "In the end," he says, "I think
I've come to a pretty good place. I mean, even in the work I do, I
spend a lot of time helping people who really need help. In some
ways, it isn't so far from the way I felt back then. Of course," he's
quick to add, "in other ways it's very different." What he means
to say is that he doesn't feel the need to apologize for his life after
Lyletown. He laughs to himself. "I did a lot better in marriage the
second time around."

"I guess," Rory says after a while, "you'd have to say I'm still
traveling my own twisting path." After a couple of seconds, he asks,
"By the way, do you have any pictures of your wife?"

Alan is suddenly on the defensive. "No," he lies. "I don't have
anything on me." Of course, he has a picture of Julia in his wallet,
but he has an instinctive aversion to showing it to Rory. It's totally
irrational, he knows. Of course there are albums at Innisfree with

plenty of pictures of Julia. If he stays there for a week he'll certainly find them.

"I'll bet she's sexy," Rory says.

"I think so," Alan responds, eager to change the subject. "Do you know what you're going to do at Innisfree?" he asks.

Rory shakes his head. "Well," he says after a while, "I'm going to have to do a lot of thinking. It's a bit like chess. I've got myself into a tough situation and I have to think my way out." Alan nods, hardly listening, happy to be talking about something other than his wife's sexiness.

South of Hartford now, they've pulled off the highway onto a two-lane blacktop heading west, and their progress here is slower. The Hartford suburbs have gradually given way to small Connecticut towns with histories of their own, evocative, on this splendid fall afternoon, of bushels of shiny apples and bright fat pumpkins lying in fields, colorful flags rippling in the wind, towns where even though the practice is no longer permitted, a phantom trace of smoke from burning leaves seems to linger in the air. The bright, wholesome scene buoys Alan's spirits.

"We should stop here and pick up a few supplies," he says as a supermarket comes into view. "We have some canned stuff at the place, we've got flashlights and batteries, but you'll need more and only you know what you want to eat. Remember, you won't have a car, so you'll have to stock up."

"I've got plenty of money," Rory assures Alan as they move down the aisles, and he fills his bascart with an ample supply of meat and vegetables, a dozen eggs, some canned fruit, a box of cereal and a half-gallon of milk, enough, it seems to Alan, for guests, if not an extended stay. Rory puts a couple of six packs of beer into his cart in spite of Alan's telling him that there's already plenty of booze at the house. "It might be a retreat," he says, "but it's not a monastery." Still, Rory insists on buying a bottle of bourbon at the nearby liquor store. "I have no intention of being a freeloader," he explains. The crisp brown shopping bags full of provisions convey an air of excitement to the enterprise, and for a moment Alan almost envies Rory his solitary stay at Innisfree. In some ways it would be exhilarating to be by yourself in a place where nobody knows you, planning to start all over.

When they leave the liquor store, the fall light gives the scene before them the sharpness of something viewed through a telescope, and a gust sends a bright tatter of golden leaves scudding through the October air. "Hey," Rory suggests as they approach the car, "how about letting me drive for a bit? After all, as you said, I won't have a car for a whole week."

Alan smiles at the notion. Maybe Rory's been intoxicated by the weather. It is a fine day for driving, though by now they're little more than thirty miles from Innisfree. "Why not?" he says.

"Nice car," Rory declares after a couple of minutes' driving. "First time I've driven a Toyota." He's going a little faster than Alan would, but there's hardly any traffic. "When I got out of the can," Rory says, "first chance I had, I got behind the wheel and drove all day. You can't imagine what it's like to be cooped up like that."

By now they've made their way beyond the cluster of towns west of Hartford and are in the higher, rolling country of the state's northwest corner, in the foothills of the Berkshires, a world away from Boston. The rising and falling road follows the contours of the land, which is steeply elevated in places, and much less densely populated here, with little between the small settlements but forests and fields. "I can see what you mean when you said this area is remote," Rory comments. "It's pretty empty here, at least for my idea of Connecticut."

"The thing is, it used to be bustling in the last century," Alan tells him. "There were iron forges in this part of the state then. It may be hard to believe, but for a time this used to be an important area, industrially. You have to try to imagine lots of little Pittsburghs tucked away in these hills, the pulsing red glow of dozens of forges in the night." As he says it, he's filled with a sense of wonder at the thought of all those vanished forges.

"What happened?" Rory asks.

"Eventually, they used up all the timber for fuel and once the trees were gone, the iron industry moved."

Rory shakes his head. "It's hard to believe there were no trees here."

"It's true, though. Most of this stuff is what grew back since then. There's more forest cover here now than at any time since colonial days."

They're traveling through a corridor of thick, colorful foliage where the land rises steeply on both sides of the road, the vivid, shivering woods closing in on them in places, opening out in others to vistas with low mountains on the horizon. Alan is still talking about the history of the area as they come around a bend, when something big slams into the car from the woods on the right. The car swerves sharply and goes into a slide, all the way across the center line. "Jesus," Rory shouts, clutching the wheel and yanking it back as he strains to keep things under control. Alan is aware of his breath coming in gasps, his senses jolted as he tries to unscramble his memory of the brown blur, the blunt thud accompanied by the clatter of flying groceries coming from the backseat. It seems ages but he knows it has to be only a couple of seconds before Rory manages to wrestle the car back to the right, but in his over-correction the tires strike the soft earth of the road's shoulder and the car sluices weightlessly for a moment or two before the rubber finally grips the pavement again, the vehicle recovering stability just seconds before a red pickup coming from the other direction flashes by them, dangerously close. A deer, it had to be a deer, Alan is thinking, Rory hit a deer, noting a pale spatter of blood on the windshield. "Hey, pull over," he shouts, "pull the fuck over."

The car has already slowed and, seconds later, Rory brings it to the side of the road, where he jumps out as soon as he's turned off the engine and yanked the parking brake. "Jesus Christ," he shouts, taking a few aimless paces toward the woods, "Jesus fucking Christ."

Alan, whose heart is racing, sits in the passenger seat for a second or two before jerking himself out, slamming the door behind him. "What the hell did you just do?" he yells at Rory.

"I didn't do anything," Rory yells back. "It was a fucking deer."

Alan's fists are balled. "You didn't have to be driving so God-damned fast." he shouts, though Rory is only a few feet away. "Didn't you see the signs?"

Rory takes a step toward him and stops, then kicks savagely at the dirt and turns away.

Calm down, Alan urges himself, and he takes a deep breath. Rory wasn't going all that fast. The deer's leaping out into the road was a totally random act. "Hey," he says, at last, raising his hand, "I didn't mean what I just said. It could just as easily have happened to me."

Rory lights a cigarette and holds it in his cupped hand as if to protect it from the wind, though there's none discernible. "Christ," he says, "we came close to being killed." He takes a deep drag and exhales it slowly, looking away from Alan, who watches the smoke drift slowly and turns away, aware that his sudden anger has already ebbed. In the clear fall light, there's an air of hyper-reality about this peaceful stretch along the shoulder of the road. Dead leaves crackle beneath his feet and he feels the breeze on his skin. His hands are trembling. "It's not your fault," he says.

Rory is standing beside the car. "It's dented. Not much," he observes icily, pointing to the crumpled fender, where more flecks of blood are visible. "I can pay for it."

"No, no," Alan insists. "The insurance will get it."

Rory says, "It had to be a deer, right? Did you see it? I never saw anything."

Alan's pulse has quieted somewhat. "I sort of saw it," he says. "It was over before I was aware of it, though. It kind of ambushed us out of the woods." He runs his hand across the dent. "But, yeah, it was a deer, all right."

"Where the hell did it go?" Rory asks, calmer now.

Both of them glance in the direction they've come from: nothing but trees and the empty road. By now they must be almost a quarter mile beyond the point where the animal hit them. "Must have gone back into the woods, I guess," Alan says. "I don't give it much of a chance to live." He drops into a squat beside the point of impact and tries to get a look under the car, and is relieved to find no evidence of further damage other than the crumpled fender and a slightly cracked headlight. He'll have to tell the insurance company he was driving, of course. And pay the deductible. The deer must have hit them a glancing blow, just striking the side of the car. It was the shock as much as anything that threw them off course. Squatting there beside the damaged fender, Alan remembers his surprise, the sudden sense of powerlessness, his recognition that everything might be ending without his being able to do anything about it, and he slowly exhales, running his hand delicately along the dent. He gets to his feet and the two of them stand there smelling the faint trace of exhaust and tobacco smoke that's swallowed up by the rich smell of earth, grass and leaves. "Jesus," Rory says. "What would have happened if that animal had jumped out a second earlier? He'd have come through the windshield."

"I know," Alan says. "I know. And if that truck had been coming down the other side of the road a little earlier, both of us would have been toast. This is our lucky day, I guess," he says. His heart, he's relieved to discover, has gone back to beating normally.

Rory takes a deep drag. "Not so lucky for that deer, I guess."

"You did a good job holding the car steady," Alan says.

Rory makes a dismissive gesture with his cigarette.

Fortunately, the groceries have survived the episode intact, and have only to be repacked. When they've finished with that, there's an uncomfortable moment before they resume their trip. "You might as well take over from here," Rory says.

"Look," Alan says, "I know hitting that deer wasn't your fault, but we're close and the last part of the trip is kind of tricky, so, yeah, I might as well drive."

Rory shrugs. When Alan pulls back onto the road at last, he keeps a tight grip on the wheel, preternaturally alert for signs of anything else that might jump out at them from the woods. Both men are silent, as if neither wants to be caught off guard again.

Before long they've come to their destination. "Here we are," Alan declares, and they pull off the paved road into the trees. The car moves carefully across the packed dirt that takes them through the gap in the stone wall and onto the middle path in the trail. Here, after a brief flat interval, they make the steep, bumpy, twisting ascent under a thick canopy of leaves, until they come at last to the top, where the road straightens and levels out as it runs alongside the pines planted by Richard Mallory, toward the elaborate stone pillars he erected decades ago. Passing between those pillars, they enter a break in the forest where, in the bright sunlight, the shingled white house with its sharp gables stands out amid a shimmering leafy background of scarlet and orange, russet and gold. The grass, which hasn't been cut since the Labor Day weekend, is high, though not overwhelmingly so, given its slower growth this time of the year, and its muted green moves silkily under a wind that sends a confetti of brightly colored leaves into the air. When the car's motor is turned off, all they can hear is the hissing of the trees punctuated by the motley calls of birds.

"Well, this is Innisfree." Alan climbs out of the car and gestures toward the house. "This is going to be your home for the next week."

Rory steps out of the car and looks toward the wall of trees that surrounds them. In the dry October air, he seems taller and more limber. "You sure were right about its being deep in the woods," he says.

"It used to be a lot more primitive in the old days," Alan feels compelled to say. "As I told you, all we had was kerosene for light. There wasn't even a phone." He points to the area beyond the stone wall where he'd once labored so heroically with an axe. "All that used to be thick with trees," he says. "We were fenced in by the forest up to the eyeballs. I hacked out a clearing in that notch." Of course, Rory couldn't know how much work it took or what it looked like when Alan first finished the job, when he and Julia were able to feel the breeze that came up the back of the mountain through the newly recovered open space. Then it occurs to him that, of course, Rory would have been in prison then. "As you can see," Alan says, "the trees are already coming back." He laughs. "All you have to do is look the other way for a minute and the forest will start to take over again."

They carry Rory's provisions inside, their combined weight on the sagging living room floorboards causing some of the glasses to ring in the hutch built by Julia's father. "I'm going to have to jack up that floor," Alan explains. "We have to do that every few years." The house, closed for weeks, is infused with its particular smell of cedar and innumerable fires that have burnt in the large stone fireplace; and when Alan opens the top of the Dutch door to air the place out, the interior's muted colors contrast sharply with the dancing outdoor light. "Let me show you around," he says, and he takes Rory on a quick tour of the place. Upstairs, he tries to explain to him some of the changes he and Julia have made. "You can see the original shape of the roof. That chimney was outside. We had an outdoor wrought-iron spiral staircase." He ends his tour with the library, where, as a final gesture, he pulls back the false front of the books and opens the panel in the wall that leads to the upstairs room.

"Your father-in-law must have had a lot of fun building stuff like that," Rory says.

"I don't know if it was so much fun as desperation," Alan says. "Apparently what he saw in the war really got to him. This place was his answer, I guess, to a world that was too much for him." He remembers Julia's stories about her childhood here, about her sister. "He tried to create a fairy tale world for his daughters," Alan says.

Rory looks on silently, a man with a certain amount of building of his own to accomplish. At the moment, Alan feels churlish about his earlier resistance to letting him stay here. Maybe, just maybe, he'll be able to figure things out at Innisfree.

He shows Rory how the stove works, how to turn on the electricity; he takes him out back to where the firewood is stacked under a tarpaulin. "Fortunately, there's lots of it. It's comfortable now, but it can get pretty cool at night. You're probably going to need a fire in the morning, at least, even with the good weather. This place has no insulation."

"I'll be all right," Rory says, an air of quiet having descended on him in the last few minutes.

"You might start to get cabin fever after a while, with no car. The radio works. It's set to WCBS in New York, which is an all-news station. You can pick up a few more stations, Hartford, a couple of others. No TV, though. And then, there's an interesting collection of books in the library."

"That's OK, I've got enough to occupy my mind," Rory says.

Alan gives him his phone number back home. He also hands him a signed note identifying him as Alan's guest. "Frankly, I'm sure everyone on this side of the hill is gone for the season, but there are some people who live here year-round; and if one of them should come tramping through here on a hike, this note will make it clear that you're not somebody who's come here to steal the family silver."

Rory nods distractedly.

"OK," Alan says, "I think I've told you just about everything you need to know. Any other questions? Now that you're here you can see how tough it's going to be without a car."

"You said there's a bus schedule up here and that a bus goes through that town we passed, right?"

"Yeah, though that's a walk of a couple of miles."

"I can do a couple of miles," Rory says. Again, he seems to have become quieter, as if he's already begun his solitary occupation of Innisfree.

"Well," Alan tells him, "the good news is that it's mostly downhill. Here's something else. This is the phone number of Billy Armand. He's an old guy who lives a little way down the road. For twenty bucks, he can give you a ride to the railroad station in Pawling, New York, if you decide to go in that direction, or any other destination within a reasonable distance. So, what else? You sure you have enough money?"

"I'm fine," Rory says. "I'll manage fine. Look, I know you must be eager to get back home, but you have to have time for a drink, right?" It's clear this is important to him.

"Sure, I can manage that," Alan answers, aware of the irony of Rory's being for the moment his host at Innisfree.

Alan gets the glasses while Rory opens the bottle of bourbon he bought on the trip, and extracts a couple of ice cubes from the clear plastic bag. He pours a couple of generous drinks in a silence broken only by a clucking sound coming from the woods. "Turkeys," Alan tells him. "You might run into a pack of them at any time."

Rory's thoughts seem to be far from turkeys, though. "You were right about Leo," he says again. "I don't seriously think he's going to spend any time chasing after me." It's suddenly very quiet in the little house as Rory turns the glass slowly in his hand. "In truth," he says, "Leo has lots more important things to concern himself with." He puts the glass to his lips and takes a quick sip of the whiskey. "It's a very complicated situation down there right now," he says. "Actually, there's a good chance that before the year is out, Leo might be through. Anyone who looks carefully can see the handwriting on the wall." His brow is knit. "It's too bad. I mean, in some ways I had a really sweet situation down there, but, as the song says, you've got to know when to fold." In the silence that follows, Alan hears the turkeys again, deeper in the forest this time. "As to Leo," Rory goes on, "he's pissed at me, no doubt about that." He looks into the glass. "But no, really I don't think he gives a shit about me anymore. Though it would be very stupid of me to go back there any time soon," he says distantly. When he turns toward Alan, there's no mistaking the urgency of his statement. "You've got to believe me, I had to get out of there. I had to."

After a silence, Alan ventures, "So this business with his son, this insult—it was your way of burning your bridges, then?"

Rory nods slowly. "That's about the size of it." Alan resists the impulse to say more, to probe, and after a while Rory resumes on his own. "It's what I do, I guess," he says. "I was with a woman named Ellie for a while in California, and that's what she said when she saw what was going to happen between us. 'You're going to make sure things can't work out,' she said. 'I know your type,' she said. 'You're a bridge-burner. Even before you set foot onto a bridge, you're already working out how you're going to burn it so you won't be tempted to go back.' She had her finger on something,

I guess. It seems as if, after a while, wherever I am, I need to get out, and somehow I manage to do something that insures that I'll have to get out." He laughs to himself. "I remember something else she said: 'What's going to happen to you when there are no bridges left?' It's a good question."

The two of them drink in silence for a few moments. The only sounds come from outside the house: bird cries, the distant tapping of a woodpecker. Rory could have gone anywhere, Alan thinks, after he burned his bridges in New Orleans, he didn't have to come to Boston and he certainly had no reason to travel all the way here to hide out at Innisfree. Still, both trips seem to have been necessary to him. "So what are your options at the moment?" Alan asks. "If you can say anything about that."

"I've got some contacts," Rory says. "Here in the U.S., even one in Canada. I've been thinking about Canada lately."

"Canada's not that far from here," Alan says.

"Yeah," Rory says. "I noticed. Anyway, I might have to make some long distance calls from here. I'll leave you the money."

Alan raises a hand. "Hey, what kind of hospitality would that be if I charged you?"

In the silence that follows they hear the buzzing of a late-season insect, possibly caught in a spider web. At some point recently, like the turning of a tide, the afternoon has begun to wane, and long shadows stretch across the portion of the front lawn that's visible through the opened Dutch door. Alan should be going soon if he wants to get home in time for dinner. "It could get chilly tonight," he says again. "You should be fine with the sleeping bag, though. And if you have a fire . . ."

"I'll be fine. And, don't worry, I'll try to keep the place tidy."

Alan realizes that he can't start for home without broaching a subject he's become very curious about in light of what Rory said a few minutes ago. "One thing," he says, "about your burning bridges."

Rory turns his head. "Yeah?"

"That doesn't seem to be the case with Lyletown, does it?"

Rory makes no immediate response. Outside the dry leaves whisper in the wind. At last he asks, "Meaning?"

Alan shrugs. "Meaning, I've seen you three times in the last few years. And our only real connection is Lyletown. That seems to mean something."

Rory gives him a sidelong look. "Like what?" he asks. "What do you think it means?"

Alan shakes his head. "I can't honestly say." He remembers the terror he felt when he heard Rory's voice on the phone three years ago, the sense of dread about Lyletown that's never completely gone away. "At first I thought you were going to try to blackmail me," he confesses.

Rory smiles sourly. "Well, I can understand that, given the circumstances."

"I mean," Alan goes on, "it was just that first time. After that, I guess I didn't really think it had to do with blackmail anymore." After a pause, he concludes unsatisfyingly, "It had to be about something else."

"Yeah," Rory nods.

"Yeah?"

"Yeah, something else," Rory says. "That's probably the best way to put it. I'm not sure I can make it any clearer to myself. But, yeah, Lyletown seems to be a bridge I could never bring myself to burn—and don't think I haven't tried. But it just seemed that, as far from it as I'd run, something would keep taking me back to that night. Maybe I thought it was the one thing I had of my own, some compass point. I don't know. I mean, it's where my life left off before I went to prison and after I got out. Hell, it's not as if I was planning it that way, but you're right: it's curious that somehow in the end I'd wind up touching base with the one person from those days that I knew." He shrugs. "Who knows? Maybe I thought you were the lucky one, maybe I thought I could get some of that luck to rub off on me."

He looks in the direction of the open Dutch door, through which a square of the darkening forest is visible. "But what I do know now is that this shit has got to stop, things have to change," he says, "or I'll just get caught up in an endless loop. It's time." He's still looking out the window. "I mean, look at you: you've traveled your twisting path, as you call it, and it seems like you've got to some place where you think you want to be. Hell, it even appears that Lily has made her peace with the past. Serena and Bobby, well, they're out of the game for good, aren't they? As for old Ben, God knows what's happened to him. Maybe he actually made it to Alaska, where he's happy as a pig in shit." He pauses a moment. "I guess I don't want to be the last of the Lyletown crowd that's still drifting around after all those years. Hell," he says, suddenly animated, "I keep thinking about what happened on the road today. What if I'd been killed when that deer hit the car? What would my life have added up to?" He lets out a long breath. "I'd like to believe that this thing that just happened in New Orleans was the end of something." After a moment, he says quietly, "It's time, man. It's just time for me to move on."

"It sounds as if you've already decided on some pretty important things," Alan suggests.

"Look, dude," Rory fires back. "Nothing is guaranteed. You know that. Just because I've, as you say, decided on some important shit, that doesn't mean we're going to get a storybook ending. It might make me feel good for a while, but it doesn't mean things are going to start going my way, does it?"

"No," Alan says, "you're right there." Hell, he knows there are no more guarantees for him than there are for Rory, and he suddenly has a strong wish to be back with his family, as if he feels them to be in danger.

"All I'm saying," Rory goes on, his voice heavy with weariness, "is that this is what I've got to do now."

The two of them are silent for a while as Alan contemplates what Rory's just told him. Of course, he wishes Rory well, he hopes he'll be able to burn the bridge that leads him to Lyletown, if that's what he needs. Though if that's so, it means that after today Alan isn't likely to see him again. Surprisingly, that fact saddens him. Is it because Rory is his own last bridge to Lyletown? He listens to the rustling of the leaves outside, he drives the beveled edge of the glass into his hand. So this could turn out to be the final scene, then, the two of them in this space in the woods created by his wife's father. This is where Lyletown has led them. And is this where the Caper will end, that action launched during those heated days in the sixties, when Alan was driven by a youthful longing and despair so ardent that it fused his political grievances with his sexual yearnings, and both were concentrated in the allure of Lily Culp? Whatever the mix of impulse and desire, it moved him to step across a line and join a couple of shady ex-cons and the others in a plan that was as reckless as it was desperate. Everybody who took part paid a price, and he could easily have wound up like Rory. Two roads diverged in a wood, he thinks, looking out toward the darkening forest.

What he feels isn't exactly melancholy, but it has an equivalent weight. As an antidote, he feels the need to jolt himself into purposefulness. "Well," he says, getting to his feet, "I really do have to go." Both men finish the dregs of their drinks and they walk to the car without speaking, the rasp of leaves accompanying their steps. The evening chill has already begun to take hold at this altitude as the shadows from the black woods surrounding Richard Mallory's fairy tale house lengthen across the lawn. Passing the car, Alan runs his hand idly along the cool metal of the crumpled fender. When he's come round to the driver's side, he holds out his hand to Rory. "Good luck, amigo," he says, to which Rory responds, "You too, dude." They shake briefly and release each other's hands. Something's missing, Alan can't help feeling. If this is in fact going to be their last meeting, this seems too casual a farewell. Certainly there's something more that ought to be said, there should be some ceremony, but what would that be? Alan has his own life to return to, after all, an unburned bridge back to Wildwood Street, where his wife and son are waiting for him, where the rest of his life is waiting for him.

Checking his impulse to remind Rory one more time about making a fire tonight, he gets into his dented car and starts the engine, backs up on the lawn and turns around. "Keep your eye out for deer," Rory calls, standing in the tall grass. He waves when the car passes between the stone pillars and onto the road that runs beside Richard Mallory's pine planting. Alongside the deep shadow of those pines, Alan sounds his horn in response as he makes his way slowly along the dirt path. First Rory's silhouette, then the house's steep gables and finally the stone pillars recede in his rearview mirror. After a few seconds the road turns and dips sharply, and Alan has to keep his eyes on the twisting, stone-filled path before him as the car begins its descent toward home.

t's not going to be the greatest weather for shutting down Innisfree, but Alan has kept putting off the necessary last trip of the season until he'd heard something definitive from Rory, and it was only on Monday that he got the postcard from Vancouver.

"Nice," he told Julia when he showed her the picture of the glistening skyline set between the water and the snowcapped mountains. "But when he said he might go to Canada, I was thinking Toronto or Montreal."

"Vancouver's a long way from New Orleans," Julia pointed out. "But what's he say?"

"Very little." Alan turned the card over, where she could read, "Thanks, Rory."

"A man of few words," she observed. "And you think that's the last of him?"

He couldn't deny that Rory's being at the far edge of the continent was comforting. But would that be distance enough to keep him away for good? "I'd like to think so. He's in another country now."

"It's time to close up Innisfree," he said minutes later.

She sighed. "Not one of my favorite trips."

"Amen to that. This Saturday?"

"Sure, let's get this business over with."

He understands exactly how she feels. Closing the place for the year means more than just saying goodbye to lazy summer afternoons at Innisfree, it means that the earth is turning toward the season of darkness and cold. Innisfree is a different place now that the days are shorter, the temperatures lower, the woods stripped of their leaves; and the entire mood of that last trip is one of somber efficiency. Once there, it takes only a couple of hours to close the place down; but, unlike its counterpart journey in the spring, when the house is being reopened, the last trip of the fall brings only a sense of things coming to an end, it's a kind of entombment.

What makes Alan's mood slightly less funereal this time is that the situation with Julia has settled down, and things are much better between the two of them, though the thaw hasn't come immediately. She's told him that it's likely to take her a little time to get used to incorporating into her sense of him a part of his life she hadn't known about. "And I don't mean what you did back in the sixties—everybody's done things in their past they might regret." No, she told him, what hurt her was to recognize that during a significant stretch of their marriage, at least from the time Rory resurfaced, Alan had been capable of withholding from her the knowledge that his job and their entire way of life could be taken away with a few words from this figure from his past. "You really believed we were in danger, and you chose to keep me in the dark—that's so hard to accept."

All he could do was to throw up his hands at these accusations. "Yeah," he said. "It was very bad judgment, I agree. Of course, I should have trusted you. That's all very clear now."

Fortunately, in the end Julia didn't really want to stay mad. "I don't know," she said after a while. "It's always easy to tell other people how to act. I don't know what I'd have done in similar circumstances." He can only guess that one of the reasons why she wants this to be over is that she herself is on the verge of an important step, having started on the scary project of writing her book, which is sure to present her with plenty of challenges; and she doesn't need friction with Alan about something that both of them hope is over at last. So, like a fire that flares up quickly but lacks sufficient fuel to grow, the discussions about Rory and Lyletown became quieter and less frequent, and then they stopped.

But now on the dismal last Saturday of October, unable to put things off any longer, he, Julia and Tommy are setting out for the anticlimactic trip to Connecticut. Tommy could have spent the day with one of his friends, but his parents have decided that he's old enough to take part in this ritual and it's important for him to learn the drill. "Do I have to?" he pleaded, not eager to be part of a mission to Innisfree that promised to be so lacking in the possibility of fun. "Take some books for the trip," his mother suggested.

His resistance to going is understandable, given the weather. The sun is nowhere to be seen as they set out for Connecticut and the streets are wet from the night's rain. Still, there's been a break this morning that raises Alan's spirits. Though the sky is a composition of gray on gray, the predicted rain continues to hold off, and the first two legs of the trip along the Pike and Route 84 go swiftly. Alan's hopes are still strong as they travel along the more intimate Route 4, though the towns they pass through look damp and dour: straw-filled Halloween displays on lawns are sodden and wet ghost-sheets hang limply from trees. "That's not very scary," Tommy says of a spineless scarecrow lolling on some porch steps like a Slinky toy. "It's dumb."

"You're such a big kid now," Alan says. "Think you'll be able to do your job when we get to Innisfree?"

Tommy looks suspiciously at the lowering clouds outside. "I hope it isn't raining when we get there," he says.

"Hey, it's not going to rain till tonight," Alan tells him. "I promise." This is a bit of bravado, though he gives himself a fifty-fifty chance of being right.

"Is this where the deer hit our car?" Tommy asks after a while. To keep things simpler, he's told his son he was at the wheel when it happened.

"No," Alan says, "that was closer to Innisfree. I'll try to show you where."

"I want to see the place," Tommy says.

"It might not be easy to find the exact spot," Alan confesses. "I doubt that they've put up a marker." The dent has been repaired and the car is fine but, once bitten, twice shy, and having been reminded of the incident, now that they've passed through the towns and are in the countryside, Alan watchfully scours the woods along the side of the road for any animal that might leap out at them.

When Tommy's returned to his reading, Julia says quietly, "That must have been something, hitting that deer."

"It happened so quickly," Alan says. "I only saw things after they were over. I'm still not sure what I really saw. Same goes for Rory, apparently."

She takes his hand and squeezes it. Alan, aware of how much difference it would have made had the deer jumped out seconds earlier, returns the pressure.

"Are we close to where that deer hit our car?" Tommy calls again from the back.

"We're getting there," Alan says. Minutes later, when he's fairly sure about the location, he slows down. "Here," he says. "It happened somewhere around here." There is, of course, nothing out of the ordinary about the scene.

"Were you scared?" the boy asks.

"I was surprised," Alan says. "It happened so fast. I only had a chance to get scared after it was over." He laughs. "It did get my heart beating pretty fast, I'll admit."

"I don't think I'd be scared," Tommy says after a moment.

"No, I don't think you would be either."

A little later, Tommy asks, "Think another deer's going to hit our car?"

Alan shakes his head once more. "You only get one."

"Good," Tommy says solemnly. Then he asks, "Do you think when I'm old enough to drive, a deer will hit my car?"

The thought of his son as a teenager, exposed to all the hazards of the adult world, gives him a shudder, but he shakes his head again. "No, it's one to a family and I'm afraid I've used ours up."

"Good," Tommy says again, and goes back to reading. Julia gives Alan a smile. How many years will it be, he wonders, before Tommy's actually going to be behind the wheel? A half-dozen? That's still a long way away, Alan assures himself.

The day remains dreary and by the time they pull off the paved road and are on the grounds of the association, Alan feels as if he's been keeping the rain at bay by sheer force of will. The rich fall coloring of a couple of weeks ago has given way to a thin fringe of brown through which the skeletal shapes of the trees are visible. Even the dark patches of pine seem muted, huddled against the encroaching winter, and the grass itself has lost its greenness. The family is silent on the twisting dirt road that climbs upward to Innisfree. Stones are flung up beneath them and packed wet leaves cause the tires to spin at times, but the car manages to maintain its traction, and before long they're on the lawn in front of the house.

"It looks sad up here," Julia says after they've all gotten out of the car, and Tommy, as instructed, has gone to get the key from its hiding place in the rocks behind the house. "It makes me think about my father."

In the dim light the shingled house with its steep gables does have a bit of a gothic air, which is heightened by the wind's sighing quietly in the nearby pines. "Hey," Alan says, "he built a great place and he had a lot of happy years here." Rain may not be falling, but there's a bite to the raw, damp air, and he's glad he decided to wear a heavier jacket.

Julia shakes her head. "My father wasn't a happy man."

Though Alan wouldn't disagree, he tells her, "He'd have been a lot less happy if he hadn't had Innisfree."

The house is musty and damp when they enter, but there's nothing to suggest Rory's recent occupancy. None of the furniture appears to have been moved, nothing seems to be gone. Aside from some canned food in the cabinets, he's left a scanty trail. "He's a better housekeeper than I thought," Alan says.

"And he seems to have done all the right things with the refrigerator," Julia points out. The little machine is empty, it's apparently been cleaned, and the door has been left open to keep off the mildew. "This guy's beginning to seem like a real homebody."

Alan sniffs the air. "I'd say he did most of his smoking outside too. We'll have to check the beds, though, to see if he burned a hole in the sheets."

It's not much warmer in the house than it is outdoors, but a little light will help. "Let me turn on the electricity," he says, "and check around the outside for a bit before we get started in here." He opens the bulkhead doors and makes his way into the tiny basement, where he throws the switch for the electricity. When he climbs back out, he goes into the woods behind the house. There, he slides open the door of the shed, then checks that all the tools are in place and the mower is doubly protected by a tarpaulin, before he pulls the door shut with a screech and makes sure that it's secure. He takes a quick tour of the area, looking for stray objects and sizing up the trees, giving particular attention to a maple that's still healthy but is definitely leaning toward the house, and tall enough so that if it were to fall it could cause real damage. He's going to have to call Charlie Bowen about taking it down before the winter storms arrive. Heading back to the house, he routinely inspects the woodpile. When he lifts the tarpaulin, he breathes in the resiny smell of freshly cut pine that blends with the subtler essences of maple and cherry. The logs are neatly stacked and he wonders if Rory split some wood to replenish whatever he might have used for fires.

"Damn," he says as he realizes what he's hearing: the soft patter of rain on the tarpaulin that's protecting the firewood. Gradually he becomes aware that the sound is being echoed in a different key on the roof behind him, and now he can feel it on his skin. It's a fine rain but it's cold and it falls with the quiet insistence of something that isn't likely to let up soon.

Julia joins him. "The inside's fine, as far as I can see. Oh, hell, it's started to rain, hasn't it?"

He nods. "Yeah, it'll be best if we move fast. You didn't find anything in the house?" he asks. "Like a note or something."

She shakes her head. "Were you expecting one?"

"I don't know," he says. "I guess I must have been hoping for something." He smiles. "A Get-Out-of-Jail-Free card from the Monopoly game would have been nice, I suppose." The rain is cold on his face.

"Why don't we take the outdoor furniture off the pergola?" Julia says.

"Aha," she observes when they've gotten there, "is that a crushed butt I see?" She points to the stone floor near the outdoor furnace.

"I was getting uneasy about your friend's housekeeping. It was putting me to shame."

Alan can imagine Rory here on the pergola, smoking meditatively as he looked down the slope of the hill toward the south, possibly hearing the deep rumble of a freight train passing through the valley. Was he weighing competing options about where he was going next? Was he trying to steel himself to at last burn the one bridge he hadn't been able to burn, finally putting Lily and Serena, Ben and Bobby, even Alan behind him? Well, whatever he may have been thinking, Rory is gone now and Alan is living his own life. "OK," he says, "call Tommy. Let's see how quick we can be about this." He looks at his watch. "It's 11:30. Think we can get it all done in an another hour?"

The rain has settled in, the fine mist being replaced by a steadier fall. "Dad, I thought you said it wasn't going to rain," Tommy complains.

"Don't worry," Alan says. "Most of what you have to do is inside."

"But it's cold in the house. Can't we have a fire?"

"I don't think that would be such a good idea. We'd just have to wait around here longer making sure it was out. Why don't we try to get this job done real quick, and we can stop somewhere on the way home where it's warm, OK?" Tommy's main assignment is to put the trays containing vivid blue pellets of mouse poison in each of the rooms. "You're smart enough not to touch that stuff, right?" While Julia stores the linens in plastic bags, Alan opens up all the faucets and drains the toilet tank, then pours anti-freeze down all the traps and into the tank. Back in the basement that smells thickly of dirt, he affixes the hose to the faucet at the bottom of the hot water tank and pays it out, straightening the kinked green plastic tube as he lays it down on the sloping lawn, stretching it to its maximum length in order to keep the outlet below the source. A pulsing silvery stream pours languidly from its mouth onto the grass. By now the fine needles of rain are falling with an insinuating persistence, and Alan is getting soaked pretty quickly. If only they'd gone last Saturday, he thinks, when the weather was dry and sunny.

"My job is done," Tommy announces proudly, and Alan tells him to go back inside and stay dry. Meanwhile, from behind the shed he gets the plywood panel they use to cover the new window in the library. The wind's picked up and a sudden gust turns the panel into a sail as he stumbles across the slippery, uneven ground with it. Pivoting to steady his burden, he feels a twinge in his knee. Only a sprain, he judges after testing it, but a warning. Careful, he tells himself and makes his way down the stone steps to the back of the library, where he nails the panel into place over the glass. The cold air stings and he wishes he'd brought gloves. Julia, her wet hair flat on her head, comes up to him as he's finishing the job and they join Tommy inside. "I'm cold," he says. "Brr."

"I guess there's no harm in starting a small fire," Alan concedes, and crumples some paper, combines it with dry kindling from the wood basket near the fireplace and lights it. The fire that blazes up is more for show than for heat, but they won't be there long. He looks at his watch. "We're doing pretty well on time," he says. "We just have to wait for the water to drain." His unenviable job is to keep going out onto the soggy lawn to check on the mouth of the hose and determine when the last of the water has poured out, which isn't easy with the steady rain. As usual, it takes him a few trips before the last gurgle is sounded and he can declare that job finished. Laboriously, he rolls up the now dirty hose and returns it to its place in the garden house. He makes a final reconnaissance of the property, checking that all the doors and windows are shuttered by giving them a shake.

Once back inside, Alan asks, "Am I forgetting anything?"

"I always think I'm forgetting something," Julia says, "but I think we've done everything we were supposed to do."

When he's turned off the electricity and closed the door, he gives Tommy the key to return to its place among the stones.

"Goodbye, Innisfree," Alan says. "Have a good winter." Before long this hill will be covered with snow.

"We'll be back," Tommy says, shivering. But soon they're all in the car and within minutes the heater is pouring out warm air.

"Well," Alan tells them, "we did it. Good job, team. Let's get out of here."

As a reward for their diligence in closing the place down, he decides to take a slightly longer way home so they can stop at an inn in one of their favorite towns and have their lunch in a room with a large, crackling fire. The inn's windows glow cheerily in the rainy street and the little family tramps across the covered porch, where the long row of wicker chairs is empty. Inside, though, it's warm and cozy as they make their way over thick rugs to the restaurant.

Julia orders a bowl of fish chowder and Alan opts for the hearty burger smothered in Portobello mushrooms. To his and Julia's amusement but not to their surprise, Tommy, with a wide range of delicacies from which to choose, asks for the super plate of mac and cheese.

"Don't worry," Alan assures Julia, "his taste will improve when he grows up." To Tommy, he says. "A good mac and cheese will warm you up any day."

When the orders arrive, they're surprised by the size of the mac and cheese, but Tommy immediately falls into eating with gusto. "How do you like it?" Alan asks.

Tommy interrupts his eating long enough to declare, "Great."

"I wish I had his metabolism," Julia says. "You did a good job," she tells Tommy. "You earned that mac and cheese."

Alan takes a sip of wine and looks at the fire that dances in the big fireplace. It's good to be inside today. Turning to Julia, he says, "When we open Innisfree again next spring, you'll have a couple of chapters done."

Julia winces at first, then nods, her face brightening. "Yeah," she says, raising her glass. "Why not?"

He sees their reflection in the nearby mirror, and at that moment, together with his family after the three of them have successfully completed an unglamorous but necessary task, he wants to stop time. The muted apprehension he feels as he looks at their reflected images is overcome by a rush of love, and he prays that next spring all of them will be as happy as they seem to be just now.